CHRYSALIS AND REQUIEM

QUINTON LI

Contact: www.quintonli.com

Cover Illustrations: Caleb Hosalla

Part and Chapter Backgrounds by Wenceslaus Hollar 1646

- Five butterflies
- A moth, three butterflies and two beetles
- Three moths, two butterflies and a bumble bee
- Three butterflies and a wasp
- Five Butterflies, a moth and two beetles

ISBN paperback: 978-0-6456815-8-1

ISBN ebook: 978-0-6456815-9-8

To my characters who endured all their changes and went with the world that shifted around them.

To every queer and trans angel reading this.

To every girl who had a friendship that they suspected was a little more gay than they thought.

CONTENT WARNINGS

This book contains references and themes to alcohol/drug use, blood, confrontation to abuse, death, emotional abuse, escalating violence, gaslighting/manipulation, gore, lifechanging injury, murder, corpses, visions about traumatic events, panic attacks, paranormal/occult content, self-harm, sexual references, suicide ideation, and trauma.

Beware of typos. There may still be a few that made it into the final version. That could be owed to the author and ARC readers being human beings, and how we miss things sometimes. Have fun!

ADRAREDON ACADEMY

1. MIRIAM MANOR
2. MUSIC & PERFORMANCE
3. INFIRMARY
4. ADMIN BUILDING
5. HEADMASTER'S OFFICE
6. LIBRARY
7. GRAVEYARD
8. ADRAREDON CATHEDRAL
9. FITNESS COMPLEX
10. LEARNING CENTRE
11. CAFETERIA
12. STATUE OF FOUNDERS
13. GATES TO THE ACADEMY

WITHIN
ACADEMY
FORCEFIELD

TOWARDS
TOWN

PART I

"Forgive me, for all the things I did but mostly for the ones that I did not."
—— *Donna Tartt, The Secret History*

CHAPTER 1
YOUR ATTENTION

Year 3, Semester 1, Week 8

Hanging from a window ledge five stories high was not how Veaer Rosell imagined to be spending her Friday afternoon.

At the same time, she knew it was only one of many intriguing things to come as the school year continued.

Even being up so high, old oak trees grew taller than her and a risky turn of her head revealed a view that inspired a feeling like sinking in an ocean. Far down below were stone pavements and shady grass patches, her fellow senior students scurrying like ants. Beckoning a dizzy spell were the worn buildings of Adraredon Academy surrounding—no, towering—over her.

Long pointed arches and spires touched the stars. Flying buttresses protruded off ornate walls. The institution orbited an intricate stone and marble art piece in the centre of the courtyard, the cardinal directions featuring a statue each—the four heroes of centuries ago and the founders of Adraredon Academy. They were surrounded by dragon saints, winged beings, and at the very top were Ter and Mian, creators of the universe.

Veaer's sleeves tightened around her biceps as she shuffled her hands along the dusty windowsill above her head. The rolled-up fabric against her elbows did not help, but in this case, she'd pay any price to get the job done, even if she had to beg her sleeves to stay put as she shifted her weight left to right, brought her legs together and let her body swing in rhythm. She eyed the balcony that was almost beneath her—just too much to the right to drop straight down.

Her legs swayed in motion. A leather satchel wrapped across her chest bumped into her side with each swing. She gauged momentum, a gritted prayer to the dragon saint of time and season between her teeth, and finally let go of the ledge.

Her body fell to the right as intended; her destination calculated. With arms tucked in, she landed on the balcony with bent knees, arms out, and gratitude that cats weren't the only ones that could land on their feet.

As she stood up and dusted off her white shirt and ironed skirt, she peered at the thick gold curtains drawing away what sunlight tried to make it into the room. Beyond these glass doors framed with wood was a world that she had technically seen before but, in another sense, never experienced in this way.

For the fourth floor of Miriam Manor was reserved for who were considered the royalty of Adraredon or, alternatively, those who had parents rich enough to pay for the upstairs rooms—not that they were much better than those downstairs, if anything they were almost the same!—but that the status and bragging rights were enough to create endless politics between families. Veaer didn't get this courtesy as a scholarship student placed on the ground floor, which she always found strange. Were smarts not more valuable than money? But then she reconsidered who her audience was.

Besides, with her smarts came boredom, and it meant that her academics led a path of undesired cruising. Where she could sit at the back and zone out during class, staring out the window at the beautiful buildings like they were paintings, and still get in the top ten of her cohort on tests. Academics were only systems and patterns to understand and then execute, which she always had a knack for.

Now she took initiative, for it was her last year at Adraredon, and she needed to make her own fun if she wanted to survive to university.

And where she was today wasn't by mistake. No—she was ready for her next, and toughest, challenge. The next thing she could call her very own, that she could pick away at, turn inside out, hold so closely that no one else could know more about it than her. And it came with a name.

Elise Excava.

Princess of Adraredon Academy, if only for being the daughter of the headmaster.

Unlike her golden brother, Elise kept her circle small. She also didn't exhibit her abilities in loud ways, such as her brother in fencing or student presidency. But she did have a motif: butterflies. In Veaer's preliminary research, she observed every art piece Elise submitted, every sketch during class, scoured every essay placed on their teacher's desk. She understood that Elise had a deep philosophy within her about transformation. About change, the Wheel of Fortune. How existence gives and takes. How every push is a pull, and every pull is a push. How caterpillars curled up in their cocoons and by the magic of nature itself, became a being of beauty and flight.

The way she spoke to her close ones in a hushed voice, always like something said too loud would escape her grasp, it ate away at Veaer. She needed to know more.

It was almost like Elise was a ghost, floating through the halls decorated with candles and portraits, an ill aura about her. Something followed her, not of this world. And not only that, but she was best friends with Tychon Alastor Galacia, renowned tarot reader and diviner, rumoured to have the ability to communicate with spirits. Two senti, people of the non-magical kind, with no distinctive physical features, yet somehow, deeply intertwined with the unknown.

And what really mattered was this question: *what do they know that I don't?*

Because people like Elise Excava had something to hide.

And to answer her question, she would gain the attention of this princess who eluded her by doing what she did best—outsmarting her peers, and taking things she didn't own.

See, while Veaer did live in Miriam Manor herself, she was never allowed upstairs without explicitly extended invitations, that included close supervision, as per academy rules. That, and faculty administered force fields that threw you back where you belonged just when you thought you had a chance. But in addition to that, she also figured out that the fifth floor belonged to Elise and her brother Izot, and that there were no barriers there because anyone who made it up to floor four would be aware of their place.

Her solution came to her through heritage and an undeniable determination. As a caemi—the magical counterpart of sentikind typically seen with brilliant coloured hair and animal-like ears and tails—and one of the wolf variety, her increased dexterity allowed her to climb the side of the manor with, not so much ease, but a less painful experience than dealing with people. Her route of choice was to reach the bottom ledge of the fifth floor balconies from her dorm room window before dropping down to floor four for a quick pit stop.

She opened the balcony door, and she slipped past the curtains into a room with brown couches and walls of books. She deliberately decided against a bedroom as they were more likely to house students during and between classes, and with floor plans replicated from the ground to the fourth floor, it was easy pickings.

She didn't loiter for long, nothing new to keep her interest apart from the slow stream of euphoria flowing through her veins. *Patrons above, it won't be this easy, will it?*

She gave herself a moment to shake the excitement from her arms, taking a long deep breath in and out. She quietly stepped out of the room and, to keep herself stimulated, sequenced her fingers to tap the inside of her thumb in succession, providing rhythm to her movements. *1, 2, 3, 4. 1, 2, 3, 4.*

Murmurs and laughter crawled through the walls, not close enough that she could tell who they were, and not far enough that she couldn't tell where it was coming from. She would need to avoid running into anyone before she made it upstairs, but that just made this even more invigorating.

Something caught her attention as she padded across the carpet, her gaze betraying her plan to keep straight ahead. She approached a wide doorway with sliding doors not dissimilar to the ones of her favourite art room in the learning centre. Within were a circle of canvases, half painted and left in a moment of time. The smell of oils and acrylic drew her in and she found herself in admiration and envy for a special studio just like this.

Goodness, strokes of paint on a stretched canvas could bring her to her knees if they really wanted to—and it was one of the only things that Veaer couldn't make herself intellectualise.

The beauty of art was the mystery—the unknown against the known, bursts of colours, myriads of shapes, composition with a heartbeat, and it undid her in the way she hoped to undo Elise.

A voice snapped her away from the canvases, someone coming her way from another corridor. She flew to the doorframe and couldn't help but listen to the mumbling, but it wasn't *what* was said that caught her attention, but *who* it was.

Adair Boudreau was quietly saying something to herself, almost like trying to memorise phrases like she usually did for quotes before a literature exam. Her arms remained by her sides, as opposed to swinging like she usually enjoyed... something was bothering her. But she was meant to be in class right now, so what was she doing here?

Veaer didn't desire to be spotted by anyone but Elise, making the experience even better to savour, something intimate enough to really call her attention—that if Elise told anyone about it, her hushed whispers wouldn't be so fruitful. But again this was her vice; her need for knowledge won her over.

"Addie!" Veaer whisper-shouted while clinging to the wooden frame. Even if her friend knew she was here, no one else but Elise would.

But the caemi girl, orange hair like a fire burning Veaer's vision, continued walking, as if the words she chanted covered her ears and took her somewhere else. If the academy didn't have their means of restricting the unique appearance of caemi animal features, perhaps she would've had a better chance at gaining Adair's attention through her cat caemi ears.

Veaer squeezed her hands into fists a few times, going back and forth on this moment of solace. Perhaps she could let her pass if the patrons above granted it so, but Adair wasn't one to break rules, and she was always so adamant on Veaer making it to class. Hypocrisy— meaning questions that could be answered just for her.

She rushed forward in wide strides and grasped Adair's arm, leaving just a moment to place her other hand against Adair's mouth as Veaer backed her into the wall. No screams, no attention. None of her plans ruined for her foolish itch of curiosity.

Adair's eyes widened, and it was like a spell broke as her gaze focused and she blinked a couple times. Veaer peered into them to draw out the questions. *What just happened? Wait, it's Veaer, what is Veaer doing here?! How did Veaer find me... will she find out what I'm hiding?*

Yes, because whatever questions are asked, you will answer.

"Veaer?" was the only word muffled through Veaer's palm before her free arm flew into action and grabbed Veaer's wrist. "What in the name of Mian... you aren't meant to be up here."

"Technically neither are you. You're supposed to be in class!" Veaer finally let go, her hands dropping to her side, but didn't step back to keep Adair pinned. She couldn't see anything suspicious in her expression or her uniform. Her gaze dropped to Adair's hands and she noticed some markings peeking out from her blazer sleeve. "What is that?"

Adair shifted the incriminated arm so that she couldn't see it anymore, which only caused her to look up and narrow her eyes. "Notes."

"Notes for what?" Veaer placed a familiar touch on Adair's hip, a slight squeeze with an urge for something more.

"I know you aren't up here just to catch me revising for a test, Ve. Tell me, what's going on? Trying to snipe something from my room this time?" That lopsided smile of hers appeared on Adair's lips, successfully lowering Veaer's guard and unlocking her from her position.

Veaer paced backwards, letting Adair close her eyes and breathe out. Just for a test... just as she assumed. She didn't know whether to feel vindicated for figuring it out earlier based on Adair's usual quirks, or if she was disappointed for nothing more.

"It's unlike you to be revising during class time when you're meant to be, you know, in class." Veaer crossed her arms and offered her own smile to shift the subject. "What happened to 'this is what your tuition pays for', huh?"

"My tuition also pays for what I define success as. *Nous sommes nos choix*—we are our choices. I simply make the most of this time to study for the test rather than sit in class, uninspired." Adair triumphantly placed a hand over her chest and began walking to her room again, to which Veaer quickly stopped her by the shoulder. She couldn't walk and talk with Adair if she had to go the other way.

"What is that phrase you like to say... *on ne change pas...* you don't change if you're on the winning team? You were doing plenty fine. Anyway, I'm not here for your room, but your brother's room on the other hand..." She flashed a devilish smile, to punctuate her point and for the gasp Adair let out.

"Great idea! Need me to come?"

Hope filtered through Adair's eyes and it pained Veaer to say, "I'm sorry, this is a solo mission. Can't measure my success if your wonderful tact is in the equation, yeah?" She tapped Adair on the nose and leaned in closer.

Adair scoffed and rubbed her nose with her palm, but the sideways glance she sent Veaer communicated otherwise. "Fine, got it. Good luck and don't get caught. I don't want to hear either my brother yelling or you falling down the stairs later."

"You got it, lovely." Veaer winked and waved Adair off as she went back to chanting her phrases.

With an exhale, Veaer let herself refocus. The sound through the walls hadn't abruptly stopped, or gotten closer or louder, which meant she was still safe. She realigned her path, going back to the intersection of corridors and through to the quarter she needed. Her next stop: the rooms of Elise's court. Fortunately, there weren't many in her little group and the likelihood she could find the room she needed was high.

She came to a stop in front of a pair of doors separated by a wall and here was where the chills ran down her spine. The name plates on both doors were way too similar, and she had only come along with a vague idea of Elise's personal underclassman companion for this week, figuring the process of elimination would serve her enough.

With an under the breath curse, she pressed her ear against the left door to listen in. She at least knew that this underclassman was in class right now, meaning if one of the rooms were occupied, she had a free pass.

Silence met her for a few beats and she returned to tapping her fingers to count the seconds ticking by. Nothing. She tried the next door, but the same result. She returned to the first door, though with frustrated misplaced feet, she tripped and slammed against the door.

Frantic ruffling from the other side and whispers. Oh goodness, someone, or a few someones, were in there.

"Who's—*ahem*." Their voice was high-pitched and as if off-balance, like after running a marathon. "Who's there?" the person asked with what sounded like a slightly deeper version of their voice, perhaps even their natural one. Heat rushed to Veaer's cheeks at the implication that she had just interrupted something important.

"Darling, come back. No one's here right now," a second, very affectionate and sultry voice answered, and Veaer knew then it was time to use the other door and take the risk that her luck would place someone in there too.

She took extra effort in closing the right door, embracing comfort in the quiet and dark room that appeared to be what she was looking for. No surprises in here, just drawn blinds, a bed on the left, a desk on the right. A closet that was closed. She had an itch to check it just in case and she swung it open only to reveal a spare uniform and other changes of clothes.

Bust statues emulating marble decorated a few shelves alongside taper candles, weathered book pages and diagrams stuck to the walls. While this was humble decor often found in Miriam Manor, Veaer did wish she could swipe some of the objects for her own room. But in this case, she was here to give rather than take.

The underclassman was always scheduled to come along to Elise's room at the end of the day to serve her duties—gathering any refreshments, tidying the room, perhaps secret activities Veaer didn't need to fantasise about. For Elise's counterpart of a brother, his second in command was usually the one to take the role, but it seemed Elise didn't want Tychon in that sense.

Veaer unclasped her satchel and pulled out two things. A raspberry muffin and a tablet. This week's assignment was a bit of a sweet tooth, and she noticed each time the young girl reached for the desserts in the cafeteria before any savoury item.

She gently placed both upon the table and looked around, her gaze settling on a letter opener. She grasped its handle, spun it around and carefully held the blade between her fingers, bringing the blunt end down onto the tablet and crushing it into powder.

What came next was quick work—taking the powder from the table and sprinkling it over the muffin, letting it get into the cracks and dusting it like sugar.

She didn't intend to hurt the underclassman, but if she wanted her plan to work, she needed the princess alone. An underclassman who found herself running to the bathroom for the rest of the night wouldn't be much use in completing her evening routine with the royal, would she?

She made sure to not leave any evidence behind, returning the letter opener to its position, swiftly exiting the room, and closing both her satchel and the door. A low rumble from downstairs was distinguishable enough that Veaer knew the end of the school day had arrived, and she had just enough time to enact the final act of her plan.

She sprinted for the next staircase and gazed upon the carpeted steps. An entire floor dedicated to the prince and princess of Adraredon was before her.

Each step up was electrifying, the next better than the last. Every piece was falling into place, and this would mark the beginning of the princess in her palm, like a flower bud ready to bloom just for Veaer. Thorns falling away, petals outstretched, bleeding red onto white roses—revelation would be hers and hers only.

This time she knew the exact door she needed, if only from nights watching Elise gazing to the stars from her balcony, Tychon chatting away in a chair shuffling his cards. The two were bonded in a way she couldn't place her finger on. As if lifetimes ago they crossed paths and now they returned to each other's orbit. But there was always something else between them that sparked conspiracy, and not in the romantic sense. Something like they were meant to intersect in every life and then continue through, leaving each other behind. It was only a matter of when this would happen, and how. She was nervous to admit she feared a similar fate between herself and the Boudreau twins, but time was the master of that, and it had a fluctuating temperament.

Her hand hovered over a golden door handle, beautifully engraved with twisting vines. Upon a closer look, she could see a name intertwined—Elise Excava. A nameplate wasn't enough for her. She wasted no more time and turned the handle, bursting through the door as if it were her own.

This was the Kingdom of Elise. A veil draped over a queen-size bed, a piano on the other side of the room, a tall mirror on another wall, with a stacked vanity. The air sung here, not that actual music played in the princess' absence, but a choir of tea tree, lavender and clove that wrapped her being and belted 'this is home!'. This bedroom wasn't just that, it was half the size of the entire floor and showed in its luxury apartment style fit with a small kitchen, and a bathroom through a door to the right.

Her immediate choice was the wall with the vanity, and she stared into the mirror reflecting a Veaer surrounded by butterflies and other small winged specimens hanging on the opposite wall.

She looked down and used a finger to gently spread a pile of jewellery in a tray apart. A thin gold chain was exactly what she needed, and she palmed it away for later.

Her ears perked up as a bout of commotion echoed from down the hallway. *Soon, soon, soon, soon.* Two voices but three sets of footsteps joined the fifth floor. Veaer took a seat at the vanity, facing the entrance. The door to the other room opened and closed, the voices muffling to almost nothing, and the three sets became one. The golden handle on her side turned and Veaer placed a hand on her bouncing knee. This was no time to be hesitant. The door parted and there she was.

She couldn't describe Elise's beauty in words if she tried. She needed a palette of paint and a fresh canvas this instant. She needed to dip a brush into Elise's golden skin and transfer it to the weaved cloth. She needed to contain those ebony strands of hair between her fingers and memorise each one. She needed those down-turned hooded eyes dusted with a dark shadow to stare at her like a flickering flame being threatened by the wind.

She lowered her eyes for a moment, almost overwhelmed by every feeling coming for her mind and throat in an instant. Oh, adorable black socks that reached her thighs that slightly overflowed creating muffin tops. She would have fainted right there but wriggled her fingers to let go of the rush and maintain her composure.

The young woman sighed to herself, quiet enough that Veaer wouldn't have heard it if she weren't concentrating on every move and sound as much as she was. Elise went over to the balcony to open the door for some fresh air, then she slipped off her blazer and placed it over one of the other chairs in the room tucked under a round tea table. Even if her presence was known, the young woman didn't react to it or find it strange.

Veaer's steady gaze was interrupted by the strike of a match and she dipped her chin at the long shadow of Elise casting to her feet. The flame was brought to a taper candle and the wick came alive. Her ears twitched in anticipation.

"I think for my next piece, " Elise began slowly, softly. Her voice cut through the silence like a dolphin leaping from the deep blue, breaking the surface into ripples. She shook the match and tossed it in the bin, then lifted her hand with careful intimacy, barely stroking the edge of a framed specimen. "Red admiral butterflies."

Veaer swallowed, her words stuck in her throat for a moment. *I know this, I know this.* She had prepared for this.

"And what do you wish to draw from this piece?" Veaer asked, her own voice sounding foreign, distant. A small crackle in the lightning storm Elise brought forth to her emotions.

Elise's fingers closed into her palm and she moved her fist away from the glass, propping it to the side of the frame. She stood straighter, not so much of a flinch but definitely a response that delighted Veaer to almost a giggle. The princess didn't turn around, though the tilt of her head acknowledged a sense of unfamiliarity.

"Their wings are a snapshot of the universe. We are contained in those delicate strands of brown, surrounded by a bubble of orange— a few dark dots... something to explore. This is what we call our home." Elise separated her hand from the wall and gestured over her shoulder, calling Veaer towards her.

Veaer inhaled sharply and her senses heightened all at once, her fingers tingling with excitement. Her gaze locked onto the golden clasp that sat pretty on the back of Elise's neck as the princess moved her hair over her shoulder.

Suddenly it was as if she were the one floating by Elise all this time, but now she was more than an apparition—she had a voice: "Tell me more, my princess."—she had thought: *I need this, I need this.*—she had limbs: her hand floated by Elise's shoulder blade before she gathered the courage to lower it and the warmth that came with the action was searing, but Veaer let it burn.

She wondered if in another life, she would've let herself fall apart then and there, thrown the plan out the window for its complication, dancing to the hum of her heart, knowing life was not reality nor imagination but what they decided was worth conscious thought. She would've decided on the mystery of Elise Excava and been happy with what they had in this moment. But that was not enough for her, not yet.

"We are so tiny," Elise whispered, like a confession that pained her. "We are nothing in comparison to the fantastic infinite possibilities outside of what we can comprehend. How am I supposed to capture that? There is only so much room on a piece of paper, or on a canvas, or even if I used an entire wall for a mural. Nothing will come close to this feeling."

In a motion faster than anything since Veaer entered this room, the princess grasped Veaer's hands and pulled her forward. She stumbled closer, her chest against Elise's back, and her mind ran in circles of wonder and fear. Elise tilted her head back slightly, her long black hair like a waterfall that rushed past the side of Veaer's cheek, covering the necklace once again.

"My dear maiden," Elise's fingertips drifted over Veaer's forearms absently, "a penny for your thoughts?"

The hairs on Veaer's arms stood at the touch and she took a deep breath before answering, "Perhaps what you're saying is not a constant that we can qualify or quantify. Maybe it's only..." Her breath hitched as Elise shifted in her arms and finally turned around, staring right into her soul. "An intangible experience"

They stood there, Elise wrapped in Veaer's arms, with a collection of frozen butterflies of all colours and sizes as their backdrop, in growing darkness except for the lit candle, and racket that came from the students on the floors below which served to remind them of where they were.

"My, you are not what I expected." Elise's calm demeanour stilled Veaer. "Rosell, year 3, senior. Art stream. Most peculiarly, assigned the ground floor. How did you end up all the way up here?"

The whimsical quality of Elise's voice made her want to spill every thought to her, but Veaer stared hard into those eyes and knew that this was a challenge.

"You know a lot about me." Her arms shifted downwards from Elise's neck and tightened around her waist, pulling her soft belly against Veaer's. "How's that?"

"Not more than the school records. And what's to say you aren't guilty of the same considering we're standing here, doing this?" Elise brought her finger upwards and ran it along Veaer's chin.

"I happen to know your underclassman is out of commission tonight. I figured I would skip the inconvenience." She recalled the two voices from behind the door, the images that came to mind with each assumption. "Why don't I serve you tonight?"

A small, entertained chuckle followed an intrigued look on Elise's face, and she stepped back. Veaer let her go.

Elise folded her hands behind her back and paced the room as she spoke. "An experience... implying that an experience expressed in writing, voice or visually is not good enough for my thoughts. You mean something that doesn't stay still... an obscure form of story-telling. Maybe *really* living and breathing. Curious." She arrived at her bed and paused, then looked back at Veaer. "Bring me a drink, will you?"

Veaer hadn't realised she had locked in place and snapped herself back into motion by approaching the tea table and pouring a glass of iced tea from an opaque decanter. She padded across the room to meet Elise again, her slightly taller stature keeping the princess' shins against the soft doonas that spilled over the bed.

"Tell me," Elise looked down at the glass then back up to Veaer, "why are you really here?"

"It's not easy to get your attention," Veaer murmured. Then she lifted the glass and brought it to Elise's lips.

Elise only hummed in response as she sipped the tea, her gaze unmoving. Striking brown with rays of gold. She had the sun in her eyes.

And in a swift move, Veaer took the glass away and dropped it.

The glass shattered into a starry sky and Elise gasped as she was pushed into the bed. With the princess buried between soft cushions and silky sheets, Veaer unclipped the gem necklace she'd been eyeing for days. The prized jewel encircled in gold fell into her palm.

"There is a lot to learn from a girl like you." Veaer tucked the gem necklace into her pocket as she held her gaze to the golden chain in her right hand—her decoy.

The princess sat straight with a changing expression—something of surprise, of anger, of excitement, of curiosity. Veaer waved the chain left to right and if she closed one eye and looked carefully, Elise's gaping expression would be trapped in the loop.

Veaer bent over, bringing her voice to Elise's ear, and whispered, "I hope to mark this the beginning of our experience together."

And as she pulled back, she dropped the false chain onto the floor, and left through the open balcony, making her grand escape downwards, leaving the other residents of Miriam Manor none the wiser.

CHAPTER 2
MY INTENTION

Year 1, Semester 1, Week 1

Veaer Rosell stepped onto the grounds of Adraredon Academy two years ago in search of something beautiful.

And she found it all. In the buildings that took her breath away as she tilted her head upwards and exposed her neck to the summer sun pouring over the campus. In the students who were as good looking as they were clever and creative. In the grass for being as green as can be. In the classrooms with thoughtfully arranged furniture, expensive desks, and a teacher dressed in the exact way she wanted to dress when she grew up and had enough money.

She was spinning along the path between the learning centre and Miriam Manor on her first day of orientation, during which she had made friends with no one and familiarised herself with where classrooms were located, how they were categorised and counted on each level of each building, and noted that she wanted to explore the performance block someday, as well as the cathedral.

Her airy daze was rudely interrupted by two girls walking from the opposite direction, the one closest to Veaer shouldering her so harshly that it sent her flying off the path and covered her skirt in freshly cut grass blades as she hit the ground. They didn't have memorable faces except for looking quite pretty, but their expressions failed to meet the same expectation.

They stopped walking, looked down upon Veaer in the grass, and didn't make an effort to help her up. Their silence told her, *"This is your fault."*

Their gazes travelled across her body: to her untucked shirt, to her rolled up sleeves, to her sneakers that she had to replace with leather loafers someday, in accordance with the uniform code. Veaer eyed them back, regretfully envying their ironed uniforms and polished shoes.

One of the girls spoke in an entirely unhelpful way, "You're the freshman on the bottom floor, aren't you?" She smiled with a tense lip and glanced at her friend who returned a wordless look. "She's already halfway there."

Veaer couldn't tell if the words were meant to be an insult. All she knew was: *they sound exactly like the girls from my old school.* But they did state fact. She was assigned the lowest floor and it didn't take long for her to realise what that meant in the hierarchy of this academy.

This isn't my old school anymore, she reassured herself, quickly, but still neglected to lift herself from the ground. *This is Adraredon Academy—where I will find everything that I'll ever want and more.*

CHAPTER 3
A CHASE OF ALTERNATIVE
MATTERS

Year 3, Semester 1, Week 9

T wo days later and no phone calls, no confrontation, and no faculty at her door.

Veaer slipped into her leather shoes and then shouldered on her blazer, and while she was getting ready for a Monday of classes, her mind was elsewhere. The lack of attention was cause for concern. But was she secretly glad that perhaps the princess didn't find it in herself to tell anyone else—to keep it a secret between the two of them?

Entering the learning centre granted nothing new either. Every student was in their usual place, every piece of dialogue lacked any knowledge of what transpired on floor five of Miriam Manor last Friday.

Veaer tapped her fingers along the leather strap of her satchel and her teeth played with her lip. Her gaze darted from side to side with each classroom she passed, remaining cautious in case someone from Elise's court was just waiting to jump out at her and take her away. But by the time she arrived at her classroom —nothing.

She stood in front of the door, staring through the tiny window for any semblance of change that she caused, but it seemed what she did really stayed behind closed doors.

A certain voice piqued her attention and she spun to her right to see Elise walking down the hall. Only a few other senti and caemi kept by her side, though not a word was exchanged between them. It didn't take Veaer long to notice that Tychon wasn't with them, who usually was chattering away about his latest reading or something to do with tarot. Other students in the senior year also seemed to notice, turning to each other and pointing towards Elise.

A waving hand appeared in her vision and she quickly shifted out of the way for her classmates to enter the room, her gaze still stuck on the princess. *Why isn't she looking at me? Have I not done enough for her to be more interested?*

And it wasn't like her attention was divided among others. This was a young woman keeping to herself and continuing to exhibit as such. The princess didn't garner nearly as much attention as her brother, who by happenstance appeared not far behind her—and had the crowd to show for it.

But even then, Elise did not acknowledge the pushing bodies that rushed towards her brother, or the student who found themself brave enough to approach Elise and ask her where Tychon was.

She continued walking and then disappeared into her classroom across from Veaer's, the hall becoming empty as Izot also took his leave.

"Everyone keeps asking about Galacia," Haiwrin Boudreau noted as he balanced his chair on its back legs, propping his feet up on the table as the last stretch of homeroom class was ticking by. "People skip class all the time, what's another one?"

Veaer nodded, mostly as a means to contribute what she had the capacity to, which wasn't verbally until her thoughts processed. She did find it strange that Tychon was absent as well, not because he never skipped, but because if he was away, then there had to be something wrong. His precognition brought him to unknown places only for him to turn up again all smiley and well the next day. He didn't do it often at all, so there was merit to the buzz, but Haiwrin may have been right in a way too.

"I know he has his habits, but I'm still a little concerned," Adair added to her brother's words, tapping the lead end of her pencil against the table leaving small dark marks. Veaer reached out and softly placed her hand on top of Adair's. "I haven't spoken to him recently... I mean, he just hasn't been around to get a chance to speak with him, even if I wanted to get a reading or something. Never saw him on Friday while I was pacing the halls."

Veaer exchanged a knowing look with the orange cat caemi, and Adair gave her a wry smile. She wondered if anyone had seen Tychon that day, because while Adair couldn't be the entirety of Miriam Manor's surveillance system, she did spend quite a bit of time on the same floor as where Tychon's dorm room.

"Hey, Ve?" Haiwrin's voice cut her thoughts off and she straightened in her chair and blinked at her friend.

"Yes?" She wiped her hands on her skirt and didn't fail to notice that the classroom was almost empty now except for Haiwrin who moved to the seat next to her, his blue and black hair teasing the corner of her eye. "Oh... did I miss the bell?"

Haiwrin chuckled light-heartedly and touched her shoulder—a grounding touch. "Your mind palace is like your second home. Just remember to spend some time in this reality too." He winked and patted her back a few times before heading out. "I'm going to catch-up with Addie, but I'll see you?"

"You'll see me." Veaer smiled. She must have gotten lost in the map that was Tychon's absence but somehow she couldn't recall exactly what that consisted of.

She looped her satchel across her chest and took some time to tidy up the room to further ground herself. In the span of silence, some frantic rummaging came from the other side of the hallway, pulling her away from arranging a shelf of books.

The classroom across from her also had its door open but she couldn't see much happening from where she was. Then, the tiniest evidence of Elise's distinct dark locks came into view, the princess focusing on a desk near the front of the room as she ran a nervous hand through her hair.

Murmured swears emitted from her being and she forced a desk open, letting crumpled papers fly out and a small box hit the floor. This was the most Veaer had ever seen Elise so riled up and she couldn't tell if this was passion or randomly placed rage.

After several moments of searching with no apparent direction, the princess crouched down to pick everything up and stuff it back into the desk, but not before her head whipped to the side and she fixed her gaze on something under the table. The paper she pulled out was white and crisp in her grip, and then a sudden air of conviction arose and she was storming out of the classroom, the opposite way from the cafeteria.

Veaer paused, her breath stuck in her throat.

And not a moment later, she was running the same way.

If the universe was out to spite Veaer, then it was currently making a circus out of her.

Elise's chase led her to the doorstep of Adraredon Cathedral, her very favourite building on the grounds and her main witness to her climb and break-in last week.

Unlike most other buildings on campus which were grey or brown, with exposed bricks or dark concrete, this one was a beautiful cream that remained clean through all weather, disasters and time. Perhaps she could credit the maintenance to caemi magic, but she also theorised that a house of the divine simply received such treatment from high above. The building was also like a small fortress, rather square in composition but with incredible depth and five wonderful spires, one on each corner tower with the centre one towering above all. The front was decorated with tall stained-glass windows, and the towers were layered with carved statues of dragons, feather winged beings and depictions of nature personified that some religions venerated. A place of worship for many across Syriphian and Kyross cultures.

Beyond these doors was a space of comfort in trying times, housing her dragon saint's chapel, on the left at the very end of the hall, and a calming atmosphere. She would sit in one of the pews, other students and faculty members coming in and out to pay their respects to the mighty dragons or to light candles in memory of their loved ones. She knew she wasn't the most consistent devotee, only coming by when she found she could make time, or when she really needed to clear her mind, but somehow every time the words flowed smoothly from her mouth and she would open herself to the statue staring at her, with its expansive wings and strong jaw. Zhu Long, Dragon of Time and Season—saint of the red caemi. What was it like to control day and night, summer and winter?

In this moment, while everyone else was studying or having lunch, she felt a proper lack of control, placing her hand upon the engraved door but feeling as if she'd be intruding on something by entering. Maybe the prospect of the saints and deities being so close and watching her caused the unnerve that sparked at her fingertips.

But then she heard something shatter, and her curiosity propelled her to slightly nudge the door open, leaving any creaks within the grains as she slipped through to the lobby.

The circular foyer room was empty except for its bowls of holy water and pamphlets of information. The select paintings in this room depicting scriptures and creation tales would normally keep Veaer in here for several more moments, but one of the doors leading to the main hall was left ajar and, in the distance, past rows and rows of wooden pews, filtering between large columns, was one short figure by the altar and another carefully creeping down the aisle, remaining unnoticed. It was nothing but suspicious, and Veaer took a different door to the upstairs balcony.

Fighting balance between speed and stealth, she finally made it close to the opposite end of the cathedral and ducked down to watch what was happening through the bannisters. The culprit for the shattering was a wine glass that's pieces spread on the altar platform.

But what made her more curious was the chalk circle drawn in front of the altar platform, and the hooded figure who was frantically bringing the glass pieces together and hissing quietly to themselves. The chalk circle had a range of geometric and symmetrical shapes and if that didn't hint anything, a few candles were placed around the edge along with other items: a wooden stick, a ritual knife, another cup that could've been a replacement to the broken one and a pile of coins. In the middle of the circle was a book, sheets of paper, a box like the one she saw with the crumpled papers earlier, and a bunch of feathers. This had to be some sort of ritual... in the middle of the day, in Adraredon Academy, but with who and why?

Then the figure in the aisle came into light and Veaer perked up at the return of her target after losing her at the doorsteps. She couldn't see a lot from where she was, but Elise's fists closed by her side and she seemed to be making an effort to remain quiet as well albeit in a more obvious position.

The hooded person still didn't notice and after leaving the pieces of glass on the altar cloth, they dug into their pocket and pulled out a stone as they stepped right before the edge of their circle. Their eyes kept to the floor as they mumbled, and the familiarity of the voice tipped Veaer off that this must have been a student... the youth of the tone and how she would know if it were one of the teachers. But the way they spoke was also different than anything she's heard, like an incantation of tongues. With the stone, they traced an arch in the air, just bigger than themself, and stepped through into the circle, before they looked up and dropped the stone.

"Elise?" the figure said, surprised, and with confirmation that they expected to be alone.

The wicked noise that came from Elise caused Veaer to stumble back and clutch the collar of her shirt. It was beauty and terror.

"Now, now... what is going on here, Tychon Alastor Galacia?"

CHAPTER 4
TYCHON ALASTOR GALACIA

Veaer couldn't help but feel she was about to witness something not meant for her eyes.

"Elise..." Tychon repeated, and he lifted his hands to his hood to lower it, perhaps in courtesy to his best friend. "You aren't meant to be here." He brought his hands to his short hair and pulled at the strands.

"That reveals nothing of what you're doing." Elise stepped forward and Tychon suddenly dropped to his knees and grabbed the stone.

"Wait—no, no, stop, wait. I need to... give me a moment." The words came in a whirlwind as he stood up again and smoothed out the front of his cloak. His hand shook as he walked to the other edge of the circle where Elise was and lifted it to trace another arch. He started mumbling the incantation again, his arm becoming still and his voice a droning yet intriguing thing, until Elise sighed and returned to the pews, idly running her hands along the wood as she paced.

"Will we really continue doing this? You running off somewhere and then I have to go find you?" Elise lowered her hands in front of her and folded them, turning straight on towards the boy.

As the incantation came to an end, Tychon seemed to snap back into reality, his limbs and movements growing softer. He allowed himself to step out of the chalk markings, but not without a nervous look at the collection of items and then at Elise.

"I'm not asking you to find me, you don't have to."

"It's not about wanting to, it's the fact that you still can't be open with me and if I don't push then you're left—" She waved her hand vaguely towards him, her fingers riddled with shakes. "You're left on your own, doing this."

"But I tell you what matters, I tell you the things that I care about you knowing. You were there when I doubted my practice, you were there when I was hearing things I shouldn't have been... patrons above Elise, you were there for my transition, when I needed support the most and I went to you and you still held my face and looked me in the eyes and told me I was a man despite it all."

Elise's chest heaved and her breaths were deep yet strained. She remained silent and her eyes became shiny as tears welled up. Only the cathedral's ambience of crackling fire and running water sounded, and they were like a frozen image for a few seconds longer.

"And you are, and I still believe that." Elise broke the silence slowly, as if picking her words. "But why must you be the one to decide what matters? Why can't I care about knowing more about you too? You're drifting away, you're leaving me. How ironic is this? Just another man who—"

"Don't." Tychon stepped forward and held up a hand. "You know I don't like it when you say those things."

Elise let out that laugh again, that irksome and vexatious laugh. "There it is again! You're telling me what matters, what should be cared about, what I should say. Where is my autonomy in this? And why does every choice I make get met with something? Like you always have an answer, but you don't. You don't have all the answers."

"And I'm not saying I do!" His voice boomed towards the ceiling as he snapped, throwing the stone to the ground, and letting it fling off to under the pews. But he didn't move, didn't inch away from his stare at Elise, who stood her ground and was even leaning in, like she was looking for a fight. "You keep acting like I'm trying to be like those people in your life. But I'm not. And you're bringing my gender into this when it's something entirely different. I want to be treated as a man because I am one, but not if it comes with all this. Not if you're only going to compare me to Izot."

"I don't even want to hear his name!" Elise shrieked, departing from the pews, and pushing past Tychon. "I'm going to—"

"You won't."

"Stop interrupting me! You're so impossible when things aren't the way you want them to be. You thought I wasn't going to find you today? You know I always will." Elise stood frighteningly close to the chalk, like she was tempting it, taunting it. For something to happen if she just—

She stamped on the chalk outline and Tychon's gasp was deep and audible.

He lunged for her, grabbing her arms and tackling her to the floor. She thrashed around and screamed, attempting to get out of his grasp and... run away? Keep going? They became a pile of limbs fighting each other, tangling and twisting, clouds of white dust and feathers rising around them. She scattered the artifacts—the wand, knife and coins reaching the edge of the broken circle. And it was a miracle that the lit candles remained upright, until Elise tossed Tychon off for a moment long enough to start blowing them out and subsequently kicking them over.

"Stop it, Elise, stop!" Tychon fumbled as he tried to get steady on his knees, for some sort of foundation as opposed to a boneless mess in a cloak. "Please stop, stop, stop, stop." Over and over, he cried until he left himself kneeling in the ruined ritual circle and just held his hands out in a disarming fashion, waiting for mercy.

Elise was an amalgamation of sobs and cries and no's and grunts. She kicked the second chalice over and it fell into pieces easily and hopelessly. And then she stood up, her back turned to Tychon as she looked at the wall behind the altar, staring into the eyes of their patron deities: Ter, god of innovation, birth and knowledge. Mian, goddess of tradition, transitions, and magic. Quiet blanketed the expanse of the hall.

Something stirred in her expression and in the way her fingers twitched by her side. The peace of the cathedral hardly returned, a whine in the air coming from Tychon who was doubling over enough to place their forehead to the ground.

"Please help me understand, Ty." Elise's voice was level, too level. "How can we have been by each other's side for so long, for you to have read my cards and for me to read your palms. For us to share an upbringing, an education and even a bed in the past, but you can't let me into this. I keep you with me, when I don't keep others, but I feel like I can never understand."

Tychon blubbered for a few moments longer until he found his voice, muffled against the floor. "But... but I think that's just it, that you won't be able to understand. This is for me and—"

"And who?" Elise cried out and whipped around, swinging her arms before wrapping herself in them. "Everyone keeps everything from me. I'm told I need to work these things out myself, that it's only fair to do so. And now that I'm standing here, having worked out where you've been skipping class to go to, I'm being told... I'm told..." Her voice cracked into a million pieces as a sob wretched from her lips. "I'm told I wouldn't understand. You're just like all of them!"

"My darling, please." Tychon lifted his head, his expression stricken from the noises Elise made as she crumpled. He paused, and then began shuffling closer to the young woman. He tried to pry her arms open but failed to do so, then settled for leaving his outstretched as an invitation. "It's just a not now, not right now, I can tell you everything, but you must trust me."

Elise wiped her tears against her blazer sleeve and took a heavy breath in, allowing herself to become swallowed by Tychon's arms.

"How about some of it?" Elise asked, and when Tychon pulled away and did only that, she continued, "Explain parts of what you're doing. I need to know my best friend is safe. To prove my worries wrong, and to know whether I should expect you in last period. I have a wonderful new project to show you."

Silence followed for a few beats until Tychon gave in, sinking back into an embrace with Elise. "You do have a way of convincing, don't you?"

"Not one that is strong enough it seems," she replied in a jovial tone but the way her eyes flashed lent a different impression.

Tychon got up and faced the pews, back straight even after what happened, renewed confidence returning to his stature. He raised his arms as if about to present a grand speech to an invisible congregation. After a moment, a smile stretched over his lips—content, grateful, peaceful.

Despite it all, perhaps he was glad to share this part of himself with Elise finally, as suggested by the cycle of their relationship. Two best friends crossing paths years ago, somehow divinely paired for their shared vigour, their desire to bring something deeper to the world. They forever walked the Wheel of Fortune, every turn bringing something new. And all they had was each other.

Elise stood up and stared at Tychon, arms dropping to her sides, that air of another world drawn to her character. She raised her right arm as if about to pat her companion on the back for his honesty. After a moment, a smile stretched over her lips—vengeful, crude, disdainful.

She plunged the ritual knife into Tychon Alastor Galacia's back.

Despite it all, perhaps Elise didn't want this anymore, trying to figure out Tychon, as led by his secretive ways. Two best friends, crossing paths years ago, somehow not meant to last, drifting away with animosity, their inability to disconnect what was meant for each other and meant for one always forcing a wedge between them. They forever walked the Wheel of Fortune, every turn bringing risk and ache. And now they couldn't have each other.

Tychon choked and brought a hand to his mouth, pulling away to find blood. No words came out, hardly a sound apart from another whine. The cathedral spun, each thick pillar turning to slush, every statue in the building jeering and mocking him. The floor disappeared and the ceiling came crashing down. He stumbled forward once, twice. And in that motion, Elise twisted the knife, pulled it out and stabbed him again, and again, and again, and again, and again.

Fire ignited in her heart, and she kept moving and screaming and crying. She refused to turn him around, refused to stare into those eyes darkening from their wonderful mix of brown and purple. Her attention remained on the wound that continued to grow larger with every hit and the pool of red that formed around her feet.

Then she stopped, dropped the knife, and got on her knees.

And Veaer joined her in prayer.

CHAPTER 5
THAT NIGHT

Moonlight pooled around her, shooting bright missiles from circular windows that formed glass halos for Ter and Mian's statues.

Crickets played a song outside, somewhere in the grass, and it was the only sign of life apart from the frantic breaths that left her.

The carpet sliced into her knees and burned them as she scrubbed a steel brush against the stains. *No one can know what I did. No one can know what happened.*

Her body was set aflame, anguish yet excitement, as she mixed dish washing liquid with cold water and sponged the area with a white cloth. Red seeped into the fibres and remained stuck. It couldn't leave even if it wanted to—there was nowhere to go.

When the blood wouldn't lift entirely, she mixed ammonia and warm water and continued to press on the area until it only appeared as if someone had spilt water.

The body was disposed of earlier, not long after the deed. It made the clean-up easier.

Each broken artifact, every half-melted candle, every piece of chalk and feather became rubbish in a plastic bag.

By the time she was finished, she could only wonder how she managed to get away with entering with a stolen key after lights-out.

Before she left, she entered a chapel room and lit a candle in remembrance.

And when she did return to Miriam Manor, throwing the bag among everything else to be taken away in the morning, and buried herself in her sheets, only the gods would know that Tychon Alastor Galacia was murdered in Adraredon Cathedral.

CHAPTER 6
DESTINED TO STAY

1, 2, 3, 4.

"I *t's just a not now, not right now, I can tell you everything but you must trust me.*"

But Elise did not trust him. She didn't. And she took that mistrust and pushed it back onto him.

1, 2, 3, 4. 1, 2, 3, 4.

"Stop, please! Stop, stop stop—"

She didn't stop, she didn't stop.

Everything was a paradoxical vortex. Crackling fire and rushing waterfalls. Voices too loud before they became whispers. Then the flames snuffed out and the water became a drought. Phantom limbs carrying me to the altar, and away to a faraway place at the same time.

Someone high above pulled the strings, dragging her through the dirt. All for entertainment, all for laughs.

Students surrounded Veaer as she sat incredibly still in her seat at homeroom. She was never one for arriving early in the morning. But to stay at Miriam Manor was to stay with her thoughts.

Her thoughts, and the ghost of Tychon.

"Don't. You know I don't like it when you say those things."

Her head twitched the side at the sound of his voice. What

would he have said if he had the chance to preach to his invisible congregation? He sat beside her now, in the spare seat to her left, inching close to her ear and his cold, lifeless breath blowing as he recited his last words like a prayer.

For a split second, she tuned into the conversations around her, a futile attempt to ignore the ghost that held her head in place, pushing against her ears, forcing her to stare straight ahead. The motion of getting lost behind her eyes without a worry wasn't new to her, but here she was very aware of how she couldn't turn her head to the door when it opened, in hopes her friends had arrived to release her. A conversation passed by her as her classmates walked to their seats.

"No one's seen him," whispered one.

"Where could he have gone?" questioned another.

"Who?" a third voice asked.

"Galacia. Tychon Alastor."

He's right here. In my eyes, in my ears. He's haunting me.

The space in front of her snapped against the force of books piling onto the table. She glanced up, with a stiffness still in her neck, to see Adair and Haiwrin smiling at her and then walking around the table to take their seats. No nerves shaking their hands, no patchy sleep drawing the dark from their eyelids. They didn't know what happened. It was just another day.

"You know if we want to assume the worst," Haiwrin began, and with the smirk on his lips, this could go anywhere between two extremes, "Adraredon is perfect grounds to murder someone. In the middle of nowhere, huge area, many places to hide someone or get rid of someone—"

Veaer squeezed her knees under the table and held her breath. Her bones locked in place, like guilt tunnelling through the marrow and leaving her helpless. Her eyes flickered to Adair, in hope that she wouldn't see the worry and secrets behind her eyes, but perhaps a call for help in such a sensitive topic.

"Hai, we shouldn't say that about our classmates." Adair's gaze briefly moved to Veaer before going back to Haiwrin, acknowledging her silent request. "At least, that's what you're implying. We should hope for the best instead."

The two fixed up their mess of books that toppled over, continuing their conversation. Adair propped her chin in her palm though Haiwrin took out a book of puzzles and started completing them. They spoke of theories as to what happened this time, a similar thought experiment to Veaer's own around an investigation Tychon may have gotten himself lost in. Haiwrin suggested, alternatively, that Tychon could be looking into someone else's murder case and that'd take up so much time. Adair mumbled about trying to find Tychon, lest he got caught up with the wrong people and got hurt himself.

"I'm not asking you to find me, you don't have to."

Veaer sighed and forced herself to shift her attention, at least something to break her away from these bounds she found herself in. She hooked a hand over Adair's thigh under the table and faced the open door and watched more classmates file into the room.

But across the hall, the few students that Elise usually wrapped herself in were on their own. In the sunlight and without being huddled in a circle, they looked like any other student, neat uniform, styled hair, a few accessories to define their individuality, but she'd never seen them as outgoing or even speak above a whisper—*apart from that one-time last Friday*. Without Elise's presence, it was as if they had always been this way.

"Maybe the two are wagging together. Lover's getaway." Haiwrin closed his book and got up to step around the table, positioning his head next to Veaer's. "She's not in class either."

Adair's smooth skin slipped away as the cat caemi moved back and Veaer tucked her hands together. "She could've gone before them? Or just a little late?" Adair's head joined on the other side, and now the three of them were staring out the door.

Before they could theorise anymore, another student stepped into the frame, immediately ripping their attention just with his appearance. His uniform was especially dedicated to his role as a student council member, his blazer an intricate mix of gold and red, instead of black, with embroidered hems and a white band around his right bicep with the school's insignia. His blonde hair was brushed and gelled back and usually Veaer thought that style silly on teenagers, especially for school instead of a formal event, but he pulled it off well enough that she could admit it.

Izot Excava walked into their classroom, his shoes clicking against the wooden floor planks, and his Vice President, Harquin Carrash, in a similar getup except with his dark skin and curly hair complimenting his deep red jacket rather than contrasting, followed closely behind with his cane.

The classroom immediately fell into silence, but it was obvious by the buzz in the air that it was not out of fear, but respect and admiration. Veaer didn't quite subscribe to the idea of his boyish charm, but she could understand why he had such a following. Conventionally gorgeous, talented, and a leader.

"Attention senior class 12B," Harq began, straightening a few papers against the desk at the front, and the teacher, who Veaer hadn't realised entered the room, stepped to the side.

Izot took over, maintaining steady eye contact with the entire class, "As student council representatives, we are notifying classes that Tychon Alastor Galacia of senior class 12B has been declared missing by the headmaster, and that he will be reported as missing and to be investigated to the authorities in twenty-four hours."

Murmurs rippled through the room and for good reason. Their beloved diviner and tarot reader hadn't been reported missing before.

Veaer shifted her hands and held the hem of her blazer tightly, trying to regulate her breathing. She wasn't close enough to Tychon to garner such a dramatic reaction about him being missing. *1, 2, 3, 4.*

"Not if you're only going to compare me to Izot."

Her gaze bore into the golden boy at the front of the room, scrutinising him. Yes, Izot was the older brother of Elise, despite them sharing a year level. Elise started her education at the same time due to her birthday being earlier in the year.

But what comparisons were there to be made between Tychon and Izot?

"We do not advise that you go searching for your classmate, as this may be dangerous." Izot nodded towards the class, and a few others nodded in return. Veaer noted his charming nature, in the words he chose to use and in his mannerisms. "But if you do have any information on the whereabouts of Galacia, or even any clues to the places he would go, please notify Harq, myself, or any other student council member. Ideally, he is found safe and sound by this afternoon."

That's not going to happen.

Veaer didn't know whether that was her own thought or the apparition of Tychon running circles around her. She also didn't know if that was about any information getting back to the council's ears or finding Tychon today.

All she knew was that Adair was staring at her for some reason, and she wondered if she let her face express something it shouldn't have, in which it wouldn't be the first time.

Izot continued with other general announcements before taking his leave and the room burst into conversation before their homeroom teacher caught their attention and quickly summarised what was said. The entire time Adair kept looking at her and she couldn't read the thoughts behind her almost unmoving eyes. A slight twitch here and there, a blink naturally. But nothing came to mind. It was as if Tychon had taken her mind and ran away with it.

Finally, once they were dismissed for their morning classes, Adair spoke, "This all seems too strange. He wouldn't go so long without telling anyone."

Veaer sighed, relieved, but passed it off as a cough to the side. Then she straightened her blazer and stood up, her chair making an ugly sound as it scraped against the floor. "Well, someone must know. Maybe they just haven't told anyone. None of us are really friends of his."

"Who, like Elise? But she's not here either. Maybe something happened to both of them." Haiwrin rubbed his chin as he picked up his satchel and tossed a couple books in there.

"I thought the story was that they were having their getaway." Adair stood beside her twin and raised her eyebrows at him.

"Let me be creative. It's what I do."

The twins bantered and an ache settled in Veaer's heart. He was gone. And they were joking. There were no jokes to make or anything to say or anywhere to look that would bring the boy back. And even now, while he was left somewhere on the grounds, he would not be remembered as he should be until they reported him missing to authorities, then launched an investigation, then pronounced it a murder case. And either Elise didn't care about the consequences, or she was ready to clear herself as suspect.

She took a deep breath of fresh air as she went over the bridge that connected the learning centre and the fitness complex. It wasn't like the twins knew Tychon was gone, and their jokes were only a form of coping with the idea that a classmate of theirs could have had something much worse than a lover's getaway happen to him.

The gnawing guilt flooded in, making her limbs stumble and her hands shake. Her mind raced and her attention flickered here and there, in and out of reality. She had to rely on her muscle memory to get herself to the changing room.

What if someone came up to her and said to her face that they knew what she saw? That they knew Veaer for what she really was. What if her stall opened this instant and not only would she be left physically bare but mentally bare, her classmates peeling her head away to reveal things she shouldn't have witnessed etched into the mounds of her brain.

Best and worst of all, they would know her most sickening secret. Not that she watched Elise do it, not that she did nothing to stop it, not that the ghost of Tychon was following her around like a piece of tape stuck to one's clothes and gone unseen. No.

They would know that Veaer would never tell anyone what happened. That Veaer felt a protective urge so strong that she would cover her eyes and claim to have never left to chase after Elise that day and watch her take the knife and commit the deed. And it reeled her guts and tossed her around in her own mind to know that she wanted to see the light flash in Elise's eyes at knowing Veaer knew all along but didn't do anything about it. It would be the two of them, together, against the world. Crossing paths and destined to stay.

CHAPTER 7
IZOT EXCAVA

Year 1, Semester 1, Week 12

As much as she didn't want to, she knew meeting Izot Excava was inevitable.

The boy was like a burning ball of fire that one couldn't stare at for long unless they wanted to sear their eyes out of their face. He strutted through the academy like a celebrity, with a perfect smile of white teeth and an everlasting entourage.

He was in the same freshman cohort as Veaer, but on a completely different level in many ways. A national fencing champion, an up and coming leader, and within the top ten students who excelled in a prestigious entrance exam at another academy, that he did just for fun. Of course, he didn't take that offer. Why wouldn't he attend the senior school that his father headed, becoming the richest, most popular, and most powerful student here?

As bright as a star, as judgemental as anything.

He stared Veaer down as she sat in the headmaster's office after being caught in the faculty room looking for gods-know-what. While the headmaster was in the chair, Izot was just as intimidating. It was a unanimous idea that Izot held even more power than the teachers themselves.

"No friends, poor taste in uniform, breaking into rooms you shouldn't be in. What are you doing, Miss Rosell?" Izot grinned and shook his head. "*What are you doing at Adraredon Academy?*" Izot probably meant to ask. "*What are you doing in my school?*"

Veaer opened her mouth, a sting piercing her heart. "I don't need—"

The headmaster lifted a hand and gave Izot a sideways glance that slightly chipped his facade. He remained silent for the rest of the time while the headmaster explained that Veaer's scholarship depended on good behaviour and great academic performance. He believed in her.

Veaer didn't know if she believed that. Especially when Izot grabbed her shoulder after they left the office and then didn't say a word. He stood there, keeping Veaer in place, like a message and a promise.

Maybe it would be smart to make a friend, so she could protect herself from the likes of the Excava family.

CHAPTER 8
A MATCH OF GREAT
EXPECTATIONS

Year 3, Semester 1, Week 9

Veaer walked the path between the changing rooms and the gym to find it empty. Perhaps she had spent too much time looking at her reflection while everyone around her headed out. She couldn't blame Tychon's ghost for tardiness, or for how long she had tried to search for the spirit in the mirror.

And then she saw Elise Excava standing by a window dressed for the same class, without a care of the time or a semblance of urgency.

Saliva built on Veaer's tongue and her throat closed up. Her feet were like a rubber band, unsure whether to keep going or not. Her mind was drawn in all directions and she committed to none of them.

Mian above, she is beautiful. Let her beauty stay eternal, even if you make her a statue right this moment it would be venerated for years and polished for all to bow to.

Get out, get out, get out.

Run away, run away, run away.

1, 2, 3, 4. 1, 2, 3, 4.

She's going to hurt me, she's going to hurt me, she's going to hurt me.

Ty—

"—chon," she finished the name aloud, stopping right next to Elise with anxiety gripping her knees and lips. She feared that her foolish tongue revealed her thoughts and everything they carried, but Elise simply continued to watch the window.

A mix of white and purple butterflies fluttered about, particularly drawn to the one window Elise concentrated her attention to. They neither got too close nor flew away.

"Rosell," Elise responded and her head slightly tilted to the right. "You're late for class." Today her hair was tied in a high ponytail and Veaer noticed a purple scrunchie holding it up as it slightly bounced.

"I wonder... I wonder what happened to Tychon Alastor," Veaer rasped out, thinking at any moment Elise could turn around and grab her and pop her like a balloon for knowing what happened and deceiving her. And it would be pain and joy all in one to be held that way.

Then she turned around and Veaer restrained from flinching even while her bones screamed. *I'm in control. There's no need to show fear. In the face of the unknown, I will pry it out of the darkness and understand.* The princess' eyes dropped to her feet and she tapped the nose of one of her shoes to the wooden floor. Then she looked up again, her eyes fixing on Veaer's face. Her lips became a thin line on her golden face. "You tell me when you figure it out."

And she took one last look at the butterflies before walking the rest of the way to class.

~

"What better way to learn than to watch the sport play out?"

Veaer slammed the gym door open as Izot finished a spiel, not intending to bring so much force to it. But the determination to dig even deeper into the mess she was in created an undeniable ambition within her, especially with Izot standing at the front of the class, a class that wasn't his, and she could sense confusion and worry radiating off Elise who came in behind her.

Izot cleared his throat at the interruption though his expression softened at the appearance of Elise. He didn't have any apparent ill wishes for his sister but this was based on limited observation and didn't consider his habit of self-preservation as student president.

"Oh, how wonderful for you to join us!" Izot smiled and clapped his hands, though Veaer had trouble knowing if it were a genuine statement or a sarcastic one. He was much cheerier than this morning's announcements and that made sense when Veaer spotted a fencing weapons rack close by a piste mat typically laid out for fencing matches. "It appears we have our first two volunteers." His smile widened in a similar way to Haiwrin and Adair's when they were up to no good.

"I think you're greatly mistaken," Veaer snapped, accepting that she could see him as aesthetically pleasing but never desire to get along. It had been this way since she enrolled, but she was never reprimanded for any underhand remarks. He preferred to play the facilitator rather than the punisher. She looked away from the expression of the young man as she joined the group of students.

"Now, now... we don't have to be afraid. There is a lot to discuss with an experienced fencer going up against a novice. You can create an example." Izot stepped to the weapons rack and took a foil from it.

With no retort from Elise at all, who silently went to the bench and picked up a helmet and fencing armour before grabbing a foil from the rack—ignoring when Izot tried to pass the one in his hands —Veaer had no choice but to follow suit.

As herself and Elise passed their classmates, she picked up whispers of condolences about Tychon being missing and hoping that Elise was alright, but deep inside Veaer knew that this act was only in the presence of the prince. They didn't really care about Tychon, not as much as Elise may have, and not as much as Veaer did now. Elise's expression was impossible to see through the mask as she pocketed the scrunchie, and she hardly turned or lifted a finger in their direction.

Izot settled just behind the centre line of the piste and Veaer lined her feet on her en-garde line. Elise stood on the right of Izot at her own line.

The helmet fit well and the armour was comfortable. She could still move with enough balance for her confidence to stabilise. She weighed the foil in her hand. The only thing she knew to do was get to know her tools, and after that her opponent. But with Elise knowing many years of experience, like her brother, and this being Veaer's first time standing on a piste, this would prove harder than she wanted.

Through the mesh mask, she locked her gaze on Elise, and something ached in her chest. Her hand tightened around the hilt. In that moment, she felt as vulnerable as ever, ready to crumple in fear of Elise's ability. How Elise had changed the world in a day.

"En-garde," Izot announced.

Elise slightly bent her knees, and Veaer did the same.

"That reveals nothing of what you're doing," Elise's voice echoed. *No, it didn't. It doesn't explain anything, nothing at all!*

"Pret."

Her empty hand quivered in anticipation.

"I don't even want to hear his name!" Patrons above, what did Izot do?

"Allez!"

The princess bounced on her feet with the foil held in front of her. Her hand was steady, and her wrist gently flicked from side to side, waiting for an attack.

Veaer's feet remained in place, as if stuck to the mat, only knowing that she had to defend against any lunges that came her way. The distance between each en-garde line was too far to score without making a move. She tried to focus on something but between the moving feet, swaying foil, and every gaze around her, she ended up on Elise's faceless mask.

"You thought I wasn't going to find you today?"

Elise went for a thrust, aiming for her chest. She tried to move back in response but her feet were far too fixed to move quickly without tripping. In an attempt to save herself, she swung her foil but it hardly bounced off Elise's as the point touched her chest and Izot lifted his right hand.

"You know I always will."

"A point to Elise. Does anyone know what went wrong there?" he called to the class, only for the students to mumble among themselves. With no one raising their hand to answer, Izot continued, "Veaer wasn't mobile enough to defend herself and was quick to flail at first attack. Common for beginners. Do note how Elise was bouncing on her feet and did not have her heel to the mat. You must be ready to lunge and leap back with a second's notice."

Veaer puffed her cheeks out and turned away, even if her class couldn't see her face. Beneath the mask she was sneering at herself, for letting her thoughts remove her. *I'm in class on Tuesday morning. I'm fencing as an example with a classmate of mine ... that classmate is Elise Excava. Elise, Elise, Elise. She stabbed her best friend. She—*

It was her first try, and she knew she could do better. The fortunate part of Izot's commentary was that each time they played for point, she would have something new to adjust and another chance to win.

I'll prove to her that I'm worthy. I'll show her how much her attention deserves to be on me—I'll split you apart and drink you whole and figure out every secret, every why and how and who and where and what and when.

She whipped around again, so fast that when she faced the students, they became a blur, blending into the walls. She had to use the space she had to her advantage. The mat wasn't fourteen metres long for nothing.

This time she slightly bent her knees as soon as she aligned herself, tightly holding her foil and awaiting the referee's signal. This was the best of five, she knew that much—that required three winning points.

"En-garde, prêt... allez!"

She bounced on her toes, wary for any sudden movements. She attuned to the way Elise moved, every limb, every twitch of her head, every swing of her wrist. A second later, Veaer advanced and beat their foils a few times, almost a rhythm developing at each tap. Each beat meant that Elise was forced to respond and realign her foil. If she timed it correctly then...

In a split second as Elise went for another beat, Veaer lunged forward, being sure to keep her weapon extended to create room for herself. While she was fresh to fencing, she knew well enough to not bring her weapon back onto herself. That risked a self-score, if there were such a thing, but more importantly an opening for her opponent.

Tell me Elise, tell me everything. How does this go? We dance and swing and I spin you around, and you'll fall into my arms. I'll catch you and you will only have me to tell.

Keeping light on her feet, she continued to push. She had to figure out a creative way to get through the princess' guard. She was against a fencer first and a murderer second. Elise knew her way around a blade. This wouldn't be a matter of practise if Veaer had her way, but a matter of outsmarting.

It was only a moment's difference as Elise thrusted back with intent and Veaer failed to keep a steady grip on her foil. The point touched Veaer's belly and Izot raised his right hand again. Another thing to amend. Another chance.

"A longer bout, but our novice didn't quite make it once again. While she established a lead, she couldn't follow through, allowing Elise to attack and score. It can be quite difficult to get used to fencing at first—your mind is focused on the movements and strategy of the other person while also working out your own."

This was no issue, she would persevere.

"En-garde, prêt... allez!"

They were off again, but Veaer was quite eager to break passivity as she advanced forward and parried the beats coming from Elise. With her more aggressive approach right off the bat, she could hear a few grunts from Elise's mask. Yes, something to reveal her human nature. That she wasn't invincible and unbreakable. A smirk tugged at the corner of Veaer's lips.

I need to understand Elise, I need to know more.

It seemed the princess relied on beating foils rather than pushy starts to almost train her opponent into vulnerability. Veaer wouldn't give her the chance and pushed Elise to the edge of the piste, metal clashing against metal.

I'm constantly running just to catch up.

Deliberate and with little care, Veaer straightened up and yelled incoherently at Elise, a battle cry ringing through the gym. Based on the slight shiver and flinch coming from the faceless mask and white suit, she had successfully shaken Elise with the sudden burst.

Veaer stepped back and created unexpected space between them and Elise then rushed forward, taking it as a chance to attack. But Veaer was ready to create right of way with a slashing motion to beat the incoming foil aside and touch the point of her foil right to Elise's chest.

The princess dropped her weapon with a clatter, further adding to the unexpected choir of noises condensed in the student spectators. Even Izot was too stunned to declare the winner.

Veaer's foil point lifted and dropped with each heavy breath coming from the princess. She tried to squint through the mesh to find Elise's face, those eyes and those lips in an attempt to read something from them, to show her an answer.

I realise, now, that I have only come to know so little about you. Why did you hurt your friend in a way so natural to your movements?

Seconds passed and Izot finally raised his left hand. "Veaer wins the point! Two to one in Elise's favour." He clapped his hands, short and twice. "The novice had taken a different approach. She established dominance from the start of the match by disallowing any passive time. Perhaps she has warmed up and is now forming her strategy unlike her losing bouts."

If she scored the next point, they would be tied.

We will not be equal until I have you at my disposal. Your mind is an entire landscape for me to explore.

"En-garde, prêt, allez!"

Veaer didn't want to fall into error due to being predictable, and so she let passivity blanket them for a few seconds longer than last time. It didn't take long for the beating to begin but then they quickly transformed into attacks that Veaer had to parry.

She pushed on Elise' blade and threatened a touch on her. While it wavered Elise's movement and her feet bounced in place, it wasn't enough to guide them back to the centre of the map.

What was Tychon doing there? What was that ritual? What was he hiding from you?

With little room to work with, she went with her next attack strategy. She waited for her opponent to make a move, then she parried the blade a few times. Timing it finely, she disengaged, surprising Elise, and dipped low to the ground to score a point on Elise's stomach.

The adrenaline was pumping now as Izot lifted his left hand and even cheered for Veaer. She gasped and grinned and pride welled up in her chest.

"A point to Veaer! While Elise managed to back her up on the strip, she was able to recover by going for an attack that would once again throw her experienced opponent off. A parry or two short from what you'd expect a full exchange to be, turned to a disengagement that allowed an opening from a touch below!"

The air buzzed with intrigue and Veaer felt like she could float away with all the excitement radiating from the class. But what really mattered was the girl she was facing. If she could see how much Veaer was willing to *try*.

The next match started in an instant and it was their fastest start yet. The two advanced towards each other—Elise with precision and Veaer with confidence. They were both light on their feet, the foils an extension of their arms. Blade against blade, fencer against fencer.

A slash here, a thrust there. If there was something she could grasp from this exchange with a silent opponent, it was that fencing was a great way to know more about another person. The way they approached a bout, from their first match to their last point, can reveal impatience, restraint, decisiveness, and the mindset they brought to the game.

It could reveal how afraid you were and right now neither of them was afraid.

"This is for me and—"

And who! I want to wind myself into the fabric you fell upon, Tychon, just to know what you were going to say. Who else is part of this? "Me and you"? A declaration to Elise? Or perhaps something more sinister?

Elise recovered flawlessly from another attempt to score against her. Veaer could only assume the princess' habit of beating the foils together came from her brother, who showed off a talent for aggravation when he wasn't being the charming student president.

What Elise lacked in force, she made up with speed. Veaer was strong but lacked the same speed. She used tactics that made up for her lack of practise. She revised her past mistakes and retried with another extreme.

It was no one's piste, their fight remaining within the centre and the spectators only shifted closer and closer. A flutter of excitement took over her arms and she needed to shout or shake or stomp or something right this moment to let it out. Elise staggered, becoming worn, but the two continued.

You've planted these seeds, these questions in my mind, Elise. And my mind will spill upon the walls and everyone here if I don't get answers soon. I will not stop until I know.

Veaer advanced and Elise parried, but weaker than usual. She didn't blame her—her own arms growing heavy. The trained fencer would have lasting stamina, that was one area they couldn't compete in. If she wanted to win, she'd need to make her move now.

She parried once, then twice, more heat, more clashing, more pushing. If she continued to strategise, continued to outsmart, continued to use her mind—she would get anything she wanted. She has done it before and she will do it again.

Elise—I, Veaer Rosell, declare this school is our kingdom, this match the last where we are opponents, and Tychon our fallen knight who will bring us together in solidarity. I will make you my queen,

Elise Excava. And when I call you mine, I will have every answer I will ever need.

A slashing motion to misalign their foils before she disengaged, dipped down and—

Both of their points had touched the opposite's chest with barely seconds between to tell them apart. By the time they stilled, and the clanging of metal ceased, no one knew what to say.

Until: Izot lifted his right arm and announced, "The final point goes to Elise!"

No one moved or said anything else until Izot started clapping and a staggered applause followed from the class.

Veaer watched the student standing in front of her take off her mask and catch her breath. Her hair was layered with sweat and her cheeks were a beautiful deep shade of red. The world moved slower and Veaer found herself watching each step taken towards the weapons rack, each movement as the foil was gently nudged back into place.

When Elise turned on her feet and marched up to Veaer, she didn't know what to do with herself.

She opted to remove her helmet too, her hair damp and stringy, and they met at eye level. Those swirling pools of hazel with a flash of gold caught her breath.

"Better luck next time, Rosell." She could see and hear the smile with that post-game remark and she engraved that image into her mind.

"Yes, next time." And Veaer raised her foil with a nod and a smirk.

CHAPTER 9
A REQUEST OF HORRID PROPORTIONS

Her veins coursed with euphoria and fear and pride and shame.

"I tell you what matters."

Veaer clutched the sides of the changing room basin and stared at her reflection in the mirror as the tap ran at full force and water rebounded against the ceramic bowl. This time she wasn't looking for the ghost—she knew it was there—she was looking for clarity in her eyes.

It's only a matter of time until she needs more of me.

She's going to hurt me if she gets too close.

Elise saw me as a worthy opponent.

How could I be capable of holding this burden of hers? What can I even do to help her if I only get distracted and sink back into my thoughts?

She was floating in a space without an up or down and her eyelids fluttered with no commitment. Nothing could be proven real even with a touch; it was all just another prop to fuel her disorientation. Her head was heavy, but her heart was light. Her knees were like jelly, but her hands were numb.

1, 2, 3, 4. The bell is going to ring any moment now and I'm stuck here.

Water spilled over the basin and drenched her shoes, and she scrambled backwards while attempting to turn the tap off at the same time. Her shoulder strained in a sharp pain, and she slipped on the tile floor, hitting her knees against the wall under the sink as her arms were buried in the basin to catch her.

"Shit..." she hissed to herself, unsure whether to focus on the injury in her shoulder, knees, or dignity. If only she had her magic to ease the pain all over her body and deep in her mind, affinity shuttered away by the academy's restrictions.

The water had time to drain from the sink and floor, and this time she only let a small stream of water out. Anything to take away the bright red cheeks of heat and embarrassment and anything to bring her back to this reality.

She shut her eyes and bent over the sink, basking in the coolness of the water, and believed for a moment that this chaos would pass. School was operating as usual, and it was her own doing that she kept mentally lashing out.

When she turned off the tap, opened her eyes, and stood up, Elise was standing behind her in the mirror.

Before Veaer could even react or verbally acknowledge her presence, Elise stepped closer, staring at their reflections, and placed a hand on Veaer's shoulder, her fingers lightly playing with silver strands of hair.

"Your fight was quite impressive today, for someone who hasn't fenced before," Elise began, with no introduction, no reason as to why she wasn't heading to class. "Tell me, what was your strategy?"

Veaer gulped and pushed down her flurry of unhelpful thoughts. She could only concentrate on the way Elise's soft fingers ran through her hair and scratched her neck. The way she could really see Elise's makeup with little eyeliner butterflies on her cheeks, blush surrounding them, and freckles made more prominent with a brown tone.

Gods above, is this another ghost? Am I losing my mind?

Her eyes fluttered shut again and she wondered, perhaps, if she needed more sleep.

Then a distinct snipping noise snapped her to a more diligent state, and she flinched this time, only to meet Elise's confused expression in the reflection and nothing other than their breaths and beating hearts. Maybe it was a sign from Tychon to get it together.

Veaer played with the response on her lips before releasing it. "I get to know things as much as I can and use that information to my advantage. By feeling the foil, I could work out how I would have to balance it, and then it was a matter of practical application. As my opponent, I could read your body language and movements, even as we moved through bouts. I knew the space we were in and how I needed to use it. I also implemented personality." She cut herself short there.

The princess paused her hand in the middle of Veaer's hair and she thought for a moment that Elise could easily grab it in her fist and throw her against the wall or sink because she knew what Veaer knew. But then she resumed, quietly humming, and then replying, "Interesting. Interesting mind."

They stayed like that for a few minutes, even after the bell rang. One student was missing, what was another two? And Veaer saw the mirror as a canvas and wondered what it would be like to paint Elise. Would that painting be tainted by sharp edges and red when Elise was so blue and brown and green, soft and plump and not at all dangerous at first glance?

"I would like to commission you," Elise said and broke the silence, now bringing confusion to Veaer's face.

A commission? "What sort?"

"I've seen your work... the kind that involves you breaking into the fourth and fifth floor of Miriam Manor despite the barriers and lack of permission. The kind that sees the way your mind is always working. The kind that makes you flexible and quick." Elise let go of Veaer's hair and stepped away, now pacing the changing room, awaiting a response.

A part of her was screaming and shaking and waving her hands about in excitement and thrill. A job for Elise, and one she was personally approached for. One where Elise had been watching her and remembering. She had half a mind to accept on the spot, but she knew she had to practise her rationality.

"And what are the details of this commission?" Veaer asked smoothly, only revealing her bubbling feelings in the way she tapped her fingertips along her thighs while watching Elise in the mirror.

"I will pay you—" She wouldn't need money to sell this proposition, but it was always a nice inclusion. "—to break into Tychon's room and gather a few items for me, before students show up, after the room is sealed off by authorities."

Veaer stilled, everything stilled. And she became very aware of Tychon's presence around them, floating in the mirror and staring directly into her soul.

"Don't do it, Veaer," the ghost says.

New words. He didn't say this yesterday. He's speaking to me, and he means it.

"It's not your place to be there."

"What do you need in Tychon's room?"

An innocent question, a detail of the commission. And quite possibly an effort to confirm that Elise shared the same goal as her— find out what Tychon was doing in the cathedral, why and for who.

"A journal, maybe. Any notes. I want hints, to figure out where he went." Elise inched closer to the exit and Veaer was frightened for a moment that the princess was going to slip away, but then she paused. "I'm worried about my best friend."

There was something chilling in that sentence that caused her fingers to freeze. She took a deep breath in and looked away from the mirror to watch Elise's back with her own eyes.

A journal and notes very well could reveal what Tychon was doing. Clearly Elise had found something yesterday under his desk as well, something that told her that he was in the cathedral. There had to be more.

"Why the specific time frame?" She needed to get as much out of this briefing as she could before the answers were locked away.

"You like asking questions," Elise noted, and turned her head only for a moment to reveal an arched eyebrow before she went back to being entirely too interested in the walls. "Complete the task before students show up because I don't need everyone seeing what I'm doing. My brother already said not to go looking for him. After authorities lock the room up... I can also say that students will be disobeying Izot and hanging out around his room with the same idea."

"And what's to say they won't find his belongings first?"

A few moments of silence passed and Veaer wrung her hands together. Elise showed no move towards answering, with her shoulders lifting slightly as the only sign she was still breathing.

Finally, Elise took a deep breath and spun around with a smile. Veaer didn't spend time on the details of that expression, for it instilled fear in her and that's all she had to know.

"I know my Tychon is very good at hiding things."

CHAPTER 10
BEING IN PLACES YOU
SHOULDN'T BE

I zot returned the next morning to notify the class that Tychon was officially declared missing.

Veaer distracted herself with folio requirements and upcoming essays, scouring her syllabus that she'd already memorised. In the next class, her professor droned on about alternate art forms and how universities would expect a unique project to really shine for the admission officers. It was something more productive to focus on than ghosts and feathers.

She sat back in her chair after a lengthy reminder about compositing spreads and avoiding cliches, but her shoulders did anything but relax as her gaze fluttered over to Elise who sat a few seats away from her. And it wasn't only the commission that shook her nerves and made her count each second until class was over, but that Elise went out of her way to move her classes within a day so she would be in the same Art 5 class as her. To be there when Veaer went on break, to be here because Veaer didn't give her an answer yesterday.

Her hand hovered over a paintbrush, and she stared at the threads of her canvas. It was blank except for staining she had done last lesson. Raw umber formed a neutral and universal stain, in this case helping as she hadn't taken the time to decide what she would paint next. All that appeared in her mind were butterflies. The ones on Elise's wall, the ones outside the window Elise stared at. And red admiral butterflies.

She wasn't proud to have not given an answer to Elise already. It may have been her only path towards getting to know Elise more. Now she only imagined Elise would be surrounded by concerned students because Tychon really was missing now, and slowly their interactions and any hold she had on Elise would fade.

Even yet, unyielding pride stuck to her chest, that she had proven herself to Elise enough for her to have gone to her for help. Elise knew that someone with magical caemi abilities who already showed they could get from the ground floor to the top was a much better contender than anyone else to break and enter a restricted room.

Half of the details were in place now. After authorities, before students. Fifth period, the one straight after lunch, would be optimal to complete the task. She couldn't do it now as others would notice her leaving, and not during lunch as some students went back to the dorms to spend time. Just before they had to go back to class, she would be able to linger around the manor and then make her way up as students left. She would be done halfway through fifth period and still make it to class without being seen in Tychon's room.

She knew what side of the building Tychon's room was, and she already plotted an upwards climb. If the window was locked, she would bring a putty knife to wedge through and break the lock.

The other half of the requirement was her taking the job. The fact that she already had a plan spoke plainly and clearly, but admittance wasn't easy, not when it could've been out of intimidation with each glance Elise sent her.

Ever since Veaer enrolled at Adraredon, she committed herself to making choices rooted in her personal reasoning and motivation. She didn't need others to guide her and when she was left at the gates, she was ready to spend the next three years on her own.

She chose her own stream, she chose what she spent time and energy on, and she made it her resolution to find out as much as she could about the things she loved because then she would have the knowledge and from knowledge came power.

Haiwrin and Adair became exceptions in her promise. They had weaved her in a web with their easy conversations and charming empathy. They always had a way to include Veaer in projects and hangouts, and with time and familiarity came friendship.

Though she kept to some habits and that included keeping secrets. And that meant those two would never know what was going on between Elise and herself.

And if she continued down this path, it would be because she wanted to, not because she was afraid of Elise.

Veaer sought a life of satisfaction. So when she stood before the wall with Tychon's window on it, picturing herself climbing the vines, bricks and balconies, and grabbing that journal to hand to Elise, she knew that saying no was not an option anymore.

I want to do this. I want to do this.

She closed and opened her fists as she went over the plan again and again.

There is too much to gain here.

"And so much to lose," Tychon says.

She couldn't bring herself to ponder on the risks and instead distracted herself by leaning against a tree as a couple of detectives walked past her. While she kept most of their words away, she did overhear that many students were trying to get to Tychon's room as well, through the door, like normal people.

She knew that Tychon was popular among students for being a diviner, who did tarot readings for others. Even the faculty indulged in the cards and were flexible during class. The cards were always right; a chant that flooded the school.

Elise appeared around the corner, floating like a shadow, and approached Veaer with a bag in one hand.

"Are you ready?" Elise asked, handing the worn bag to Veaer. "To hold the items. I doubt you can climb down easily while holding whatever you find."

Her words were full of assumption. Correct assumption, but nonetheless without inquiring with Veaer first. Perhaps Elise already saw it on her face during Art 5, or when she turned the corner to see Veaer standing in position, just as requested yesterday. Maybe her actions spoke for themselves.

"I'm ready." She looped the straps around her arms and waited for the class bell to ring.

Her hands were caked in dust as she got to her feet on a third-floor balcony. She clapped them together and surveyed the remaining journey, then looked back down to make sure Elise was still there. The princess stood against the tree, in the shade and keeping quiet. Her eyes remained on Veaer but her expression didn't reveal any thoughts. Somehow this felt more like a show than a necessary climb to Tychon's room.

She stood upon the balcony railing and jumped to grab the next ledge she could get her hands on. Then she shuffled across and let her left hand go, temporarily holding her entire body weight by her right hand. This time she wore a short sleeve shirt as to not threaten any rips that would give her a hard time. As much as she loved climbing, she would be happier once her feet were on the carpet in Tychon's room.

Once she got to Tychon's window, she steadied her feet on a narrow edge and tried opening it. It was locked. She slid the putty knife out of skirt pocket. It took a few attempts to stick the knife under the window frame while balancing on the side of the building, but eventually it stuck without her help and so with one hand holding onto the sill, she leaned back and then forced her other hand to push the putty knife further in and snap the lock off. It flew across the room and onto the carpet, and she stilled for a moment, ready to duck if anyone on the other side of the door caught the sound.

No one burst through which gave her permission to lift the window and dive into the room, her arm hitting the floor as she avoided the curios and boxes stacked under the window. With a hiss, she rubbed her shoulder and sat up, eyeing over the room. Even with the window open, everything looked darkened, like the room knew Tychon wasn't going to return.

She stood up, knowing she had three goals:

1. For her sake, get to know Tychon as much as she could, based on his dorm room

2. For Elise's sake, find his journal and anything that would give her answers to "where Tychon is"

3. Do both as soon as possible since the longer she stayed, the higher the risk for someone to walk in on her

A bookshelf to the right of the window was stuffed with books and other decorations like prayer beads, crystals, and candles. A few deity and saint statuettes were placed on the shelves, and she noticed others around the room as well. A group of small ceramic butterflies sat on the bedside table, and she pocketed one with another gaze over the room. If there was any correlation between the cathedral and Tychon, it was that he heavily dipped into religion and spirituality.

She started with the bookshelf for potential ritual books that could be grouped with personal journals too.

She ran her finger across the spines as she read them. Many were old textbooks for different majors in the academy, some were simply fiction novels, and then she came across a set more akin to Tychon's interests. Meditation, tarot cards, energy reading, angels.

Angels?

She hardly knew much about them, but something rang familiar. Perhaps it was the white feathers from that day or some of the winged statues around the room. She slid the book from the shelf and weighed it in her hands. She could only carry a few things in the backpack, so she'd have to keep focused. For now, she placed it on the desk and scoured the rest of the shelf.

Crouching lower, she found a worn leather journal and had hope that this was it, but when she opened it, the pages were full of small sketches of tarot cards, the names of other students at the top, and scribbles of analysis and interpretations. This must have been his tarot journal rather than a personal one. She placed it on top of the book of angels.

On the walls were different tapestries, one a large version of The Magician tarot card, one that seemed to be a full map of the school, and another was a palmistry diagram. To the left of the window was Tychon's bed, made and pristine, and above the headboard was a landscape painting of The Sun and The Moon tarot cards, except the figures on both emerged from their card frames and held each other's hand. She stepped closer and ran her hand along the brush-strokes lightly and then lifted the canvas to see E.E inked on the back.

She dipped to the floor on all fours to look under the bed. There were only so many places his journal could be, and Elise seemed sure that he hid it in his room. She didn't find the journal under there but an index card. There was some writing on it, so she reached out and grabbed it, but didn't have time to read when she heard something fall in the closet. Her limbs locked in place which wasn't ideal for the position she was in. No one else was meant to be in here—she wasn't meant to be in here.

A person, a rat, a detective, a ghost? Tychon's ghost? Telling me to leave, telling me this is a bad idea.

The closets in the manor were big enough for someone to squeeze in if they wanted to, but it wouldn't be very comfortable to stay there for long. If it were just the ghost then everything was fine, but ghosts couldn't really knock things over, could they?

She had to be sure and so she inched towards the door, placing the index card on top of the tarot journal, and continuing forward slow and steady.

The door flew open and someone barrelled towards her, pinning her to the ground and covering her mouth. Veaer stared, wide-eyed, at the student wearing a white full-face mask dressed in painted eyes, so many eyes, on top of her. She had little way to identify this person as a hat covered their hair, and they wore a school uniform just as she did. The only further difference was that this student wore pants rather than a skirt like her.

The mask is such a smart idea...

Her own identity was on full display with her bright silver hair and brownish-red eyes.

Then they spoke, quietly enough that she couldn't tell much about their voice over the thunder of her own heartbeat, "What in Syriphia are you doing here, Veaer?"

You know my name.

Voices from the other side of the door came into focus, talking about if anyone was meant to be in the room or if those guarding had seen anyone come in.

A chill took over Veaer's arms and her breathing became staggered. Whether it was because she was about to be caught or because an entire student was sitting on her didn't matter. Her mouth dried.

1, 2, 3, 4. Tap, tap, tap, tap.

The masked person audibly swallowed and then mumbled, "You need to get out of here. The closet is mine."

Veaer glanced past the person and into the dim wardrobe; Tychon's uniforms and clothing were hung up neatly, boxes and old bed sheets were stacked on the top shelf. A few things were knocked over, the culprit of the noise from earlier likely some empty shoe boxes and—

A stack of vintage books was toppled to the side but in a strange arrangement. As if all of them were stuck together by their front and back covers, not separating even after being kicked over.

Veaer pushed the student off and gunned it for the weird books. The voices outside increased in number, and the student quickly recovered and grabbed her ankle.

"I said the closet is mine!" the person hissed and Veaer kicked her leg up to loosen their grip. She just needed the journal and then she could leave.

She wrapped her hands around the stuck pile of books and shook it, then realising something was knocking around a hollow interior. She ran her hand across every edge to find an opening and the cover at the bottom of the stack snapped open, like a magnet had come loose, and she shoved her hand inside.

She didn't have any time to check what she had taken out and ran for the other two books on the desk. She opened the bag only to find it full of random scrunched up papers and cursed herself for not emptying it first. The bag was turned upside down, then upright, and then stuffed with the three books and index card.

The chime of a keychain—someone was coming inside.

The masked student had disappeared into the closet.

Veaer looped the straps around her arms.

A key was pushed into the lock.

She ran for the window, climbed over the sill, held on tight, and then dropped.

CHAPTER 11

FRIENDSHIP AND
SOMETHING MORE

Year 1, Semester 2, Week 4

Haiwrin Boudreau and Adair Boudreau were the kindest people in the entire world. Veaer declared it so after a week of knowing them.

They offered her snacks when they took too much from the cafeteria, which she associated with great happiness. They brought water to her room in the evenings while she was working away at new projects that were scattered across her carpet. They sat on either side of her during homeroom and wouldn't let her move after her first, and final, attempt at changing seats.

She liked the twins, and they were caemi people just like her. Solidarity in this academic world where they couldn't really tell caemi apart from senti unless they actually told each other.

One day when they arranged to meet her after classes at Haiwrin's favourite theatre on campus, she gave them flowers. She made a loud and dramatic show of friendship, using the stage that enabled her gesture.

Though it didn't take long for Haiwrin to start having rehearsals when they would usually meet, so Veaer and Adair spent their time alone, learning about art and literature for their respective majors and, one day, deciding that the swirling heat in their chests and poorly-hidden, frequent glances towards each other would lead to something a bit more intimate.

CHAPTER 12

THE ADRAREDON LIBRARY

Year 3, Semester 1, Week 9

By the next evening, Elise still hadn't told her what was next.

Veaer sat on her bed as she wrapped gauze around her knee, having scraped it on her way down the side of the building the previous afternoon. It bothered her to have to change it every few hours.

And when she had managed to make her way down to the bottom with the goods in tow, Elise was nowhere to be seen.

Did I do something wrong?

Her gaze hovered to the worn sack on her desk, heavy with the index card and three books. She didn't want to check the hidden book she grabbed without Elise.

But if Elise was going to ignore all her attempts to talk throughout the day, then perhaps she deserved this much for what she had achieved.

Once the gauze was fastened, she tested her leg off the side of the bed and then made her way to her desk. When she opened the bag for the first time since yesterday, she noted two leather bound journals and a hardcover. That was promising.

She stared at the books for a while. *Does Elise already know I failed? Surely a book hidden like that would be something personal.*

The alarm clock by her bed ticked by. It had been around 60 hours since Tychon originally went missing. Soon, this would turn into an abduction or murder case. The true case.

Elise's long silky hair flies with each thrust of the knife and her smile is just as sharp.

Conviction in her eyes, vengeance in her bones.

I can only watch in awe, in disgust, in fear, in admiration.

How can a young girl be so brave? And so cruel?

What is going on? I should leave.

But a laugh rings in my ears from somewhere distant, and she just keeps going as if it doesn't bother her.

If it takes a pain this horrible to be wrapped in her arms like that, maybe I will take it.

Veaer snapped back to reality when a knock sounded at her door. A sheet of paper slipped under her door and that was enough to make her get up and pick it up.

Library. 20 minutes. Key is under the mat.

Short and succinct, right to the point. The thought of Elise drove a bolt of heat to her cheeks yet an image of the masked intruder took hold of her. Whether this instruction was delivered by Elise, or the mysterious student had found her again, she hoped to the gods that it was Elise.

The library at Adraredon Academy was not just a room with half-filled metal shelves and some dingy carpet flooring. It was entirely unlike the one Veaer had at her public schools before getting into Adraredon.

For when she retrieved the small key from under the welcome mat, and used it to unlock the library, those large wooden double doors opened to an arrangement of dark tables with old glass desk lamps surrounding the centre of the complex which housed a raised librarian's counter. Bookshelves took up almost every inch of wall except for the door and a staircase which led to two more floors upwards, and there was enough space in the middle to look straight up to the dome glass roof. The glass wasn't so clear to allow blistering sunlight through during the day though at nighttime, it was transparent enough to see the stars.

Considering how vast the library was and how she was supposed to be in bed, a creeping feeling settled in Veaer's system. She played with the hem of her jacket and thought herself fortunate to have put on her running shoes over her school loafers in case she had to make a break for it—she thought the same for wearing track pants over her skirt.

She had only seen the library during the day when there were people to occupy it. Not when anything could jump out of the darkness at any moment and take her away. There was nothing to even signify that Elise was even here yet. Or was someone else expecting her?

"You came."

Veaer whipped around as she clutched the leather journal tighter. A desk lamp switched on and she noticed Elise sitting at one of the tables by the door, bending over a small specimen frame and using tweezers to gently adjust a butterfly's wings. She was shadows and starlight at once, the warm bulb emitting enough light to recognise the young woman, but the library continued to be shrouded in darkness. Her dark hair was done up in a bun this time and she still wore her uniform but with an Adraredon Academy branded hoodie on top. Even with just this small detail, Veaer held her breath. She hadn't seen Elise casually before, hadn't considered she ever would. But here it was just the two of them and maybe she would be greedy enough to want more.

Veaer ran her tongue between her lips. "You asked me to." It came out more as a question than an answer. Then Veaer continued, in an effort to recover her uncertainty, "At least have the light on before I come in, next time." *But either way your beauty shines. I would paint you onto a dark canvas, and the canvas would be grateful for the light.*

"Imagine if someone else found the key." She held her hand out and lowered her eyes to the book. Her eyelids were still covered in eye shadow.

Veaer pursed her lips and stepped forward. She wanted to draw more words out of Elise, not just simple answers. More than just their short conversations. Or maybe she only spoke more to closer, familiar people—such as Tychon.

Veaer couldn't feel his presence right now.

She wanted to be someone Elise found comfort in sharing with, though she had to be patient and play her cards right. The first move would be handing over the book. She still wanted to know what was inside, and to find out with Elise.

Elise placed it carefully on the table, her hand running up and down the spine, her eyes fixed on the gold writing on the front cover that Veaer didn't notice previously. "Alright, thank you. Just leave the key here on your way out."

No.

That can't be it.

In a flash of irritation, Veaer was glad to have left the other clues in her room, not knowing what was to come from this session, desiring some semblance of control. She was right for not setting expectations, because Elise truly treated this job as just that. If Elise wanted the wares of Veaer's experience and knowledge, she would need to let her in first. They both wanted the same thing, right?

"No." Veaer avoided eye contact with Elise until she walked around the table, pulled out a chair and then took a seat. Then her gaze was all over Elise's confused expression. "We're not done yet."

Elise's lips twitched, like she was about to burst out laughing. She tilted her head. "Well, yes. I asked you to do something for me, and you have done it. Thank you."

"I'm not here just for a thank you." Veaer placed her hand firmly on top of the book and kept her gaze on Elise. She noted how the rays in her eyes disappeared when they weren't in the light.

"Okay, what are you here for then?" Elise asked and Veaer's cheeks flushed. "Oh, right, the money. I can have it wired to your school account so you can purchase what you like on your student card. Or I can hand it to you in cash?"

"No, no, not the money either!" Veaer said all too loud in the empty library. She grumbled and shrunk in her chair. She couldn't bring herself to admit the words now that she was here.

That I want to let someone in.

Or I want them to let me in.

I want to solve this, and it should be with you.

But you're interesting and clever and creative. And I am not very much at all.

"Don't you want someone else to help you with this?" Veaer decided on, but instantly ran through the implications that she was just like so many other students trying to stick their head into this as well. She wasn't just one of the others.

"There is plenty of *help* already." The sarcasm wasn't lost on Veaer. Elise didn't open the journal.

"I mean real help. Someone who absorbs information and thrives in it. Someone who won't stop at anything to get answers. Someone who's going to do more than sit around Tychon's room and wait." As she spoke, her words became smoother and more confident. Her gaze flickered between the journal and Elise. Her hand shifted to the edge of the princess' hand. "Someone as curious as you."

Something in Elise's expression fell away and her mouth moved a few times like words were floating through but never materialising. She closed her eyes and looked away and Veaer thought she might have done something wrong, but the next moment her right hand was being taken into Elise's.

"Your right hand is your dominant hand?" Elise asked, giving her a serious stare.

Veaer blinked and forgot herself in Elise's eyes. Then, when the silence became too much, she answered, "Yes, it is."

Elise turned Veaer's hand, drew lines across her palm and measured Veaer's fingers against her own. The books were like a warm cocoon and the singular lit lamp meant she couldn't look anywhere else but Elise. Not at the stars above, or the pure knowledge that surrounded them, or the darkness that threatened to take them away.

She was afraid that if she did look away, and for too long, that a star would fall from the sky and crash through the glass ceiling, spraying them with shards and they would lose this moment and their future forever.

And then, with a stroke of Elise's finger along the middle of Veaer's palm, a beautiful smile bloomed on the princess' face.

"You're smart. A drawback or an advantage as you find yourself using your mind to get your way with things and people. Your self-motivation is infectious—it can make you a good leader. You consider how others acknowledge you important but at the same time, you keep your feelings so close to you that, in a moment's notice... you're quick-tempered or fast to depress." Elise inhaled and Veaer held still. "You're a planner. You love details. There's something about the way you act... like you would rather ask forgiveness after doing something than permission beforehand. It's the way you counteract planning forever. Being robust is important to you, to have things you're exceptional at, to have many solutions, to observe and indulge. Finally, you say with utmost confidence that you owe everything to yourself. I think you're right." She glanced up, a twinkle in those deep brown eyes. "You are very curious."

Elise removed her hands and the warmth left with them. Veaer shivered and let out a breath slowly and sharply. She soaked in the feeling of emptiness that came before she inhaled.

Elise, Elise.

Patrons above, I want to grab your shoulders and pull you tightly into me. I want to grasp your hair in my hands and see your eyes widen as I bring myself closer. I want to run my hands down your arms and hips and hold you there. I want to press your back against your chair right now and—and...

She exhaled.

"You are magnificent," Veaer whispered, and her heart beat

louder than anything as she crossed her ankles under the table. "That was beautiful." *You are beautiful.* "How did... Is that really just from my palm?"

"You recently turned eighteen, in April, which means that your lines have developed well. Though, lines do change and typically every six months you will notice." Elise was back to looking at the leather-bound book but her face glowed more than Veaer had ever seen. "I read the shape of your hand, the shape of your fingers, how your index and ring finger measure, if your middle finger curves slightly a certain way, any ringed lines under your fingers, your life line, your head line, your line of fortune, if they intersect, affection lines, travel lines..." She used her right hand as a demonstration and traced and pointed at each aspect she listed until she fell silent and dropped her hands, immediately going to open the notebook.

Veaer blinked at the abrupt change. "Why did you stop?" *You speak like music.* "I would love to learn more some time. Maybe I can read your palm."

Elise softly chuckled, suppressing it with the lift of her hand against her lips. "Maybe, someday. But for now, the rest of the world thinks we're sleeping the night away, so why don't we make the most of our time?"

And she turned to the first page.

PART II

"I killed a plant once because I gave
it too much water. Lord, I worry
that love is violence."
—— *José Olivarez, Citizen Illegal*

CHAPTER 13

DIVING FROM A PEAK HIGH ABOVE

"Ah... he loved to encode his belongings," Elise mumbled, picking apart the letters with her eyes. *Loved.* A slip of tense. "Mirrors, mirrors." She reached under the table and pulled out a few sheets of paper from a compartment alongside two pens.

"So why *are* we in the library so late?" Veaer asked as Elise drew W and then a line through it to make two Vs, then B and sliced it horizontally, though it didn't exactly create anything except two short Ds. It was when she did H and gave the paper a confused look that she crossed them out and rewrote the letters with no strikes. "Shouldn't there be some sort of key for this?" Veaer waved her hand vaguely at the page, as if the fog of confusion would part and the message would make itself clear.

"This is how I take back time. There is so much to do during the day, so many people to be around. I wonder if I sit here in the dark, I'll have some sort of epiphany. If not, then I have a few hours to be with me, by myself." *Oh, but now I'm here. We're by ourselves together.*

Before Elise continued scribbling on her scrap paper, she lifted the book and flipped through it, too fast to read anything, but Veaer could see paragraphs of text that looked like the first page—a mess of letters with no obvious system. As her thumb reached the last page, she opened the book to the front again and laid it flat. "And there is a key. It's the mirror. It's how Tychon works."

"Is that how I work?" Tychon makes a snarky remark. He's back.

But just like the fog, I wave him away.

"I'll give it a shot." Veaer took a sheet of paper and a pen. Perhaps the puzzle wasn't only on an individual level with each letter, but something wider.

She wrote the alphabet out, noting there were twenty-six, and made two rows of thirteen so they would align.

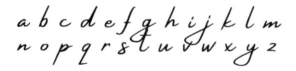

She glanced between the book and her paper and latched onto B and S. If she were to split a mirror down the middle of her letters...

b 8
o f

"Of." Elise leaned closer. Her hair was jasmine scented. "That's a word, and a start." She made quick work of the rest of the sentence, and Veaer sighed in relief at the decoded answer.

JOURNAL OF
TYCHON
ALASTOR
GALACIA

"Wonderful, we have the right book. Where did you find this? In his room of course, but more specifically." Elise was already turning to the next page and decoding sentences.

"It was in this contraption, like a stack of empty books used as a hidden compartment. It fell from his closet when—" She paused and realised Elise was watching her as she recalled what happened. A flash of white, being pinned to the carpet. "I opened the closet door, and it toppled over. Someone, an investigator must have been rummaging through if it was that easy. I thought it was strange how the books all stayed together."

"You're lying."

I'm avoiding unnecessary details.

"Why are you afraid of her knowing?"

"Contraption. Interesting." There was something unspoken in her words.

Veaer needed to do something with her hands, tapping her fingers wasn't enough as she waited for Elise to finish. She was writing before she realised.

e l i s e

r y v f r

"Alright I got this one." Elise lifted her paper and turned to Veaer who used her arms to cover her writing. "It's from a while ago, based on what he wrote. We'll need to go further in." She handed Veaer the paper and swiftly flipped to the middle of the journal.

Why is it always hard to write in a fresh journal?

Today is a good day. I walked into R&M 3 with the boy's uniform on and it felt amazing. I can't believe it took so long for me to do this. I owe it to Elise, she spoke to her father

And the decoding ended there. Religion and Mythology 3. That placed this journal entry to a year ago. She did recall seeing Tychon switch to a male uniform, but at this point she couldn't imagine him without it.

"Next one, still too early," Elise said, keeping her eyes to the pages as she flipped with one hand. The other hand was fitted with a pen to start writing.

> Crows are our friends, that's what my mother told me. That's what my ancestors before my mother told her.
>
> Sometimes I wonder about that, considering they keep trying to swipe my cards. I've asked Elise to add a shield on her balcony. How can she expect me to work under these conditions!

"She never did get around to that. Oh well."

Several pages were skipped and the sound of pen against paper overtook the silence of the library. Veaer's eyelids had grown a little heavy by the time Elise's chair thumped to the floor as she stood up with zeal and shook the paper in her hands. "Yes, yes, yes," she repeated. She only breathed for a few moments and Veaer snapped her gaze to the paper, trying to decipher anything that was going on without ripping it away from the princess. "*Yes,* this is—this is new..." She double-checked by lifting the back portion she had yet to flip through and seemed to mentally note its placement in time. She slapped the paper back on the table before rushing towards a book-shelf in the darkness.

Veaer took the chance to fix the chair, then grabbed the paper to read it.

> The Order of Ascension.
> Creation is our highest form of
> privilege and existence.
> To create is to be alive.
> We love art. We are art.
> Why shouldn't we go further?
> Self-creation — perfect
> creation.
> Most angelic, most divine.
> I have gathered the choir. The
> Tree of Life yields fruit. We
> meet at Heaven's Peak.
> Angeli tecum eant.

"May angels go with you," Tychon whispers.

There were plenty of codewords in this entry that Veaer couldn't place. Self-creation, what did that mean? And where were the connections to angels? A choir, a Tree of Life, Heaven's Peak? Too many things to wrap her head around, too much for this late at night.

Instead, she waited for Elise to return by flipping through the rest of the journal. At face value, she couldn't tell if there was anything useful, until she started seeing Elise's coded name mentioned more and more. On one of the last pages, her name was written in large letters, scratchy and frantic, like he had written her name over and over on top of each other to indent it into the journal.

Her hand ached as it held the bunch of pages.

Potential answers. Potential learnings.

She ripped the pages from the book and stuffed them in her jacket pockets, then forced her shaking hands to the loose papers they'd been deciphering on to tear them apart—to avoid suspicion in the wrong direction; she'd rather her selfish impulse stay in her mind only. She left their latest and most important deciphered message intact. As the last shred of paper hit the table, she sprung up and attached herself to a nearby bookshelf, grabbing aimlessly in the dark for something to occupy herself with, and found a stack of cards held together with a metal ring. Flashcards of bugs and insects.

She shivered, not typically enjoying the crawling, many-legged images, but she flipped through and found the one on butterflies near the back. It was a standard orange and black monarch butterfly, but still mesmerising enough that she wanted it. With a quick opening of the ring, she slipped the butterfly flashcard into her pocket and then placed the cards back into place.

Elise returned with a worn hardcover book as Veaer stuffed her hands in her pockets, trying not to make the crinkling paper obvious, and walked back to their table.

Don't worry about it now, I'll look at them tomorrow. Don't worry about it now, just concentrate on Elise.

The book was dropped on the table and the title read: The Order of Ascension by Brielle Haldar.

Veaer perked up and her eyes widened. A match to the entry.

"I have reason to believe that this Order, his choir that he's gathered, has something to do with his disappearance." *Are you trying to convince yourself, Elise?* "This book, I've never read it, but Tychon and I came across it when we started at Adraredon. In this very library, we sat upstairs and tried to read it, because he was always after something new, spiritual, mythological or theological. But everything was way too dense to me and… it was like I was missing something, as if the writer and every other reader were continuing a conversation but I had only just joined." She opened the contents page.

"Creation, ascension…" Veaer mumbled, leaning forward to read and then glancing towards the decoded entry. Despite knowing the truth, this was too good of an opportunity to pass up. A piece in the grand scheme of things, a clear vision to what Tychon was doing that day, how the actions of others could have led to this very moment, even if it was Elise who took the knife. "They have to be connected."

"And I know they are." Elise briefly glanced at the ripped papers with a pause. Her lips parted and then pursed. Her gaze flitted across Veaer's face. "Such haste to get rid of our evidence. Why is that?"

Veaer drew a breath in and held it as excuses circled her mind. Though, Elise didn't leave room for a reply as she sat back down and flipped to a page in the middle of the book, as if the scraps of paper were nothing of relevance anymore.

The spread displayed drawings and writings on The Tree of Life and Heaven's Peak, not with a lot to understand as much of the page spoke of history and recounts of events, a heavy absence of anything to apply in their situation, but what was most interesting were the two index cards tucked inside.

Just like the one still sitting in my room.

"This is Tychon's handwriting." Elise slid the two cards onto the table. Some sort of equation with fractions was written in blue pen. Ter and Mian, she hated maths. "He must have come back to this book and..." Her fingers picked at her lips as her mind turned gears.

Veaer took a closer look at the numbers, wondering about the correlation between her card and these ones. Did they have different equations? But with that, she felt useless in this situation. Elise was practically doing everything. Veaer didn't know whether to stay or go. Her limbs felt too light and her eyes too heavy. Whenever she shifted to do something, she didn't commit lest it interrupted something, or it wouldn't lead to anything. Was this selfish? To force time spent with Elise, to be another weight, to hide things from Elise?

Everything was too far away, all in the air, spiralling towards the glass dome, too much to grasp or comprehend. The corners of her vision became vague. She shifted in her chair and made herself take a deep breath. She stuck the soles of her shoes to the floor so she couldn't be anything but grounded. Her thoughts floated to the Boudreau twins and how they were sleeping right now. She thought of Adair, how after tonight she needed her company to erase untouchable feelings, an untouchable girl. She thought of Haiwrin, how he always knew the answers to her anxieties of holding onto so much yet nothing at all.

Then new questions appeared like a flash in the dark.

Where do people hide more information? Where do people keep their secrets?

In their minds, in their journals, in bookshelves, closets, under the bed, tapestries...

She blinked, drawing herself out of her mind, and the darkness came back to engulf her. Elise was mumbling to herself but she didn't tune in as fatigue was making its way through her system. Tychon's room would have clues, and she had already been there. Tychon likes puzzles and riddles, what about a quest?

The map of Adraredon Academy was put up on the left wall of his room, above his bed. The Magician was on the opposite side of the room, above the desk. One hand pointed to the Heavens, one hand pointed to Hell.

As above, so below.

Below the bed was the index card. Haphazard mess, or purposeful placement?

Above the bed was the map. Convenient, or just like the mirror to the letters?

A map meant coordinates. Coordinates meant numbers.

Numbers, she had numbers.

Three sets of numbers. Why the equations? He liked his coding.

Map and coordinates meant a location.

We meet at Heaven's Peak.

That was a location.

"We need a map." Veaer stood up and scooped up the index cards. "Like in Tychon's room, do you know the one?"

"Yes, large, sepia tone, bird's eye view of the school. Why do we need a map?" Elise closed the hardcover book and Tychon's journal.

"These are coordinates." She gestured to Elise with the index cards. "We can find Heaven's Peak."

"What has you so sure? We haven't worked them out to know if it could produce a coordinate."

I'm not sure.

"But I am."

"These belong to Tychon and if he's hidden something in that book, then it must be related to his journal entry. The only thing I gather is location. I don't see how it has anything to do with art or other people, this 'choir'. The closest thing they replicate are coordinates. Heaven's Peak... if his choir has met there, they may have left something behind. If they continue to meet there despite his absence... our questions will be answered." The rest of her deduction remained stuck in her throat. Her analysis of his room and the card she found would only reveal that she didn't trust Elise as much as she wanted Elise to trust her. "We need a map like Tychon's, I think that's what he would've used."

The princess showed the slightest hint of surprise in the dilation of her pupils and how her jaw relaxed. "Why can't we use Tychon's map?"

"I can't go back." *Someone knows I was there.* "We won't be able to go together, and I won't be able to take the map without someone noticing afterwards. And the more I go, the higher the chance we get caught." Veaer tried to smile, a small pit of pride in her chest for getting this far, but Elise didn't smile back and Veaer wondered if it was because her smile was too soft or because Elise thought it strange.

Like a mask snapping back into place, Elise didn't answer for a while, and she returned to the bookshelf to put the hardcover away.

Veaer tapped her fingertips to thumb in her pocket. *1, 2, 3, 4. 1, 2, 3, 4.* And the need for sleep destroyed the wall that kept nighttime thoughts away.

She hates you now. She doesn't want to talk to you. She thinks it's a bad idea. You're intruding between her and her dead best friend. She's questioning you because she can see through your lies. She's going to hurt you like she hurt them.

"Rosell," Elise said through everything else. Veaer brought her palms to her ears to soften the noise, but then there was only silence. Then Elise repeated, again, softly, "Rosell."

"Yes?" Veaer swallowed. She needed sleep. She hadn't been getting enough sleep. The ghost kept her up at night. The memories that she could never forget. The words that found their way into her mind when she least expected it.

The princess was by her side again, her chair closer. Her hand hovered over Veaer's wrist. "Meet me tomorrow at admin. My father has a map."

"He has one?" Quiet voice, small voice.

"Yes, and we'll go there together. Get some rest, I'll see you in the morning."

CHAPTER 14
ELISE EXCAVA

Year 2, Semester 1, Week 7

In her second year at Adraredon Academy, Veaer found a girl sitting in her favourite art room.

She was gorgeous in the way that made Veaer shiver and stuff her hands in her pockets to count her fingers. Long black hair, concentrating brown eyes, golden skin, freckles, wearing her uniform like it was specifically designed for her.

The girl gently pressed a brush into two dollops of paint and mixed the colours in the bristles together against a wooden palette. She lifted her hand to the canvas and did a single, thick stroke without a waver in her arm, without a twist in her wrist, without any smudges or gaps in the line. Perfect.

Veaer held herself against the rolling door so she wouldn't catch the corner of the girl's eye and interrupt her enamouring entertainment. A butterfly spread its painted wings across the canvas. It was created as if it had been a million times beforehand.

Practised.

It would explain the flawless line art that the girl continued to grace the canvas with.

I did not find it all. Veaer squeezed the edge of the door. *You have been hiding from me. The beauty of this academy has been incomplete.*

The girl moved to inaudible music. It flowed through her arms and chest, in the way her hair swayed to a tempo unknown to Veaer.

The next time she saw the girl, they were walking towards each other in a hallway. The girl had Tychon Alastor Galacia with her, a boy Veaer met in the courtyard once while he was reading tarot cards for other freshmen, and she knew that his older brother Stelios was a popular senior. As they moved past each other, Veaer waved.

Tychon smiled and waved back. He was holding a fresh leather notebook in his other hand which Veaer was tempted to grab and inhale.

The girl kept walking, even without Tychon as he paused to ask how Veaer was.

"Intrigued," she answered, her gaze following the ghost of a girl. "What's her name?"

"Oh." Tychon mirrored the direction she faced. "That's Elise. Elise Excava."

"Elise Excava," Veaer repeated. *Like Izot Excava, her brother.*

CHAPTER 15
FRIENDS WITH BENEFITS

Year 3, Semester 1, Week 9

Veaer forgave herself for making friends with Adair a long time ago.

When Veaer was three, she had her first play date. That date stole her favourite doll, and she could never remember their name.

When she was six, her teacher punished her for using markers to do pretend make-up, and the teacher didn't believe her when she said a classmate told her it was okay.

When she was ten, she lost her best friend. What exactly happened that day continued to elude her, and she blamed that on growing up. She blamed it on the fact that friends weren't meant to be forever, such as enjoying a song wasn't, and every book eventually ended.

When she was twelve, she learnt that walking behind everyone wasn't just being polite. She learnt that getting to class and finding a seat early wasn't just being punctual. She learnt that always needing to face the door when she settled into a room wasn't just a fun habit.

When she was fifteen, she stepped onto the grounds of Adraredon Academy, and swore that she never needed anyone else.

Caemi and senti alike failed her, and to let people in was to fail herself.

So perhaps her past self was displeased about the current situation.

Laying in her bed, the curtains drawn in the middle of the day, and the hips of Adair Boudreau in her hands.

Adair perched upon Veaer's lap, looking down at her with a smile that matched her kitten heritage. Her gentle fingers trailed Veaer's arms and wandered over the buttons at the top of her shirt. It was study period for both of them, and how fortunate that was, as they could use this time to study each other.

"Something's on your mind," Adair murmured as she leaned down and pressed her thumbs against Veaer's eyebrows.

Veaer hadn't realised she was scrunching them and relaxed under Adair's touch. She closed her eyes and relished in the feeling of Adair's hands shifting to her hair and massaging her head. "Yes, you're on my mind."

"You know that's not what I mean." Adair's knees pressed against Veaer's sides as she adjusted her position. Veaer's eyelids lifted in time to see the checkered pattern of the cat caemi's skirt waver, the material spilling out around her. "You can talk to me, I'm here to listen."

But there are things I can't tell you. Things I shouldn't tell you.

Veaer lifted her palm to Adair's cheek and used it to bring her face closer. The scent of coconut moisturiser was welcome, and there was a subtle hint of strawberry in that shiny lip gloss too. "Am I going to get the 'this is what friends are for' speech?" Veaer chuckled and the warmth of Adair's skin drew into her.

"I know you're only trying to distract me with that reply." Adair had her eyes closed now, and her lips were a ghost on Veaer's. Barely touching, almost there. Closer but holding back until Veaer was honest.

Her mind was still running circles from last night, even in wonder if it all actually happened. The palm reading played like a broken record and that memory also came with warm feelings, in her chest and below the waist. She wanted to feel Elise again, or she wanted Elise to feel her.

She pictured the library, the tall interior yet shrinking box that only her and Elise were in. The light that illuminated Elise's face just enough to see her round features and beautiful eyes but left a lot to imagination. She remembered how badly she wanted to push Elise against that chair and do more with her palms than have them read.

"Or maybe whatever is 'bothering me' is all a distraction from you." A corner of Veaer's lips tugged upwards and she moved her hands to Adair's sides before tilting the girl to the side until she fell into the soft mattress.

Adair laughed and playfully wacked Veaer's hands away. She took the opportunity to dive into Veaer's arms and bury herself there. Veaer couldn't help but join in the amusement, raking her fingers down Adair's back, a well of appreciation for her closest friend in a long time building within her.

"Okay, charming." Adair shook her head and moved her hands to Veaer's collar, beginning to unbutton her shirt. "Maybe I can convince the answer out of you."

Veaer let it happen as her gaze drifted up and down the curves that made Adair Boudreau. When she arrived at the peak of her hips, her attention snagged onto the chair that she didn't tuck in during her rush to the library last night.

She grabbed Adair's wrists, which earned a little gasp from the other caemi, and then pulled Adair up as she got out of bed with only two more buttons to go on her shirt. Adair's gaze flicked between Veaer's chest, in a look of anticipation, and Veaer's face, in a look of confusion.

"What are we doing?" Adair tilted her head with a humoured smile, a smile that always delighted Veaer, as she gently placed her feet on the floor.

Veaer cleared her throat and guided Adair backwards until her shins hit the wooden seat on the chair and the caemi fell into it. "Maybe I'll convince you that my answer is not worth it," she said in a low voice that was only for Adair.

Her hands were instantly on Adair's shirt and she unbuttoned it in a familiar fashion. Her fingertips floated to just underneath Adair's arms and the cat caemi lifted them before sliding her arms out of the sleeves and letting her school top drop behind her in a bunch.

Veaer stepped forward, enough that she wasn't suffocating Adair against the back of the chair, and so her wide stance trapped Adair in position. She admired Adair's skin like a marble sculpture, letting her touch run all over and inhaling fruit and paradise. Adair shivered beneath her with squirming hips.

Adair hooked her arms around Veaer's neck which made the wolf caemi lift her head just for Adair to pull her in, quickly and with purpose. It was then that their lips crashed together and Veaer tasted strawberries at once. She let herself get lost in the little noises that Adair made, and her hands went from Adair's orange hair to her arms to her soft chest and to her thighs.

Their lips separated to catch a breath and every part of Veaer was on fire. She stared at the flushed girl in front of her and once again, like every other time they did this, like a ritual at this point, praised the gods for making her a lesbian. Adair smiled at her, and fireworks exploded in her mind.

Oh, Adair, whoever receives the fortune to call you their true partner should pray thanks every night for your beauty and kindness. What have I done to deserve intimate company with you?

And just as she wanted, just as she desired, she lowered herself and used her mouth on Adair's breast to push her against the chair and hold her there. Hold her steady, hold her tight, hold her close. Hold her like she wanted to hold Elise last night.

Adair held her in return, softly, her fingertips tangled in Veaer's silver locks. She lowered one hand to draw circles right between Veaer's shoulder blades, above the clasp of her bra. She whispered encouragement and satisfaction and while the words were incomprehensible as Veaer's mind was taken over by a need to pleasure, she could feel the intention behind it all.

In a rush of blood and blush, she began to sob, and attempted to mask the crushing sadness with kisses along Adair's collarbone and breasts, because Adair was able to love so much. How could a beautiful young caemi like Adair love everyone with so much heart?

Two years of this intimate ceremony brought reflex to every move Veaer made and she knew what coaxed those sweet sounds out of her friend, but at the same time her fingers trembled and she was angry that she'd taken Adair's love, even though they were just friends with these moments that brought them closer, because someone else deserved it more and she could never give as much in return.

She was struck with grief that one day this light would disappear from the world, just like Tychon, and that maybe it would be at the hands of someone like her, just like Elise. And she was afraid as she lowered her hands to break Adair in half, that really she would break her heart. So she just weaved her fingers to satisfy and brought Adair to the sky and she watched the girl's face flush and her eyes flutter open for fleeting moments to look at her with so much affection and gratitude.

She cried because Adair was so much, and she cried because she was doing a good job and she cried because she didn't want Adair to call her 'mine' and she cried because all she could think about was Elise. And maybe in another world, this orange feline girl could've been hers and they would've been happy, for now and forever. But instead, Adair reached heaven and spread her wings and a billion eyes and rings glowed because she was an angel. And Veaer could only get on her knees and confess between Adair's thighs until she was forgiven.

CHAPTER 16
GALACIA FAMILY

They told Veaer there was little chance he'd come back. That they had searched all his favourite places, and all the ones you'd never find him. They looked for signs and asked questions, but there was always something missing. They released the investigation to the public, but the network of students that came together when there were rumours to share said that they only did it as a courtesy.

They weren't looking for Tychon anymore. They were looking for closure.

They knocked on her door to reassure her, because three floors up was where Tychon lived his last days.

"We're going to find him, but it'll be hard."

"Cases like this have slim chance, but we have hope."

"Best case scenario, this is only a misunderstanding."

Veaer stared at their noses and nodded so they would leave. But inside she scratched and teared at the walls of her brain and wanted to plummet from the top of the cathedral and land where Tychon held his last breath because maybe then they could find something left behind.

She wanted to scream in their faces: "Why don't you just tell the truth! Why won't you say he's gone, and he won't be back?"

But she knew if they did, with lowered caps and a muscle memory frown, that chances were, she'd spill the truth she knew just as well.

She got around to emptying her pockets from last night and threw the scrunched journal entries on her desk. They laid next to the index card, tarot journal, and book on angels, taunting her, seeing through her. She lifted her index card and placed it next to the ones from the hardcover. They all had the same kind of formula with different numbers and a few letters, but she had elected to forget all those equations she didn't need when she came to Adraredon to study something she enjoyed.

I don't have time to decipher them right now.

"You're just telling yourself that, aren't you?" Tychon's ghost laughs, shifting in and out of existence.

She closed her fists and opened them again, and then repeated the action as she mentally ran through her plan for the rest of the afternoon. Admin building, Elise, headmaster's office, map, coordinates, locate.

The numbers on the cards blurred together and she looked away. She would only be prolonging the investigation if she continued to hide her card, wouldn't she?

She slammed her hand on the cover of the angel book, dragged it towards her, opened to the middle and threw her index card inside.

Maybe we only need two. Coordinates have two points. Maybe mine is fake, to mislead.

Maybe it's okay to leave this here. Maybe I will be fine.

If she gave the index card over now, then she'd have to admit she was hiding it all along. Her trust with Elise would be broken and she'd lose the princess.

I can imagine what she'd say now... "Veaer, you ask so much and give so little. How am I meant to let you in when this is what I get in return?"

If she added it to this book, just like how the other card was found in a book, she could hand it over with the idea that angels were now related, and so this would be useful. Elise would find the card as if Veaer didn't know it was there.

But then, in this theory, she would've gone off to the library by herself to look for something, when Elise made all the emphasis that they would go to the headmaster's office together, because they were doing this together.

Or she found it in Tychon's room like she really did, and it would be the same as if she handed the card over by itself. Distrustful, closed off. A double standard because she asked for so much from Elise already.

She couldn't do that to Elise. Couldn't do that to what was blossoming between them.

She opened the book again and bore her eyes into the index card. If she wasn't going to take it, she could at least memorise the numbers in case they did come in handy, and she could run them through a formula if Elise had looked into it since then.

Then she closed the book, pushed it away and left her dorm room without it.

Miriam Manor after classes was as busy as a village. Students in kitchens making drinks, groups of friends sitting around tables playing cards or doing assignments, the common room shelves ransacked for past time reading, and that didn't consider all the sitting rooms, game rooms, bedrooms, bathrooms and more.

When she stepped outside, the cool wind touched her face, and she took in the ring of buildings that formed the academy grounds. In times of scattered thoughts, it always helped to turn back the clock and put herself in the shoes of a younger Veaer who wasn't used to such grand buildings and fantasy. There were advantages to this character she embodied—always something new to be in awe at, that rising excitement of knowing she was a student at this prestigious school, knowing that everyone else here was a contemporary just like her, ready to take on the world. A disadvantage came in the form of waking up early in the morning with a spinning head and a spike of anxiety, until she looked through the gap in her curtains and realised where she was.

But for now, she indulged and tilted her head back, circling in her steps as she needn't worry about having to leave all this behind one day. The gothic buildings struck her with their tall and proud facade, an imposing presence but one that brought her closer still. They commanded her attention while weathered and worn, glass windows foggy and showing age and history. Embellishments and carvings decorated the exteriors, bringing their own stories, like a breathing entity imbued with wisdom. She inhaled the damp autumn air, letting her throat burn from the chill.

Her foot crashed into the stairs of the admin building before she snapped back to reality. The pain shot up to her knee, but she sucked in her breath and told herself that it was temporary, that it didn't have to matter, and what did matter was that she was here.

She rolled her sleeves down and untied the blazer around her waist, bringing it behind her and putting it on. She did another check over her uniform, rubbing out any creases she could and running a hand through her hair.

As if on cue, the doors opened and Elise appeared at the top of the steps, her hair done in two buns this time with her uniform also looking more pristine than usual. The daughter of the headmaster had to also look her part.

A surprised expression appeared on Elise's face before it subsided into a gentle smile that made Veaer even more giddy.

"I'm surprised you haven't run into Izot yet," Elise said and beckoned for Veaer to join her.

Veaer cleaned the soles of her shoes on the doormat and then embraced the warm and peaceful lobby. Deep red carpet created pathways to the reception desk, infirmary, and offices, while leather couches lined either side of the entrance. Quiet piano music floated through the area, gradually growing louder as they stepped towards the reception. Stuffed bookshelves lined the back wall, full of documents and information she'd never get her hands on.

"What's your brother got to do with anything?" Veaer slid the index cards out of her pocket and handed them to Elise.

She took them and then folded her hands behind her back. "He has a habit of shining his star child tendencies all over my friends." Elise made a bit of a scrunched face but quickly returned to a composed expression when she noticed someone else in the lobby. Veaer revelled in the attention. Elise continued in a quiet tone, "He has eyes all over the school, he's student president after all. He knows when I let someone new in my circle and he follows that up by introducing himself. Then who would you like more? The charismatic leader of the school, son of the headmaster, special blazer, fencing champion, loverboy perfectly contrasted with the reserved but smart Harq, vice president with a cane. Or a girl who spends her days following butterflies, painting, and trying to find her missing best friend."

Silence stood between them like a wall. Elise didn't show much interest in saying more as she folded her hands on the reception counter, so polished that they could see their reflections in it, waiting for someone to attend to them.

Eyes all over the school. But he didn't see you.

Star child, golden child. Even yet, you're so much better than him.

Let into your circle? Am I really part of your court now?

Missing best friend. Missing, missing, missing.

Elise cleared her throat, getting the attention of the girl behind the counter who was deeply invested in her novel. Veaer couldn't see much from where she was, but the tag on her blazer read 'Library and Information Assistant'.

"Sorry about that. How can I help you?" The young student bookmarked her novel and placed it to the side.

Elise squinted and read the tag. "I'm here to see my father."

"Oh, hm, he's been in meetings all day. Benefactors, detectives..." The assistant lowered her voice and leaned forward. "With Tychon Alastor's family... my condolences."

Veaer frowned, but Elise didn't bother to respond to her words.

"I'm going to wait in his office, then." She turned on her heel and marched towards the corridor that separated the lobby and the headmaster's office. Veaer was stunned out of words, her body moving on its own.

"I don't think you—"

Elise flashed a glare behind her and Veaer was shaken to her heart's core despite it being for the assistant and not her. She was taken back to the day at the cathedral and the wicked sounds Elise made and the expressions that contorted her beautiful round face.

The implications of the situation came rushing through her synapses and created the sludge that made it hard for her to walk with the confidence she desired.

Now that everyone thought... *knew* Tychon was gone, they would approach Elise with the truth, enough of the truth that she would be reminded of her deed every day. With sorry's and condolences from loved ones and classmates, Elise would suffer a perpetual cycle.

Veaer wanted to reach through Elise and smooth out her skin like Adair did her eyebrows. She wanted to unwind the frown on her lips and the tension in her shoulders. She wanted to explore Elise's heart and gather every piece of guilt so that she could take it away.

They passed two wooden doors where a mature voice exuded from beyond.

"You cannot tell me that my son is...when it's only been three days! He went missing on Monday, it is only Thursday. How much more do I need to emphasise this?"

A banging fist against a table accompanied the spiel before another voice piped up, "You money-sucking idiots are incompetent. We did not send him here to go missing and now you're telling me that he's *probably* not coming back?! What do we even pay you for? Our son was loved and he was protected."

Veaer shuffled closer to the door, leaning the side of her face against it. Her gaze met Elise who nodded towards the door at the end of the hall, the headmaster's office. But curiosity was devastating and wrenching, and there was always something to gain from these conversations. Elise gave in but didn't lean in, propping herself on the opposite wall with her arms crossed and watching Veaer's expressions and body language.

Then a third voice, authoritative yet with a hint of nervousness. It wasn't the headmaster. It must've been a detective, foreign from the academy. "Mr and Mrs Galacia, there are kilometres between here and the next town—"

"We know! We drove from there!" the mother cried, exasperated and desperate.

"*And* that means if he hasn't been in any cafeterias or dormitory kitchens, and if he hasn't been to the faculty room, then we know he hasn't eaten. And I'm sorry to say but a boy growing up on your lifestyle would not survive that long without food! So, unless he walked over there, and even then we haven't had any appearances outside of the school since Sunday..."

"Food. You're basing our son's whereabouts on food?" The father's tone was low and deadly, cutting through the air and everyone listening, including Veaer herself.

"Let me finish. *No one* has seen him, even when we offer your generous donation for any information. They simply have nothing to supply. Any semblance of a lead has been dead-end."

"Then the students are lying!"

"Students, staff, cleaners, visitors... and I'm sure you're aware of your son's popularity among the student body—there is no reason for anyone to withhold information."

"Someone must have had something against our boy. He wouldn't just disappear."

"You say three days, now climbing to four, but we've worked day and night per your request, spreading our force across the grounds and beyond. If there was something to find, we'd find it by now. It's as if your son planned his disappearance days beforehand, distancing himself, students claiming that he refused to do his usual tarot readings at all. He attended class and left soon after. He cleaned up after himself so we wouldn't come looking."

"He still could be alive. If he's so clever, then how in the patrons' names could he get tangled in some mess where he—he..." The mother shrunk into a disarray of sobs, and mumbles of the father's comfort floated through the door.

The scrape of a chair, a solid slam of two hands against wood. A voice younger than the father but notably more mature than Tychon's finally joined the conversation.

"If you don't find my brother in the next week, we are pulling every single coin and dollar from your shit-eating face and this institution will crumble just as your Excavan administration did in the past. We know you; we know your history. We are not afraid to use it as precedent to ruin you."

And in reply, even more familiar, was Headmaster Doallan Excava, "Stelios Galacia, one of our best." Veaer vaguely remembered Stelios, an academic prodigy in his senior year when she had just started at the academy. "You should be aware of how much we value our benefactors, deeply so. And one that has been with the academy since—"

"I will not forget that you took this from my ancestors. The quartet in the age of The Separation deserves to reclaim their position, yet when one of us goes missing, that is your chance to hide the past, isn't it?" Silence for a few beats. "I *was* one of your best, so you should know my prowess is not to be reckoned with, nor the connections we have to the Boudreaus, Carrashs and Thawans."

Veaer held her breath at the mention of each name. She knew them, knew them well. One enough to call friends, others in familiar passing. There were webs of history that took the Galacias, Boudreaus, Carrashs and Thawans back to The Separation era. She swallowed the possibility of her family being involved, but she was far from the noble line that the Rosells once had.

The further silence that followed was enough to even hear Elise hold her breath.

"Okay," the headmaster said.

"Okay?" Tychon's mother, father, and brother said at once.

"We will find your son. We will return him to you."

More scrapes of chairs, a group of people standing in a rush. Veaer peeled away from the door and the corridor spun. The utter sorrow of the mother coated her thoughts, the panic of the father stabbed through her heart, and the unbridled rage of the brother overtook her senses. She could feel the lies that wrapped the headmaster's words and the false comfort the detective provided.

Someone's footsteps approached the door and Veaer froze. She knew too much, and she was going to burst. Her arms were shaking so much they were going to fall off. Her feet were cemented into the carpet and the world was incredibly heavy on her shoulders.

"So much to gain, too much to lose."

The last words she heard on the other side were whispers of Tychon's brother. "If it's just his body you turn up with, if he's *dead* by your hands, then I will kill you next."

Elise forced her into the headmaster's office and shut the door behind them.

CHAPTER 17
A TEST, OR A PROMISE

If Veaer had the face of a guilty person, then she wondered what one would describe Elise's as. The princess refused to meet Veaer's gaze and, instead, stared at the map they needed on the wall. Veaer sat in an armchair in the corner, counting her breaths, tapping her thumbs to fingers, opening and closing her fists. *Grab and let go, grab and let go.*

The door to the office opened and the headmaster burst in, causing Veaer to jump and turn to Elise for what she should do, but the princess had no such reaction, continuing to eye the rulers of coordinates at the top and left edge of the brown map.

"Ter and Mian above, bring peace upon me," the headmaster grumbled and raked a hand through his dark blond hair bespeckled with grey before focusing on his daughter. "Elise, dear. Did the reception not tell you to wait outside? I'm rather busy today."

"It's nice to see you too, father." Elise weaved her hands together behind her back.

He walked up to her and wrapped an arm around her shoulders, looking at the map as well but unknown to her intentions. He failed to acknowledge Veaer in the room, and she didn't know if it was because he hadn't seen her yet, or because he didn't bother to. She was still a scholarship student after all, her position in the academy was charitable and to emphasise that charity.

Watching with a sidelong gaze, she could see that Izot got his hair and eyes from his father, and for Elise, the shape of her nose and chin. Their other parent must have supplied Izot's face, and Elise's hair and eyes.

"I'm just about to grab afternoon tea with Mirelli. If you want to chat, how about this evening instead? After dinner?"

Veaer earned a glance from Elise though the princess didn't offer a choice from her expression. Now that the map was here, they were going to stay.

"Thank you, father, but Rosell and I just wanted to stop by to take a look at this map."

"What for?" He patted her shoulder two times before walking around the desk to place some paperback down, and then open a drawer to pull out some fresh papers.

"Reminiscing, I'd say." And Elise left it at that as she gave herself permission to take a blank paper and a pen from her father's desk.

Headmaster Excava nodded solemnly, with some empathy for his daughter, but he was quick to straighten his tie and make his way out.

"Lock it up when you're done. I don't want any others to be prying around." His gaze briefly swept over Veaer sitting in the corner, though she didn't feel the need to shift like she did under Elise's stare. Instead, she got up and looked at the map herself, now with a critical eye that wondered where on Syriphia a secret society would meet. The school was huge—good for Tychon to have chosen a location, bad for Elise and Veaer if they didn't manage to find what they needed here.

Outside, an engine came to life and rumbled for a few moments, loudly taking over the atmosphere and prolonging the silence hanging between Elise and her father. Then wheels moved against gravel, and a car only the rich could afford appeared in the window frame.

Veaer stared at the tinted windows that shielded the faces of the Galacia family. Even if her eyes didn't see through, her mind could. The devastation of a soul lost forever, life twisted from this material plane with no knowledge of Tychon's demise. No control—only confusion and anger. Trapped within one's mind relying on one decision at a time to cope. The decisions she made spat at the feet of the Galacia family's grief.

"Protect Elise. My closest friend, my soulmate."

Do you really think that of her, Tychon?

The vehicle disappeared past the gates soon after.

The headmaster closed the door behind him, and they were left to their devices, Elise taking a seat in her father's large chair and scratching a few notes down. Shortly after, she pulled Tychon's journal out of her pocket and held it towards Veaer.

"Hold onto this for me. I don't know when we'll need it again, but I find it an ill reminder to keep it." Elise kept her attention to the paper and Veaer took it as she peered over the desk to see the equations being written on the paper. "Looks like we're working with some fractions. Maybe rational equations?"

$$\frac{48}{2x^2 + 11x + 9} = \frac{1}{x+1} + \frac{3}{2x^2 + 11x + 9}$$

$$\frac{9}{x} = \frac{x}{4}$$

$$x \succcurlyeq 6$$

"How about I do one and you do the other?" Veaer suggested, her arms tensing by her sides.

"Here you go then." Elise held up an index card and passed another paper and pen. Veaer stared at the numbers and breathed a sigh of relief when they seemed easy to work with. "Do you need me to run through how to do it?"

Veaer took a seat opposite from Elise and tapped her pen against the table. She didn't have a clue on where to start, but she shook her head. There were only a few numbers and letters.

Elise got to work on hers, writing LCD in small letters on her paper. She started solving hers in a mess of fraction lines and brackets, filling up the height of the page and needing to start again from the top until she reached x=18.

Veaer followed along, with fewer steps to the other equation.

"Negative fifty-three over negative fifty-three... Negative three hundred and eighteen over negative fifty-three. That's positive six!" Veaer beamed, spinning her paper around and shoving it towards Elise. "Our coordinates are x18, y6, right?"

Elise stared at the paper in silence before shaking her head and gently guiding the paper back. "No, that's not right."

Veaer's cheeks flushed with a burning heat, and she had half a mind to sink under the table and disappear. Her confidence just a moment ago rivalled her younger self, eager to be correct, never quite to her expectation. She should've known, only being taken back to her primary school years—she didn't belong with numbers and sometimes letters.

"What did I do wrong?" Veaer more so breathed out than said, slowly bringing her working out page to her chest.

"Nothing." Elise stood up and walked around the table to take the paper from Veaer. She flattened it out on the table and pointed, reassurance coating her words. "Just that your restriction is positive 6 and your answer is positive 6. That means this equation has no solution."

Veaer swallowed her spit. She was merely a kid now, being taught how to solve numbers, having to fix her mistakes because maths was something that did have right answers. How could she have let her excitement to impress Elise over something like this get in the way of realising the simplest solution—that there was none?

She sniffed and leaned into the paper to hide the slight water in her eyes. The failure weighed heavy on her back, but if Elise were in her place, she likely would've taken it in stride. Nothing bothered her, not even her best friend being gone.

The both of them turned to the map at the same time.

"It seems we're at a standstill," Elise noted, vocalising their thoughts.

"Maybe it wouldn't have been such a bad idea to bring that other card..."

Veaer stood up and eyed the entire line down x18. It slashed through a couple buildings and the courtyard. Several possibilities, many wrong answers. Even if they had the y coordinate, every point it could've been was too large, too general. They would need a map of individual buildings, or even the central courtyard if one existed, and would they need another set of coordinates then or would they use the same?

One step at a time; she had hope in her card. She could salvage this.

"Elise, we'll need a map of the learning centre, the courtyard, the main library... just those." She let the newfound adrenaline flow through veins. "Even though we don't have our y, we have an x to work with. This really narrows us down, though we'll need to get even more specific."

As if Veaer's request was an everyday ask, Elise strolled over to a cabinet on the other side of the room and pulled out a folder, smacking it on the table as she returned to the desk.

"Maps of Adraredon Academy's sectors." Elise tapped the top. The folder wasn't huge, but it was thicker than just a few sheets of paper. "I only remember it from before I attended, having spent some evenings here as father finished work. Maybe you'll find something interesting." She slid the folder closer to Veaer—it felt like a test, or a promise.

Veaer picked up the folder and held it close.

"Leave this with me."

CHAPTER 18
A WARNING

Year 2, Semester 2, Week 1

"Please stop staring at my sister."

A voice came from behind Veaer as she approached the stairs to the learning centre.

"Izot, I have a class to get to." She didn't turn around and busied her hands with readjusting the satchel across her chest. She also decided to wrap her blazer tighter as the winter chill bit her skin.

"I appreciate the persistence in you. No student at Adraredon Academy is without persistence." The boy was like a walking advertisement. He trailed Veaer up the stairs and met her at the double doors. "Veaer." He grabbed the door handle before she could, trapping her in his presence. She looked up at him and his frown. "I hope you'll listen to your student president."

CHAPTER 19
GRIEF (LOVE)

Year 3, Semester 1, Week 9

The autumn wind rushed through Veaer's hair, and she spat out the strands that wanted to make friends with her mouth. She stumbled up the front steps of Miriam Manor, balancing the folder of maps and Tychon's journal in one arm, shielding them from the prying gust as she reached for the doorknob.

From the other side of the foggy door window, a shadow moved across and the door opened, revealing Haiwrin, changed into slacks and a turtleneck, with a look of surprise.

"Oh, Ve, what's up with you?" He gave her one of those lopsided smiles that looked just like his sister's as he stepped back to hold the door open. Veaer noticed a butterfly brooch made of metal wires hooked on his sweater.

"Gathering research material. I'm working on something big." Veaer stepped through, grateful and ready to get rid of the cold attacking her legs. Just as sleeves bothered her arms, stockings did for her legs, but sometimes she wished that wasn't the case. "Can you help me with something? Wait, do you have somewhere to be? I could ask someone else too."

Haiwrin hummed for a few seconds with a wandering look, but the way he shut the door without leaving seemed to answer her question already. "I can do something quickly, what have you got? I hope not a problem Adair usually deals with."

A light red dusted Veaer's cheeks but she knew it was all in jest. While his sister didn't acknowledge gender when it came to her attraction, Haiwrin preferred romance with boys.

"Of course not. It's something much easier than that—maths." She strode over to her dorm and burst through the door, slamming it hard by accident and earning incoherent yelling through the walls. She elected to ignore it and waved for Haiwrin to follow behind.

"Maths and easy in the same sentence, that doesn't sound like you."

She dumped Tychon's journal and the folder of maps on her desk then forced the angel book open and slapped the index card against Haiwrin's chest.

"True, but I'm sure your mind is perfectly capable." She pushed everything to the side, continuing her charade. She didn't think of the strange scrunched coded journal entries, or the journal that belonged to a dead boy. She didn't think of how she was letting someone into her mystery, even though he didn't know it himself.

Haiwrin took a seat at Veaer's desk and picked up a pen with a click.

$$\frac{20}{4y^2 - 25} = \frac{4}{2y + 5} + \frac{8}{4y^2 - 25}$$

"Okay yeah, I can do this. Rational equation. But what has this got to do with you?" He turned his head, but Veaer grabbed the sides of his face and turned him back.

"You obviously have somewhere to be and I'm entirely grateful for this, so I can explain another time." *Another time when I can think of an excuse.*

"*You make a lot of excuses these days.*"

He mumbled something under his breath, but she'd picked up on Haiwrin's mannerisms for long enough that she trusted herself to step back and sit on her bed as he worked away.

"Can I have your brooch?" Veaer said so suddenly, she didn't realise until the metal wires were placed in her palm.

"I have another one in my room, so sure." He went back to the equation without a question or a flinch, which only served to make Veaer feel more guilty about taking his pin.

She listened to the strokes of the pen, the way he drew brackets and fraction lines. There was a sense of confidence to them that was different from Elise. He wrote like he played the piano. Elise spent more time doing her lines, like she was perfecting a painting. Even though maths wasn't a subject offered at Adraredon, Haiwrin liked to keep his mind busy with his puzzle books and newspapers.

She wondered what it would be like if Haiwrin, instead of music and performance, engaged with the fine arts. She imagined him working on sculptures of clay and metal, taking a block, straight edges with a lack of character, and turning it into something so purposeful that it may as well have started that way.

Then she blinked as Haiwrin held out a piece of paper towards her.

"There we are; y equals 4. Hope this helps... whatever you're doing." He laughed and then sat down beside her.

Veaer appreciated that about him. He didn't just leave because he had somewhere to be. He took time with his actions and allowed others in. Perhaps that very same admirable trait would one day be what caused hurt for Haiwrin. But she knew when that day came, she wanted to be there to help—for all the times he had and was going to continue to help her.

She leaned into him and rested her head on his shoulder, and Haiwrin instinctively brought his hand to her hair.

"Haiwrin, I need help with something else," Veaer whispered, and Haiwrin gave her room to continue. "Or maybe... I'm concerned about something."

"Let's hear it," Haiwrin whispered in return.

"Everyone keeps everything from me!" Elise screams and Veaer covers her ears.

"I need to know my best friend is safe." But the way her body moves isn't right.

Nothing that is happening, has happened or will happen is right.

"What should it feel like when someone dies?" Veaer asked, keeping her hands close and playing with her fingers. When the few seconds of silence became too much, she added, "Empty? Like your limbs are going to fall off? Like you're suddenly aware of how quickly you could go too?"

Haiwrin paused and used his palm to lift Veaer's face. "Is this about Tychon? We don't know if he's... you know. They're still looking."

"That doesn't answer my question though." Veaer frowned. *They aren't looking anymore. I know what happened to him.* "I don't understand how it can be so heavy. Or how it may not be heavy for another person." *Why doesn't this bother Elise as much as it does me? Am I not strong enough?*

"I think that sometimes it feels lighter to the people who are still hoping. Who can't quite accept yet that someone is gone. Maybe they try to convince themselves. Try to sit by the door and wait for that person to walk through, all okay." *Elise knows what happened too, so she shouldn't hold her breath.*

"The police said the best case is that this is all a misunderstanding. Are they so disillusioned too?" Veaer rubbed her thumbs together. Her voice was quiet, and she was afraid of Haiwrin thinking her immature for this conversation.

"We shouldn't call them disillusioned." Haiwrin glanced away for a moment and tapped his fingers against his thigh. "It's what happens when grief takes us. I consider it a bit of a paradox. A feeling so foul, so bitter, so lovely, so peaceful."

Veaer ripped herself away from Haiwrin and stood before him

with arms held out, shaking, boring her eyes into Haiwrin's mind. "How can this be lovely and peaceful? Someone's life has been taken and now we're left to pick up the pieces. We're left with all this fear and doubt. And is that all you and I are going to leave behind too?"

Haiwrin closed his eyes and took a deep breath. "We leave behind love when we die."

"Love... love?" Veaer's voice cracked as her breath got caught in her throat. "How can love come from death?"

"Sometimes it's hard to know, it depends on the person. Such as Tychon—we weren't all that close to him. We won't feel the same as his family, or his close friends. It'll still affect everyone at Adraredon, because in the end he's just like us. A student making his way through senior year. But maybe when you get a girlfriend, or a wife, and she must move on to the other side, that is when your unspoken and unmoved love will come out. Grief shows us our love left behind. And sometimes we won't want to let go, because our grief is proof that this person was in our life and mattered then and matters now."

Veaer's mouth opened and closed. Her mind whirled and the room became a timeless void. Her heart turned to dust and her soul belted in agony. It was all so much, too much. So much to gain, so much to lose.

All the powers of the universe moved her forward and her knees hit the carpet and she fell apart in Haiwrin's hands as she clung onto his legs.

"Haiwrin," she cried.

"Yes, Veaer?" he whispered.

"I will never let go of my grief for you."

CHAPTER 20
THE MOST IMPORTANT QUESTION

Year 2, Semester 2, Week 14

W hen Veaer arrived upstairs, her art room was shut tight and deadly silent. Silent enough that she knew someone was inside and up to no good.

"And so what?!" A broken voice whipped through the door and against her cheek. Sudden, unfamiliar, full of emotion. She hadn't realised she had been loitering to eavesdrop.

"You aren't the only pebble on the beach, Elise. Don't be so selfish." Izot's voice floated into her ears, sounding like he did when Veaer used to sit in the headmaster's office for counselling.

She had never heard or even seen the siblings together. She was so taken aback that she leaned into the door even harder. *What are you hiding?*

"I don't understand why you're blaming me for this." Elise's voice levelled out, becoming whole like her strokes of paint. "If you care so much, maybe you shouldn't be parading around... you should be... I can't— I don't understand?" There was a resounding huff and the clatter of a brush being dropped on a table. "Surrounding yourself with every other student. Going to father's office constantly. Acting like you're a king when your role means nothing after you graduate. You keep leaving me alone, keep blaming me, keep coming to me like this as if you know what is right for me. We're supposed to be starting at this academy together." A chair being pushed and two shoes hitting the floor. "No one will ever know what is best for me. No one will know me the way you think you know me. You don't trust anyone and you especially don't trust me. I will never trust you either, Izot, and you will never know what I've been through."

Izot sputtered, his words buffering, pieces of words being thrown to the walls. Veaer couldn't grasp anything of what he wanted to say as footsteps drew closer to her. Veaer held her breath and thrust herself into the next classroom away from the staircase. She filled her lungs with dusty air as the art room door slammed against its frame and more footsteps followed, walking away from her.

Her heart slammed against her ribs and her skin prickled with excitement and wonder. Questions flew to every crevice of her mind.

A challenge. A challenge of great beauty.

"No one will know me the way you think you know me. You will never know what I've been through."

Veaer laughed to herself as she went back to the art room and Izot was gone.

What do you know that I don't, Elise Excava?

CHAPTER 21
EXCERPTS DECODED

Decoded Note 1

In raising this to the angels, they have denied my request to join hands in the ceremony. Having two came alongside me would bring strength to the spell. I don't understand what they expected when they joined me. If they thought they could draw the line here but not what we have done so far. I can't help but think we wouldn't have needed to do so much if Elise hadn't done that years ago. It's as if she has a precognition to these things

Decoded Note 2

The society draws closer to our objective. In finding the requirements, are place at three of four. Naturally in our collaboration, it seems too easy, but perhaps the spirits above have brought us together for our higher purpose.

But Elise. Her nature. As we know in her blood - has come to delay the operation. the crypt is a constant reminder of what has been done.

What Elise had done.

What can't be brought back.

And what we still need.

But earning favour, we can manage to make things right

Decoded Note 3

Elise asked me again today. Like yesterday. And last week, and before that too

I am days away from changing it all. She can't keep asking me

Sometimes I wonder if we're still the same as we were as little kids

Patrons above, is this what happens to best friends?

Or maybe what it means to want to protect someone so much that we end up hurting them too

Elise continues to compare me to iZot. It's quite irritating but I suppose it's not her fault.

If I discover how to undo what has been placed upon her, then I can let her in.

But not now.

CHAPTER 22

SUN AND MOON

Year 3, Semester 1, Week 9

Veaer's second favourite place on campus was one of the smaller art rooms on the learning centre. Every Friday, except for last week's gem necklace heist, she would spend her lunch and afternoon working on her folio projects.

The space was brightly lit by a wall of wide glass windows above long work benches. Around the room were seating arrangements that accommodated different kinds of groups and individuals; tall chairs and low chairs depending on how a student felt more creative, cushions for the floor and even standing desks that many students requested. A few easels were placed to the side, housing half-finished pieces with labels stuck on them to indicate who they belonged to. The scent of oil paints, clay and the floral perfume stuck to the ceiling and walls. In rummaging through a pile of unclaimed work, she had found a small painting, dated back more than a year, with the initials E.E written on the back. She slid it into her folder.

She sat in the middle of the room, surrounded by a labyrinth of papers and canvas, with her folio binder sitting on a table a short distance away to make the most of the floor.

Every piece was like looking in a mirror. Their folios had to consist of self-portraits throughout the semester, to gain an understanding of how material worked with creator, and how creator served material. So far, she had completed an acrylic painting using a real reflection as a reference, colours as accurate as she could get them. Then there was a paper collage portrait made from magazine cut-outs, her eyes looking strange, her hair struggling, and her lips never quite right. She had an odd liking for the pointillism piece, as the process was relaxing and she didn't quite mind how it turned out as long as she didn't look too deeply into the gaps between the dots.

Her fingertips were stained with charcoal as she worked on a side profile, her ear cringing into her shoulder as she attempted to block out an alright-looking nose.

She considered peeling herself away from the centre of her folio to turn the music box on, at least to occupy her auditory mind, until the clamouring of what sounded like a hundred footsteps filled the hallway outside and her curiosity grew tenfold.

Then a voice she knew well spoke louder than anything, "Pardon me, friends. I do have some council duties to attend to now."

"But—in the art room?" Many voices joined the one in agreement and Veaer immediately rolled her eyes. "That's not very... in art they just—"

A beat of silence said enough before Izot spoke again, "All students of Adraredon are students I care for. It's part of the job, of course."

Some mumbles of disappointment and others in awe. Typical, typical.

And before she could decide if she wanted to set up camp in the supply closet to see if the prince would just leave her alone, the wooden sliding door was thrown open hard enough for it to bounce back and almost shove Izot into the door frame on the rebound.

"Veaer Rosell! What a pleasure to find you here!" Izot Excava, prince of Adraredon Academy, shut the door behind him and strode in with outstretched arms.

In her opinion, Izot and Tychon didn't have very much in common at all.

"And to what do I owe the pleasure?" Veaer grinned with the intention of sending a message. *Go away.*

"I cannot just visit one of my classmates?" Izot returned the smile, with no apparent message, and paced around the room. He seemed to be searching for a place to sit, but they were either the wrong height for him or caked in paint. His lack of commitment was entertaining enough for Veaer to crack a proper smile.

"Not after what your sister told me." She shrugged and looked back down at her piece, disappointed to find a dark stroke of charcoal that she must have struck upon Izot's aggressive entrance.

"No, no. This isn't about Elise." He finally settled on leaning against the teacher's desk and looked out the window. Something of a smirk flitted over his lips before it morphed into his smile. "There's no need to bring her into the conversation."

She decided that she could work the strike-through in, dashing more black across her eyes and lips and neck.

"Alright," Veaer acknowledged. "How can I make this clear?" She went back to blocking her features on the paper. "I don't want to be friends with you."

Out of the corner of her eye, she noticed that golden boy smile drop from Izot's face.

"Listen, Rosell." She preferred it when Elise said it. "I know what you do on Thursdays with that Boudreau twin. I know where to find you on Fridays. There is much more I'm capable of... discovering."

She pursed her lips into a straight line and lifted her head to stare at the boy. "So what?" Elise had warned her of this already, though it was a wonder someone would snitch on her activities while they likely did the same. On that note, "It's not like you're much different. You and that Harq—I bet you like it when he makes use of his cane—"

"That's enough." He lifted a hand towards her but then brought his palm to his face in an attempt to cover his red cheeks. "How are you to call me all of that, and you're spending your days attached to the hip of my sister?"

Veaer averted her gaze, landing on a piece on the outer edge of her folio hurricane. This one was a full body lead sketch with smoke twirling around her drawn self, faces amalgamated into the design. The faces looked familiar—familiar enough that one of them followed her everywhere. In her ears, in her eyes.

"So, this is about Elise." Her recent whirl of thoughts and speculations about Elise were reinforced behind a barrier, but she feared that the dam would soon flood. She didn't need all that while she was working on her folio. She didn't need to wonder about those journal entries and every question that squeezed her heart and gripped her mind.

"That doesn't answer my question!" His voice went up an octave and he gave her a strained smile with a clap. "Perhaps I should make myself clear as well."

He pushed himself off the teacher's desk and crouched just outside the circle of art, close enough to whisper to Veaer.

"There's a reason my sister isn't like me. A reason why my sister only has a few around her who she uses for break time activities. A reason why I'm the sun and she's the moon. She needs my light, because otherwise she's only a rock in the sky." He pointed up, vaguely, and something of a smile danced on his lips, awkward like finding balance in a pit of soft sand.

"What are you trying to say?" Veaer's arms seized in her lap, and she didn't know if her face was doing what she wanted, but she imagined herself unaffected and calm, because Izot Excava couldn't chip away at her. Izot Excava didn't know what he was talking about.

Izot shook his head like a parent would at a child who was without the context that adults kept from young people because it helped them feel superior.

He stood up and straightened his back, turning his feet towards the door which only said he wanted to leave as soon as possible now that he had planted his seeds.

"Miss Rosell, I think it will do you well to be cautious. After all, we still don't know what happened to Mr Galacia."

And as he approached the door and grabbed the handle, the door slid open and revealed Elise on the other side, the melting face of Tychon's ghost hovering over her shoulder.

CHAPTER 23

SELFISHNESS

Elise led Veaer through the corridors of floor four of the learning centre. They were looking for room eighteen.

"Only a theory," Elise said, her back turned to Veaer who was only a few paces behind. Veaer watched Tychon's ghost pulse in opacity. He looked different... almost impossible. Usually, he took the form of his student self, what Veaer was most familiar with, but now his uniform was shredded, and cold lumps of white feathers hung from his back. His face melted like a wax candle and dirt tracked along his hands and arms. "No one can tell me it's only a coincidence that x 18 y 4 on the building's map points to room 18. He did this on purpose."

The ripped journal entries Veaer decoded left her uneasy and, she found hard to admit, spooked, especially in the presence of Elise, and even more so with Tychon following their every step. Elise didn't seem to notice the boy she stabbed floating around her.

Though it did help to have the journal as a scapegoat. With so much encoded, it wasn't out of the question that she 'decoded' another equation that led them to y 4. Elise was satisfied enough with that answer, and Veaer tried to convince herself of the same.

If there was ever a feeling of dismay towards questions and mysteries, she chalked that up to the feeling of inadequacy. Tychon had taken many answers to the grave or passed them on to Elise who held the answers to the universe, quite hard to unwrap, quite hard to stay away from—despite it all. Veaer was left feeling hollow and strange, like holes had been punctured in her soul now that she allowed herself to freely read Tychon's words. They were some of his most recent ones. Still fresh.

"Have you ever done anything bad?" Veaer asked, before she could catch the words and force them back down her throat. She stumbled to a stop when Elise paused in the middle of the hallway and Tychon's attention was drawn to the windows.

"Bad? What sort of bad?" Elise responded and gave Veaer the courtesy of turning around. Her expression was expected, if she were any other student, a tilt of the head, slightly furrowed brows in curiosity. At this point, Veaer wanted to find a tool and wedge it between Elise's skin and bones so she could see the reality of her thoughts and feelings.

"Bad like... you don't want to tell anyone, ever. Not even the patrons or saints." Veaer hooked her hands together behind her back and counted her fingers.

"The patrons see everything, silly." Elise laughed and waved her hand. Veaer scolded herself for the rush of blood that filled her cheeks. "Plus, if I have, I wouldn't tell you. You're part of 'anyone'."

Veaer frowned—part for the lack of substance in the reply, part for just being another 'anyone'.

Questions continued to flash in her mind, like a frantic lightning storm.

Did she murder you so you couldn't confess for her? So you could shield her from her reckless decisions in doing something she shouldn't have?

You were only trying to protect her—you had plenty to hide.

"We should find out," Tychon replies.

Instead, we're enabling her.

"Did Tychon have many caemi friends?" Veaer ripped herself apart inside for the desperation that came with her questions. Either Elise would figure out what she was doing, or...

When she has no use for me anymore, I'm next.

"He does," she answered, cool and smooth, like Tychon was just next-door having lunch in the cafeteria. "Well, our circles don't mix very much. The caemi girls I spend time with aren't the same caemi he spends time with."

At least there was that; Elise knew Tychon was involved with other people, though whether she cared much or not for that wasn't clear in her tone. Did she ever wonder if those caemi were also keepers of secrets? The same Tychon had, that she asked about too often?

Elise resumed her walk and Veaer tried her best to keep pace, so she wouldn't have to look at Tychon.

Finally, they arrived in front of room eighteen, floor four.

Mounds of dust were gathered upon boxes, cloths and weathered gold frames—enough to coax a chorus of sneezes from Veaer.

Looking at the sign attached to the door—gallery storage—things clicked into place.

The learning centre featured its very own white walled, open floor gallery section to showcase art student folios at the end of every semester, plus other fancy events that brought potential enrolments in. It was the art stream's theatre, for music and performance students; or gym, for fitness and sport students; or podium hall, for international studies. There were more comparisons she could list, but she wondered why the school would build a storage room all the way on floor four when the gallery was on the first floor. Everyone else must've thought the same, as the storage hadn't been touched for months, with cobwebs and a noticeable colour difference between these planks and the ones in the hallway to show for it.

As Veaer rubbed the tip of her nose with her palm, Elise held a handkerchief up. She didn't realise the princess would carry one—personally Veaer thought it unsanitary and weird—but the offer was like a bouquet of flowers. Beautiful, a gift, and welcome, if from Elise herself.

She grabbed the small cloth and sparks flew up her arm as their fingertips touched for a moment, lingering, Veaer's warmth against Elise's cool. She returned to the week before, where in a few hours it would be exactly a week since then, the afternoon that she spent breaking into Elise's room, into Elise's arms. And it wasn't until now that she realised how much she missed that. They had been so close, chest against chest, thighs against thighs. Veaer could've kissed her then, but the thought alone was blasphemous. She had deceived Elise that day, and for that she was proud, but she knew she wouldn't earn such affections that way. The next time it happened, would Elise beckon her again? Hold her wrists and guide her arms forward to wrap around Elise from behind?

Elise let go of the cloth and turned away to explore the room, choosing a few shelves to the side of the entrance to look through. Cans of paint, sets of brushes, rolls of tape, spare paper and canvases. The hallmarks of touch-up and restorations supplies.

Veaer stuffed the handkerchief in her pocket and wrung her hands together. The room was quite large to fit big paintings and other art pieces. She stepped over to a statue that seemed to have been cared for during its creation. Clean edges, a vision in mind. But then discarded to this dusty room afterwards. What did it take for an artist to do that?

Sitting opposite from the restoration supplies was a dark wall with the paintings of past students. Veaer didn't allow herself to go closer, with a thought that they might come to life and take her down in a room that no one visited anymore. It didn't help that Tychon's ghost stood in front of each one for several seconds, in his contorted way, staring closely like he knew exactly what they were about. The paintings may have been talking to him.

Veaer swallowed her spit. "There's something about this room..." A confession remained stuck in her throat. She didn't want to be afraid; she didn't want to give into fear.

"I agree. But at least I'm with you," Elise replied as a bottle fell from her pushing things around and she caught it in her open hand.

"With me?" Veaer arched her brows and distracted herself from the speaking paintings by staring at Elise nudging the bottle back in its place.

"I'm safe. Since you're here. I enjoy your company." Elise's voice was so quiet that Veaer wondered if she imagined those words, and it took everything to refrain from calling *What?* so she wouldn't ruin the moment.

Elise enjoys my company. She's happy I'm here. She feels safe. Safe. Safe. Safe. Is that not the highest privilege one can have with such a beautiful girl like you? Safe.

"I enjoy your company too." Veaer let a smile stretch over her lips though she was more than aware of the creeping feeling between her shoulders. The walls spoke to her, "*You are not safe*", because Tychon wasn't safe at all. She paced over to Elise as the young princess circled the room again and began looking between paintings that were on the floor and stacked against the wall. A large rack of more paintings sat next to them. She watched the shadows dance over Elise's cheeks, darkening her already black hair. She reached out and—gently, so gently—lifted a few strands with her index finger. Silky and soft, well taken care of. She'd known luxury her whole life, with a father that could provide and a brother who was successful.

And as if Elise heard her thoughts, she said, "I'm glad Izot didn't sweep you away with his words." She didn't bear to turn to Veaer, but enough light bounced from the open doors that a sheen was clear in her eyes.

Veaer's smile drew into a smirk, leaning to one side, clumsy but feeling right. "How do you know that's true?" Veaer knew. She would never be whisked up by that prince. They were too different in many ways; they simply wouldn't be found in the same social circles at all. It was never a matter of being good enough or trying to get Izot's attention. And with the twins as friends who didn't care much for that either, it didn't make their earlier conversation a dilemma at all.

Except for the fact that he knows something.
"He knows something you don't."
I'm going to find out my way, and I don't need him.

Elise sighed and stepped around a pile of boxes covered in a large white cloth, pressing her palms down on them to test her weight before taking a seat. Veaer joined her, like her aura had melded into Elise, dragging her along, despite Elise not having the heritage for an aura herself.

"Well, you wouldn't be here right now. You would've left the second you saw me in that doorway." She paused and Veaer held her breath in her throat. Technically she wouldn't have, as she was doing her folio work, so she had no reason to leave, but she gained an understanding of what Elise meant the more she pondered on it. "I don't know what Izot said to you except for his word of caution, but it's the same he says to everyone else. Nothing new. It's nothing new if you want to go."

"I don't want to go," Veaer said too quickly, realising too late for her words but soon enough for her hand that was reaching for Elise's. The princess' eyebrows were drawn together, and her shoulders slouched forward to make way for her arms to wrap around herself. "I'm not leaving."

"There always seems to be something. My brother, my status, the way I act. Sometimes people see me too much as my family members, and others see me too much for what they *think* I am, which is wrong. And no matter what, I always feel a bit... reluctant. Afraid. Unmotivated."

Veaer opened and closed her mouth, knowing with every fibre that she wanted to comfort Elise, but still unsure how to do it. She didn't understand what Elise was saying except for the sadness that strung along her words. Like something was missing or hadn't come home for a long time.

Elise continued, "To try again, I mean. To keep reaching out to people and bringing them close only for them to turn away from one little thing. And I feel like I try my best and express my gratitude for them and enjoy my time with them. I listen to their worries and if they need something, I'm there. But why, the second I want something for myself, is it taken away? Am I that selfish?"

The first time Veaer watched Elise's chest heave as it was now and heard her express so much of herself and her emotions in confidence, was the day Tychon died in her arms.

And the first thought that came to Veaer now was: *I don't want to cry.*

Because pressure built behind her eyes and a well of tears drew up from a sparse oasis. And the emotion that rushed into Veaer was overwhelming and heart wrenching. And she wondered why it was so easy for her to absorb all of this, to hold it inside of her, thinking that maybe she was helping Elise this way. Just like on Monday, just like today.

She cried too much this week already, into her pillow, behind her door, in Haiwrin's lap, and times she couldn't remember. And she told herself that things like this deserved tears, but she didn't like how they made her put her entire body into it and then left it sore even after patching up her emotions. The numbness that came after crying was only a reminder of her mistakes.

She scrunched her hands into fists to keep the tears back. These were Elise's emotions, not hers—she couldn't just make it about her. It was not her place to incapacitate herself just because she somewhat understood what Elise was saying despite being unable to recall exact memories that her words could be applied to.

"You're not selfish," Veaer whispered, because speaking too loudly gave room for voice cracks and weakness. "Some people don't get it. They take advantage of nice people and don't look back. And they get rid of others so easily. All you can do is give your best and it will hurt sometimes but when things do work out, too, then that's even better. We should be good even if others aren't." Veaer gathered the courage to grasp one of Elise's hands and pull it towards her, meeting in the middle. Elise didn't need to shield herself from the world. "You're not selfish." She held Elise's hand closer, keeping her fingers together. "I'm not leaving." Veaer pressed her lips to Elise's knuckles, meaning nothing and everything at once. "Let's be good together."

Elise blinked, her tears running to the corners of her eyes and sliding down the sides of her face. A shaky inhale, then another, until Elise wrapped both her hands around Veaer's and squeezed. "Thank you."

And Veaer was happy with the silence that followed—

—before the room filled with rattles and clanks, and the wall in front of them opened into a mouth of chains and metal.

CHAPTER 24

AN UNDERGROUND DESIRE

When the wall stopped groaning, Veaer and Elise had hidden behind the pile of boxes and cloth. The wall wasn't completely transformed, but a large panel had shifted open on old hinges, and peering through the dark revealed a metal box indented into the wall.

It appeared to be some sort of storage space, but very mechanical like senti technology from years ago.

A small gasp escaped from Veaer and she clamped her hands over her mouth. Elise crouched nearby and lightly placed her palm on Veaer's forearm.

Someone stepped out of the metal box and then shut the panel with both hands. They walked over to the rack with paintings and reached between two of them. A switch snapped into place and the clanking from earlier returned. The box took its time to do anything but, when it did, it moved downwards and showed its guts of moving chains and gears again. It wasn't just a compartment—it was some sort of large dumbwaiter lift. Then the wall covered back up.

Veaer couldn't help but stare at this mysterious person, until she caught a glimpse of their mask. A full-face mask covered in painted eyes. Eyes, eyes, eyes. The same as she saw that day in Tychon's room.

This time the person was wearing a cloak over their uniform, which they stripped off and laid in a cardboard box that they covered back up with another box. But she still couldn't be sure if this was a different person or not. They left the room and closed the door before she could gather any more information.

"Did you know that person?" Elise whispered, bringing her hands back to herself.

"What?" Veaer turned to her and then turned away, putting on as straight a face as she could. "No, I don't." Tychon's ghost hovered by the door, looking through its tiny window, refusing to peel his hundreds of eyes away from the corridor.

"You were staring at them like you wanted them to turn around and say hi. And your eyes widened. And your body tensed up. You're either afraid of them or know them—or both." Elise listed the observations on her fingers.

"Wouldn't you be afraid if you were just alone in a room and then someone walked out of the wall?" Veaer stood up immediately to avoid her point being further questioned. She marched to the shelf where the switch was and tried to look between the paintings, only to find more darkness. "I don't remember which paintings they reached between..."

"You want to bring that lift back up?" Elise asked and investigated the wall instead. She prodded her hands around for some sort of open edge, but everything seemed flush against the wall. Perfect for hiding. "This is what Tychon wanted us to find," she whispered with rising realisation.

Veaer hadn't known herself to figure something out before Elise, or at least she could only remember the wonders of Elise's inquisitive mind. A well of pride filled her chest and made her even more determined to find this switch, even if the rattling irritated her ears and made her want to pull her hair out. Even as Tychon lurked over her shoulder and ran his feathered hand across the shelf.

She decided that taking out the paintings would give her a better chance at seeing the switch, and so she began to pile them on the floor, until she pulled one and it didn't budge. The next one didn't either. The third one moved smoothly and joined the others.

Veaer tried to lean deeper into the shelf so she could push the painting from the back before she looked upon the piece. A burning tree. She whipped around to the other one, fast enough that she accidentally knocked over the mountain of paintings she was making. A blossoming tree full of fruit. Both artworks were two sides of the same coin.

The Tree of Life yields fruit.

"And it burns with the fire of wisdom and grace."

She reached between the paintings and a rough switch pressed against her palm. With no hesitation, she hooked her fingers and slammed the switch into the other position, and the sound of turning gears washed relief and anxiety over her.

Yes, she'd done it. She had proven herself useful.

But now, she had to commit, and perhaps this lift was nothing at all and they had just wasted their time.

But the spark in her eyes just then. It meant something. The patrons above wouldn't hand me such beauty and keep a glorious resolution from me. I can make her smile; I can make her proud. I can make her feel loved.

The bell signalling the end of lunch shook Veaer inside out, but Elise was unfazed, waiting for the panel to make an appearance again, and that was enough for Veaer to take a few deep breaths. *1, 2, 3, 4. 1, 2, 3, 4. 1, 2—*

The lift arrived on the wrong beat, but she distracted herself with a closer look at this contraption. The inside was indeed made of metal, and it was large enough to fit two people if they held their knees to their chests. Looking around the room, it appeared to be suitable for transporting most of the artworks and supplies needed for the gallery.

"Storing gallery items on the fourth floor must come with good protection." Elise leaned into the metal lift, her voice sounding hollow. "It means valuable pieces are less likely to be taken. If thieves can be stopped before they even get up here."

You're so clever.

One question answered, many more to go.

"Shall we find out what business Tychon had with this?" Veaer put on her bravest smile for Elise and stuffed her hands in her pockets.

"We shall, Rosell."

~

Curled up in a metal box, going down, down, down, through a shaft she didn't know existed before today. Her knees shivered in resistance to being held in one position for too long, and her arms shook from everything else.

The stench of chlorine stabbed Veaer's nostrils, but what set her on edge was the musty undercurrent of something rotten. Whenever a shred of light passed through, bleached spots of metal flashed in her eyes.

She couldn't tell how far they'd gone, but the lift suddenly slowed, and she began to rock side to side.

"Are you cold?" Elise asked in the dark. She was incredibly still, and maybe she wasn't even there. Just another ghost.

Veaer swallowed and wrung her hands together. "No, why do you ask?" *It's actually quite warm in here. It'd be more so if you were sitting with your back against me and I could wrap my arms around you.*

"You're shivering. Or at least your arms are. Which I find strange because I can feel your body heat."

She can feel my warmth.

Veaer's gaze darted around, but there was nowhere to look. "Nerves, I think. This space is small and I don't know where we're going. What if this lift breaks down? Will anyone hear us if we get trapped?" For all she knew, she was venting to nothing. The clanking around them made it hard to have a conversation anyway.

I wonder if she hides a knife in her jacket.

Or if her hair clips are incredibly sharp.

Or if she could pull a sheet of metal from these walls and slice it across my throat while my body turns itself inside out. The stretches of my muscles would be on display, and she could play music with my bones.

Then the lift stopped and Veaer clamped a hand over her mouth. Stopping could mean anything. Broken lift, stuck in the middle of the shaft. Back on the floor they started on without them knowing... Worst of all, did they arrive at their destination?

A whimper fell from her lips, and she wanted to pull her hair out.

"Rosell, we're okay," Elise's hushed voice carried through the dark. It was breathy and real. "You're doing so well. Thank you so much for doing this with me."

Veaer shook her head even if Elise couldn't see, but she seemed to understand her response when Veaer felt a hand touch her knee.

"Listen, we're currently on the first floor. I can hear the new lights they installed and based on how many people are nearby... we're not in the main gallery. A room, off to the side. Like a storage room. Their voices are muffled past this lift panel. Like there's a door or another wall there."

"What do we do?" *Was this for nothing?* Veaer regulated her breathing and tapped her fingers. She moved her hand from her mouth to above Elise's. Equilibrium. Warm palm, cool skin.

For the next moments, Elise spread her free hand across the walls, floor and ceiling of the lift. When she pawed one of the corners in the ceiling, something loosened and a piece of metal moved to the side.

Veaer's chest tightened as Elise used a knee to push against the lift's main panel and opened it slightly, just enough to let light stream in. She struggled to find the right words—she loved that she could see a stronger outline of Elise because of the light, because she could confirm Elise was real, but she hated the idea that everything could fall apart here if they made the wrong move. Or if she really wasn't smart and the coordinates were all wrong in the first place.

"Look at this," Elise whispered. From the hole in the roof was a cord that threaded downwards and in Elise's hand was a small remote with a few worn buttons. Level 4, Level 1, Maintenance, Return...

and then a button that's symbol was scratched off. "There's no reason we wouldn't hit this one right?"

A sour taste coated Veaer's tongue.

"I'm not asking you to find me, you don't have to."

Veaer grabbed the remote, shut the panel, and hit the button herself.

CHAPTER 25
BE CAREFUL WHERE
YOU STEP

T he lift came to a stop again and this time the panel opened on its own, revealing a small room lit with flickering oil lamps. It only lent Veaer the idea of others coming down here to maintain the lighting, meaning something of significance had to be down here too.

Veaer closed her hands into fists by her side as she waited for Elise to unfurl herself from the metal box. Her heart pounded in her chest —dread for what was to come next, excitement for having Elise all to herself in what seemed like a forbidden place.

Cool dampness stuck to Veaer's skin as she climbed out next, and not a moment too soon as the lift suddenly closed and sped out of their view, leaving the empty shaft in its wake. She couldn't tell if that was normal, or if that masked person had discovered what they'd done and urgently called the lift back, but either way she knew she had to get moving.

With a glance towards Elise, she could see a reflection of the flames in her eyes, giving them an otherworldly glimmer. The warm light served to make Elise's skin look softer, enticing.

Her lips parted to say something, but she was unsure what. Then, Elise spoke instead.

"I never knew they had something under the school." Elise

didn't turn away, and heat rose to Veaer's cheeks. "Do you want to keep going?"

Before them was a narrow spiral staircase, so the lift didn't even bring them all the way down. The steps were made from polished oak and the ornate handrail was carved with the shape of twirling vines. This rang strange as the walls were a mossy stone, unrefined and designed for the underground.

The ghost of Tychon hovered by one of the lamps, holding his mangled hands towards the heat. He opened his mouth and bits of dirt fell to the concrete floor. Patches of feathers adorned his skin and this time he was wearing some sort of robe, different from the one he wore in his passing. It was white with a rope belt and no hood, showing off part of his chest and the scars underneath. Then he disappeared and appeared again by the stairs.

"That's what we're here for, right?" Veaer avoided revealing her prayers to the red dragon for protection, instead opting for a small smile.

Veaer and Elise descended with the sound of creaking growing louder and more frequent as they went lower. Every so often there was another lamp lighting the way, but there were moments of full darkness that had Veaer reaching for Elise's hand but unable to find it.

They reached the bottom of the stairs and the ground flattened out. Beyond the steps was a dimly lit chamber, lined with ancient stone coffins and statues, a few more doorways along the walls like the one they had just come from.

Veaer's skin prickled. The air was dusty and full of decay. She stared at the coffins and wondered if their ghosts would rise and follow her too, and then shut her eyes in fear that she would manifest it if she thought too hard.

But Elise became one with the macabre surroundings, moving gracefully through the chamber, picking up an exposed lamp that cast light and shadow across her beautiful features. Veaer couldn't help but admire the way her long black hair fell past her shoulders and the way her eyes sparkled with curiosity and excitement.

"This crypt must have been here since they first built the academy." Elise's voice was that breathy tone again, awe-filled and just for Veaer to hear. "So much history. Perhaps we'd even find the four heroes down here."

The idea of the tombs of the four heroes being close left Veaer with a mix of feelings again. She often avoided the thought of someone she knew being in a coffin, and the last time she attended a funeral was so long ago that she wondered if she associated her memories with fabricated images and movies.

The four heroes were powerful and venerated like saints. They weren't often integrated into religion, but she had heard of groups across the world maintaining shrines and praying to them. Even the big statue in the courtyard reminded her of a relic of blessings. If they were down here, would all her prayers and dreams come true?

Elise moved forward, choosing an archway at the other end, and Veaer trailed behind her. She didn't contain her gasp when she looked upon a square room with four pedestals, two on the left and two on the right, and a statue of each hero upon them. Against the far wall was an ornate chest, covered in intricate carvings and adorned with jewels.

Her body moved with her mind, yet she hadn't registered it so, an urge to investigate further taking full hold of her focus. She carefully pried open the lid, and inside was a collection of ancient scrolls bound in leather and tied with twine. Between scrolls she could make out a silk bag filled with cards, a key and pocket watch linked together, a handful of coins that didn't look anything like their own currency, and a goblet with some gem rings in it.

A little bit of air remained like a rock in Veaer's throat, and she didn't know whether to cry or scream or shut the lid. She was overcome with a sense of love and power, like the four heroes were alive and standing right beside her, placing a hand on her shoulder and telling her they were here, and they would bring justice to the land.

She decided to close the lid, afraid that if she touched anything more, that she would be attacked by every ghost in the crypt.

Elise made a small sound like a squeal while looking at one of the statues on the left side of the room. She examined a delicate parchment encased in thin glass, placed on a short podium in front of the statue.

Veaer's heart burst as she watched Elise bounce from foot to foot, unable to stay still as she traced her finger just above the glass to read the text but seemed to skip too quickly and had to start again to really read it, this time out loud.

"Iris Galacia of Vestirr, Kyross. Having joined the quartet of heroes at the beginning of The Separation, she had lent her abilities of tarot and the wisdom that came from the heavens above through her divine transmutation. Her participation in the return of the sorbra cemented her allegiance to the Rosell throne, and from there—"

Veaer forgot all about the potential dangers of ghosts, or if the masked person would find them. Forgotten that this place was likely forbidden and not for a mere young caemi's eyes. She was captivated by the beauty and mystery of this crypt, and the enchanting presence of Elise by her side.

Rosell. That was her. Her name, her legacy. Her ancestors. Every Rosell who came before her, in allegiance to the four heroes. She had never felt so connected to her heritage as this moment, and never prouder.

But Iris was Tychon's ancestor. And while his line hadn't ended with him, his piece of history, his potential to follow Iris' footsteps as a blessed tarot reader, was gone. And that left a hole in her chest, and she made her turn away to glance at the other statues.

Kalaya Thawan of Equala, Syriphia of the Purple Cat Caemi was placed across from Iris. She only let herself stare for a few seconds before marching out of the room and forcing herself to take a few deep breaths. This was a lot, maybe too much.

So much to gain, so much to lose. So much to gain, so much to lose. So much to gain, so much to lose—

Only now did she notice a weight upon her head—and not of the mental variety. Her hand flew up, touching soft fur in the form of canine ears. Animal ears, caemi ears. Those didn't belong here, at least not with Adraredon Academy's policy for uniform appearance among senti people and caemi people. The last time she had felt these ears was the moment before she stepped onto the academy grounds, forcefield zapping her caemi distinction away.

Silence broke in the presence of dripping water somewhere deeper in the crypt, and a breeze she didn't understand the origin of brushed past the tail that decided to appear now too. She combed through her hair, allowing the silver strands to neaten around the base of her fluffy ears.

Perhaps the field didn't reach the underground. Or the tombs of the heroes were just that magical.

She flinched with Elise inching up to her and whispering in her ear, "Will you come with me to the next room?"

Veaer didn't need to respond, only follow. The next archway they found led to a labyrinth of corridors with narrow paths and crumbling stone pillars. The further they winded, the less frequently the lamps were lit, and the more statues of unrecognisable senti and caemi were damaged.

Her heart hammered and the lack of light in many sections only served to disorient her, like she was suddenly pulled into a daze. The walls were thick and suffocating and their footsteps echoed loudly against the ground that was part stone, part weathered floorboards.

Her solace came when they paused at a corridor not unlike the others, but this time there were banners hanging from the roof and small podium displays between pillars along the wall.

Elise's eyes widened as she examined one of the contained scrolls, her fingers tracing the air above the calligraphy. Veaer didn't bear to look as she didn't want to overwhelm herself once again, more than she needed to while she was alone with Elise.

"This is incredible," Elise mused, and nothing more needed to be said between them as they hovered by each case.

Veaer couldn't help but smile as she watched Elise. She had always admired Elise's passion for knowledge, demonstrated in every assignment she submitted, and every time they did have to present their findings to the class. Insatiable curiosity was a feeling she could understand.

It's one of my strengths.

"You should hope so."

Tychon's ghost was at the end of the corridor, but Veaer wasn't able to tell which way he was facing, even with his feet pointed towards her.

She wanted to take Elise's hand as her finger continued to draw a path between each line on the parchment, to lend her support in these discoveries, and to avoid the gnawing feeling that they were being watched, every spirit tracking their every move.

Unseen eyes, unseen eyes.

She grasped the princess' hand, and their eyes met in an instance. Veaer became captured by Elise's rosy cheeks and smiling eyes with an inner glow, and the alert of danger slipped away, exhilaration she had never experienced before taking its place. A small burst of laughter erupted from Veaer and it took all her might to neither kiss the young woman nor push her far, far away.

Elise and herself were the only ones in this world, Tychon and crypt spirits be damned. She only needed her ruling queen by her side, exploring a sanctuary others would never be able to see or fathom. The past laid in agony and elation in these walls, and while she wasn't in the right mind to consume this knowledge at this time, it was theirs forever, and always would be.

In a continued effort to find even more to this catacomb, they kept walking and walking through each ghastly or awe-striking display until, finally, they came to a small alcove, tucked away in the deepest part of the crypt. Inside was an intricately designed statue of what appeared to be... an angel.

A plaque was displayed on its pedestal labelled *Angelus*. Four arms struck out from its sides, one hand holding up a scale, another with an orb decorated in a golden frame, the next with a thick tome that had loose pages sticking out here and there, and the last empty with the palm against its heart. Three sets of mighty feathered wings protruded from the statue's back, and rings of eyes surrounded the being's head. Whoever this was, Veaer could not tell, and she wondered over and over what the story of this angel was.

What concerned her the most as they stood there, bathed in the eerie light of a lamp soon to run dry, was not the deep connection she felt to this statue, but how Tychon's ghost, with a blood covered toga and a pair of wings, broken and wet with mud, bowed deeply, deep until his forehead was being pummelled into the ground, and cried and cried and cried.

And when she turned to Elise for a semblance of clarity, she caught only a second of her world—her queen—being dragged away by a masked, hooded person, before she was knocked in the dark and Tychon mocked her with whispers and taunts.

PART III

"& so what – if my feathers
are burning. I
never asked for flight."
—— *Ocean Vuong, Devotion*

CHAPTER 26
WINGED DREAMS

Veaer (Elise) dreams that she's a butterfly of purple and red (red and black) wings, blended, not distinct. Butterfly wings in these colours rarely (often) appear.

As a butterfly, she indulges in the sporadic and random movements, while also knowing, deep inside of her, the position of the sun, the planet's magnetic field, the landmarks that surround her. She turns right (left), or at least as right (left) as a butterfly can interpret.

A patch of grass and a swing in the distance tells her that she's near (far from) her childhood home. A suburb that is (isn't) important to her (—at least, she tries to avoid thinking about it).

She knows that something happened here, but time doesn't exist for butterflies. So maybe it was in the past, or maybe it's something yet to happen.

When she was ten, she lost her best friend (she found her best friend). What exactly happened that day continued to elude her (continued to haunt her), and she blamed that on growing up. She blamed it on the fact that friends weren't meant to be forever (the fact that she was stuck with him for good), such as enjoying a song wasn't (a song never left her mind), and every book eventually ended (every book always left questions).

Veaer sees a red and black butterfly (Elise sees a purple and red butterfly). They know nothing except to crash into one another and see who is able to fly away with their wings still intact.

The purple and red butterfly drops and falls into a white specimen frame, and then the glass is shut tight.

(The red and black butterfly has its wings ripped apart and it's so fragile.)

Elise wakes up first, and she realises she is blindfolded. She remains still, like she is still sleeping, and waits for Veaer to wake up.

CHAPTER 27
POISON AND DIRT

Veaer emerged overwhelmed and sweating. Cloth over her eyes, wrists and ankles tied together by rope, something hard but not cold beneath her—maybe a wooden bench. Someone was next to her, she felt it was Elise. She could tell by her breathing.

Water was still trickling somewhere, so they were still in the crypt. But it was close enough that they had to be in a new place. Warmth filled the edges of the room. There were a few more people in here—she noticed her aura was stronger and able to detect the presence of others, and she wished it worked earlier so they wouldn't be in this situation. One other aura was particularly comforting, though this situation was everything but.

"Veaer, you're awake." A new voice, but she couldn't recognise it no matter how hard she tried. Something prevented her from doing so, and it felt like magic.

She remained silent. She read enough novels to know asking 'who are you' or 'what do you want' or 'why am I here' wouldn't be productive.

"Your friend has been asleep for a while," the voice continued, and it was enough to make Veaer struggle against her ties. *Elise, Elise, Elise, are you hurt? Are you okay?* But then she felt the soft, soft touch of Elise's fingers on hers, only a brush. Elise was awake too but made an effort to keep it between them. "No matter, we don't need her for you to make a choice."

Veaer yelped as someone forced the blindfold off her and the light in the room, even if by lamp and candle, pierced her eyes and forced them close before she could even take a better look around.

She blinked for a long time to adjust her eyes, and the voice waited. When she could see again, she counted two other people in the room with her and Elise, and she detected several people outside of this room. The two in front of her were caemi, based on their strong, but muffled auras, and while she assumed they were students, they weren't wearing their uniforms, not even cloaks like the ones in the gallery storage. They dressed in tunics and luxurious flowing linen robes without hoods.

Jewellery made of golden chains and crystals hung from their necks and ears, and around their heads and wrists and ankles. Amethyst, clear quartz, rose quartz, and selenite twinkled in the dim candlelight bringing a mysterious but beautiful appearance to these strangers. One of them had dark brown braids and the other had their red hair cut just above their ears. Many students had these hair colours and styles, and she wasn't any closer to understanding who these people were.

She would've been more enamoured with them if they weren't wearing full face masks with eyes painted onto them.

And she would've looked around the room more if a sudden dizzy spell didn't overtake her senses and make her bend over, almost slamming her head against the table in front of her, her hands restricted to her back and unable to support her.

"We've given you each a bottle." The one with the voice, the braids and smooth dark skin, gestured towards the table. Indeed, there were two thick amber glass bottles with some sort of liquid inside. No labels. "We took the liberty of giving you something else during your nap."

Veaer's skin itched, and her ears started to ring. A wave of rage had her fighting against the restraints, to get out, to get anywhere, to get in this person's face and punch it. But her body wouldn't cooperate. The side of her head helplessly twitched towards her shoulder.

The one with the red hair stepped to the side where a small round table had a tray of more glass bottles of different shapes and sizes, and a few shot glasses. Two glasses were taken and placed in front of Veaer and Elise.

"Simple terms—we've poisoned you for trespassing. You should have turned back. Or... not have followed one of my angels."

She flinched, causing a spasm along one of her arms. They knew, they knew. How did they know? Her gaze hovered to the red-haired angel who turned to their leader in some sort of surprise—she couldn't see any proper expression. Was this the same angel-stranger who left the lift from the storage room, the same who pinned her in Tychon's room?

She had no doubt about the leader's claim of poison, in how her body responded to each thought and movement, and how her mind continued to draw fuzzy at the edges, her lack of urgency being a reason to stay even more alert.

"Fuck you!" Veaer screamed and thrashed even more, or she thought she was. The air was making her move in a sluggish way and she was afraid of bothering Elise with her tantrum. But hot fear and confusion pulsed in her heart and mind. "Your idiot should've thought about leaving a different way if you didn't want people finding you."

The red angel bristled but the leader held his palm out. "We have measures for when this happens. This bottle has the antidote to your poison. You can have it. It takes a full bottle to take care of the poison—"

"Then shut up and give it to us. Give it to her!" Tears cascaded down her face and she turned to watch the still blindfolded Elise. Poor Elise, her poor Elise. Her charade was impressive but concerning, was she already dead, or suffering in silence?

"You're a fast responder. Your body must be trying to fight the poison. Sweating, weakness, dizziness, heightened emotion. A true wolf caemi's biology. It's a wonder that Elise's weak senti body hasn't collapsed." He carried on and snapped his fingers, and the red angel unscrewed the bottles and poured one shot from each, then closed them again.

"Are you going to help us or not?" Veaer hissed, her voice clamped in her throat. It didn't occur to her that she was asking the help of the ones who hurt her in the first place.

"As I was saying, one full bottle, but you can only take one shot a day. If you have more, then you're only setting yourself up for something worse, understood?"

"Yes?! Oh, in the name of Ter and Mian, what do you want from me?" Veaer wailed and was about to thrash around again when—

"Calm down, Veaer," Elise said, her voice raw but there and real and alive.

"So, the princess is awake," the leading angel said with a twinge of wonder. "You seem very fine for someone who has poison coursing through her veins."

She did appear okay, mostly. Veaer glanced behind and saw that Elise's hands were shaking at a shocking rate of movement. They needed that antidote.

"You want us to join you," Elise said, instead, and Veaer's gaze snapped between everyone else in the room. "You know what we've seen down here, and you will give us a choice. Join you or die."

"You're so clever." The leader's tone was upbeat but laced with malice. There was something about him that felt familiar, recent, but nothing was connecting while the room spun. "Join our legacy, and you get the shot, and the bottle."

"Legacy? We're just kids, what legacy is there?" Veaer shot back and a pain in her stomach made her actually hit her head on the table this time, spilling a little off the top of her shot glass. She grimaced and whined.

The leader laughed for a long time, letting Veaer curl up, and even Elise was starting to react with spasms and more shakes.

"The four heroes have existed for a long time in memory. But why should they stay there? Or why should their power remain buried in history forever? They have the ultimate ability to transform and transcend, stronger than anything since they passed away. Every angel carved in marble came from the quartet's image. Iris Galacia's image. *Angelus Caelum's* image."

The horrible irony of her awe and wonder towards the displays earlier, to how they were so connected to these people now racked her with anxiety and more tears.

"*The power of the past, the vision of the future.*" He had said it in a language she didn't understand but repeated it in translation. Then, "Everything we do, and every ritual will bring us closer to their power."

"Including killing us?" Veaer frowned. She didn't know how plausible this legacy was to achieve, but she did know magic was stronger here than anywhere else in the academy. Tychon's ghost hovered over her shoulder, and she refused to face him.

"Yes. Because now you know this, and if you can't join us, your existence will be troublesome. And..." He glanced between Veaer and Elise. "Excava and Rosell. What an interesting combination."

"There's nothing stopping us from refusing your offer. We can just leave this world behind." Elise's low voice shook Veaer's core even more. "This isn't only about us. There's a reason why you're pitching us a position in your little society. Your Ascension Order."

Tychon's wings wrapped around Veaer and held her tightly. His bones dug into her back, and she crossed her arms as her skin pulsed in pain.

"Hm. You already prove yourself useful. You know more than we think." He turned to the red angel, and they left for another room.

"I do." Elise tilted her head, as her form of expression.

"*You do...*" *Tychon's cold, cold voice.*

"We're down a member and could use a couple more. Core members."

Clanking came from where the red angel went. Creaking old wheels against uneven floorboards. Tychon hovered next to the leader and his face was hollow and suffocating.

"Down a member?" Elise asked, erring between caution and curiosity. "What happened to them?"

He didn't reply, but he did approach the table, slow and steady, and stood across from Elise.

Veaer twisted her wrists to try and loosen the ropes, and stomped the floor when her ankles wouldn't separate. "Get away from her!"

He grabbed Elise's blindfold and tossed it on the table. The princess kept her eyes closed though her eyelids twitched and her eyebrows furrowed. It only took her a few moments to adjust.

The leader sighed and turned away.

"We found him buried." (A dirty shovel, with splinters in its handle.)

"Covered in dirt, a hasty job." (Pile and pile and pile.)

"Shards of glass and stained feathers." (Throw it all away.)

"Desecrated. Disrespected. Our poor, poor archangel."

Elise stiffened. Veaer shut her eyes with prayers to the patrons under her breath.

Spots of red butterflies appeared behind her eyes and stayed when she opened her eyes again.

The other angel returned and wheeled in a long stone box, not unlike the ones found in the crypt.

"Our dear leader is dead," he said with a booming, convicting tone, and lifted the coffin's lid. "Tychon Alastor Galacia found in Adraredon's graveyard."

CHAPTER 28
FINALLY

A t first no one said anything and nothing happened.
Then their noses were attacked by a putrid, sour, musty, and rotting scent.

Veaer wheezed and desperately struggled against her bounds so she could at least bring her hands to her mouth and nose. The smell made her head spin, and she was ready to pass out, but she saw as Elise doubled over with cry, and knew she had to stay awake.

"Tychon!" Elise wailed, crumbling into herself, puddles of tears forming on the table as she thrust herself forward but could barely move, barely get closer. "Tychon, how long have they had you? Oh, my dear Tychon... who did this to you?"

If Veaer hadn't watched Elise do it, she would've been convinced that Elise didn't kill him.

What is going through her mind right now?

Seeing the corpse of her best friend.

Taken from his resting place.

The only thing worse than being followed by his spirit in purgatory.

Tychon's ghost stared at his corpse and screamed, so much that his body distorted and ripped in places, his wings cracking, the feathers falling out. And then he disappeared, and the red angel placed the lid back on.

"Thank Ter and Mian..." the leading angel mumbled, and then walked over to what looked like a vent in the wall, opening its shutters.

Veaer's vision only continued to worsen, and she attempted to lean over the table to suck the shot glass closer to her, but it was just out of reach. Her stomach began to ache even more now, not for the poison but the pure hunger that came with skipping lunch for folio work.

"So now that we've gotten that out of the way," the leader continued, grabbing a cloth and wiping his hands, "You can see how serious our situation is. No one can ever replace his aptitude for the spiritual, or his hereditary advantage, but we will make every effort to complete our ascension in his memory."

Her eyes watered and she blinked slowly. She looked at the leader, and then to Elise. She had done this to Tychon, and they thought no one else would ever know what happened to him. But the gods came forward and delivered him to those who must have known him best. These people and this place, a living reminder of who he was. Not even his body could be forgotten, kept in the morbid possession of these angels for whatever reason, and perhaps in their way of honouring him, in the most valuable crypt she had ever known, and alongside his powerful ancestors.

This legacy could be her penance.

"How do you expect us to contribute?" Elise asked, cracking voice reaching from the crevices of her throat, and tears reflecting in the candlelight. Veaer stayed quiet and was glad of it.

"Our rituals work to increase our power and connection to the angelic realm. While you, a senti, may not be able to contribute an auratic ability, the more core members we have, the stronger our circle. We complete rituals once a week, recovering and studying on other days to avoid suspicion," the leader explained, flawlessly. He seemed to have sufficient knowledge to take his position after Tychon.

"Nothing else?"

Veaer stared into the side of Elise's head, hoping something would be revealed. Because Elise's question didn't come from a search for something new, it came from knowing something and wanting the angel to confirm it.

"I can only remind you that this choice is between dying before the end of the day or returning to your dorm for a good night's sleep and the potential for great power."

As Elise pondered on this, Veaer took advantage of the time to focus her vision and observe the room, which may lend an advantage if needed. There were no windows, which made sense if they were still underground, and two doors—one to the room that housed Tychon's tomb, and one that she assumed was a path back to the crypt. What didn't make sense was how pristine this room was. Circular stone brick walls, a hardwood floor. Two big, full bookshelves flanked the left and right side of the room. At the opposite end, there was a long table covered in cloth against the wall, on top a set of small wooden drawers pushed to the back, and before it a pile of items that looked vaguely familiar, but nothing she could specify from where she was.

"I'd like to join your order," Elise finally said with her chin held up, which earned a satisfied, slow nod from the leader and a flinch from Veaer.

Neither Elise's expression nor body language lent any clue to why she would want to join, or at least anything other than wanting to live. Because if it were just that, then she wouldn't have needed to question, or take so long to answer. There was something else, and Veaer wondered if they shared the same intention.

"I'm so pleased to hear this." He turned to Veaer. "Will you follow her?"

His mask of eyes bore into Veaer, and she already knew her choice. Even with every lurching and uneasy feeling taking over her —whether the poison, or her judgement.

"Yes, I will," Veaer answered, and she didn't hide how her gaze dropped to the shot glass in front of her.

The red angel hurried around the table and took a small knife from their belt. They cut the ropes on their wrists and then gestured to the shots.

Veaer cupped her glass in two hands, cautious of spilling anymore, and sculled it. She whimpered at how it tasted like childhood, like undertones of sugarcane juice, sweet but slightly spicy, and a note of caramel. The pain across her body subsided, leaving a dull cramp in her legs, but her mind cleared, and her senses were returning back to normal.

When she finished savouring her temporary cure, Elise had already placed her glass back down and was having her ankles untied.

"Please note," the leader said, as he walked to the door just behind them, "We have eyes—everywhere." The masks didn't help Veaer's unease. "We will know if you betray the order, and we can do much worse than poison."

Veaer swallowed the spit that gathered on her tongue. The leader knocked the door twice, and from the other side emerged two others, notably a similar height to everyone else in the room, and while they had the same painted eye masks, they wore the thick dark hooded robes.

The leader instructed the hooded people to lead them back to the surface, and then added, towards Veaer and Elise, "Return here on Sunday evening, eight o'clock, and we will conduct your initiation rites."

The tension in Veaer's shoulders finally lessened when one of the hooded society members presented a secret exit from the crypts in the forest behind Miriam Manor. She had wondered at some point, during their winding navigation of even more corridors than before, if this was just another ploy to knock her out and drag her back, like a sick trick of entertainment.

When the two members brought their arms over their heads and moved a thick slab of stone in the roof aside, afternoon sun struck the darkness around her. In her state of hunger and soreness, she vocalised a question on how no one had found this place before, which actually earned a proper response, unlike any other question she had asked on the way here.

"How do you think the angels recruit protectors?" one replied as they climbed up and looked around, before gesturing for her and Elise to follow. "Anyone who is good enough to find these entrances and then the crypt, are deemed good enough to be part of the cause."

Veaer nodded, vaguely, concentrating mainly on putting her feet and hands in the right places. Her palms slapped the cool, wonderful grass of the surface world and she would've kissed the dirt but held back as her gaze caught the legs of Elise. She wouldn't want to embarrass herself like that.

"So how come you aren't... core members?" Veaer tried for another question, steadying herself on the forest floor and then managing to stand. Dirt painted her knees, and her uniform was in disarray, plus the afternoon sun made it hard to ignore how sweaty she was.

The protectors remained silent, and with one more look between Elise and Veaer, left the same way they came and covered the entrance again. Only now Veaer realised that the top of the stone slab was disguised with grass and moss, allowing it to remain flush against the ground. She couldn't even work out how they'd open it from the surface.

Finally absolved of being watched by strange angels and finding herself in the familiar sight of Miriam Manor, Veaer groaned loudly, her muscles deflating and her mind spinning with a desperate desire to sleep.

She ran a hand down her face. "Patrons above, I'm ready to just—"

Elise stared at her with those sunray filled, deep brown eyes as Veaer's back was thrown into the rough bark of a nearby tree, her feet slightly slipping on loose leaves and damp grass, and her entire being trapped between two soft arms. She was left completely vulnerable, mouth hanging open, hand flying to her chest. Somehow every colour in the forest melted together with Elise and framed her in beautiful greens and browns.

"Elise...?" Veaer barely managed to whisper, her breath unsure of which direction to go, where to go. She didn't know what to do with her hands at all, finding it ill timing to tap her fingers, and settled on scrunching them together in front of her chest.

An incredible smile burst across Elise's face, her lipstick smudged from their underground ordeal, her straight hair sticking out in places that only made the expression seem fanatical. Not to remind the fact that Elise was slightly shorter than Veaer too.

"Veaer," Elise breathed, and her eyes widened.

My name, Elise, that's my name. That's me, entirely, without the past and without the future, that is me right now. I've only been Rosell to you, but now I am Veaer.

"Elise," Veaer repeated, a short, questioning chuckle punctuating the name. She found the courage in her to unfurl her hands and bring them to the princess' face. Her rose-gold cheeks were soft and lightly freckled and the perfect fit for her palms.

"That was incredible. You were incredible!" Elise laughed and that quickly put Veaer out of sorts, her head hammering and her legs growing weak. But she knew there was a good reason, and she knew she was happy to be alive and with Elise right now. *Alive.* "I was afraid that we were going to lose everything."

"Everything?" Veaer perked up, and for a moment she felt her caemi ears and tail following suit, before realising that they had hidden themselves again on their trip back.

"We have discovered ancient history beneath our very feet, in the presence of great heroes. We found those who want to follow in their footsteps and test our limits, maybe even break past them. The world feels like it can fit in my hands now, like... like we can really do it. Be part of the world, not be so tiny. Not just a dot on a butterfly's wings. Finally, be part of something with Tychon—" Elise drew in a deep, deep breath and leaned in closer to Veaer. "Everything we have. Everything that is ours."

"Ours," Veaer echoed, and she couldn't help the way her gaze lowered to Elise's lips, slightly chapped, stained with dark lipstick— and maybe she could call them hers too. Electricity shot up her arms and her mind buzzed with the song of Elise. "But what about... shouldn't we..." She wet her lips with a flick of the tongue. "They hurt us." *And they have Tychon. They found him.*

"They can't hurt us." Elise's voice grew definite, as if she had just spoken a fact into existence, and Veaer knew it to be true as the warmth of Elise's body pressed against her own, forcing the grains of bark into her back, into her thighs, into her calves. "They can't hurt us when we're together. You and me, Veaer Rosell."

"Do you mean it?" Veaer pulled Elise's face so close. Jasmine flowers and sandalwood and myrrh. Layered and complex, a mystery to undo at once.

And in a flash of another lifetime, she wondered if they would've been ordinary. Not followed by ghosts, just two girls growing up who loved each other, and that was all.

She would've painted portraits, written heartfelt letters and left flowers on Elise's desk by morning. She would've told herself that she did deserve the romance she read in books and saw in shows. Their love may not have been remarkable to anyone but them.

"I mean it."

Elise didn't need any more words as their lips met and a spark erupted between them, waking every sleeping cell in Veaer's body. The kiss was hesitant at first, treading gently and afraid to break something, anything. But each passing second, each press of their declaration grew a spring of comfort that deepened the kiss, now urgent and full of feeling. Their bodies drew even closer, melding together and dancing to the wind in the trees and the fire in their hearts. They lost each other and then found one another again, tender, and careful but intense and entirely overwhelming, as if this wasn't just a second of desire bursting at the seams, but something that had to say everything. All without words, all in the darkness behind their eyelids as they just had to feel, feel, feel.

And when their lungs demanded air, they pulled apart, just enough to see the mix of awe and disbelief swirling in their eyes, a shared sense of understanding holding them together.

CHAPTER 29

ADAIR AND HAIWRIN BOUDREAU

Overnight, a small sheet of paper slipped under her door and upon seeing it in the morning, Veaer's heart hammered in her chest. The last time this had happened, she almost couldn't help the overwhelming desire to take hold of Elise, in several ways.

But the handwriting was a striking resemblance to Haiwrin's, asking her to meet him in the Music and Performance Block, at theatre one, at 10am.

She turned to her alarm clock which read 9:48am so she barely woke up in time to get the message and had to change out of her pyjamas as well. With a rush to her closet, she grabbed the handle, only to lose her footing to pain sparking up her thighs.

As she crashed into the desk that saved a bad fall, she groaned and clutched her stomach. Her arms didn't get far before a new pain stung her and her arms seized up. Sweat beaded on her forehead and everything felt exceptionally warm despite her knowing of today's autumn forecast. Detailed flashes of the crypt reminded her of the poison that still lived in her veins. She didn't know where it was, where it would go; if it had reached her mind already and if the antidote did anything to stop that.

Pins and needles attacked her feet and she silently screamed into her palm as her soles refused to lay steady, threatening her balance. A final brushstroke in this baroque canvas of twisted arms and grandeur. She swayed to the side and toppled to the floor, her side saved by the edge of her bed.

She clawed at the carpet as she inched towards her desk again, where the amber glass bottle sat in the far corner near the wall, so as to not accidentally break it if it fell upon her chair or somehow the carpet shattered it instead. Tears ran down her cheeks when her bones felt like they were on the verge of breaking, but silent she remained. No sound, no alert.

A flute played from somewhere else on the ground floor, and a violin joined in upstairs. Usually, she found music practise to be a suitable addition to the manor's depiction of prestige and speciality. In these times, the instrumental only layered upon irony.

When reaching up from the floor, her body held up by a shaking forearm despite its protests and creaking, she could barely scrape the desk's top. She would have to climb her chair first. Her ounce of optimism came from the idea of having a proper seat and resting her aching back while she administered the shot.

Eventually seated and out of breath, she concentrated every synapse into her arms and unscrewed the bottle, poured a shot into the lid and then threw her head back as the caramel liquid slid down her throat. Calming, healing, sanctuary.

Everything numbed and cooled down. She could feel her limbs again and knew that her heart was beating.

Somehow the experience lasted forever, but the clock read 9:53am.

She took a deep, shaky breath, hoping that Elise had taken her medicine upstairs, and then resumed her routine to meet Haiwrin.

The Music and Performance Block was impressively polished and decorated with a grand circular lobby, details never missed in even the ceiling. Each of the other three doorways, apart from the entrance, led to a different section of the block. Even peering through the wooden doors with tall glass windows revealed a beautifully dim-lit hallway lined with lamps, beckoning newcomers and familiar faces to indulge in the space and get lost for many, many hours.

Veaer was determined to make it to Haiwrin punctually, but she feared that she was already past the designated meeting time due to her oversight and lack of early wake ups on Saturday mornings.

She continued straight through the lobby which brought her to a wider corridor than the rest. Theatres had more foot traffic than the instrumental music studios, or the theory classrooms, and so the academy made room for loving parents and lasting academy patrons to attend presentation, play and screening nights. She especially enjoyed the water features indented into the wall, which always reminded her of swimming pools. The smell refreshed her mind and motivated her to get a hurry on to the end of the hallway where the sign for theatre one was lit up, indicating it was occupied.

When she burst through the double doors, she was pleased to find Haiwrin at the other side of the theatre, pacing the stage from end to end, only a couple stage lights illuminated. She couldn't tell much else from here, but she did note Haiwrin as a blue and black blob, his very own marker of caemi heritage as a blue fox even without his ears and tail.

As she drew closer, agitated muttering joined his sharp steps across the wooden plank stage. He stopped every so often to hum a scale of notes, but then fell back into the frantic set of actions. He didn't seem to realise that she had arrived.

"Hai?" Veaer called and waved her arms, her shoulders slightly shrinking into her centre from a second-hand feeling of... something. Embarrassment, sadness, confusion?

It was then that he really stopped and swung around, a smile suddenly dawning on his face, which appeared strange at first, but the relief in his loosened eyebrows and ultimate flow in his movements in climbing down from the stage calmed Veaer as well.

"Oh, Veaer, you made it! I was worried that I put the note in the wrong door, or if you weren't in your room, or you slept in..." He paused and placed his hands on either shoulder of Veaer, like he was making sure her entire being was there. Then he shifted her left to right, glancing behind her. "But Adair's not with you."

"She's meant to be here?" Veaer's immediately switched back to alert, knowing that Adair wasn't one to be late to these things. She hoped something hadn't happened; the number of ghosts in this academy seemed to increase every day, she felt it. But only Tychon followed her.

Haiwrin's frown only deepened. "We need to have a very serious conversation."

Often Haiwrin said that as a joke. Sarcasm was one of his quickly equip weapons. But in this sudden call to meet, and Adair running late, she had every right to believe this was a proper serious conversation.

"Do you want to talk about it before she gets here? Maybe we can run through what you're going to say." Despite Haiwrin and Adair being twins, their minds were not the same. A writing and literature student versus a music and performance student. One who wore light, breezy clothing, and one who wore dark, thick outfits. Even in mind, Veaer played mediator to ensure the two wouldn't consume each other like twins sometimes did in the womb.

Haiwrin took a deep breath and shook his body from top to bottom on the exhale. Then he stood with his feet together and clapped his hands together once. "Uh..." He stammered for many more moments before throwing his head into his hands and mumbling something. The tip of his ears brightened.

Veaer chuckled and stuffed her hands in the pockets of her jacket. She could feel her collar way too much but refrained from fidgeting for Haiwrin's sake. "Sorry, could you repeat that?"

"I..." His eyes darted. Veaer's did too, lest Adair appeared out of nowhere. "I want to leave the academy and take you and Adair with me."

Tychon's ghost started to cry in her ears as if an alarm set off. Her eyes widened and her heartbeat raced, just like it did when she was being attacked by poison. A hand flew to her chest. Her folios and classes, the years she spent perfecting art styles she hated and writing essays on historical artists in preparation for the Adraredon Academy entrance exam, and now she could see the finish line where she would go on to another prestigious art university with a revered diploma in hand.

Tychon stopped crying, but he hid in a dark corner of the stage, wrapped in webs and silk.

"You want to leave the academy," Veaer repeated, slowly. To buy herself more time for thought, or because she already knew what she would say and didn't want to admit it. "With all three of us. Why would you take me? Where would I go?"

The easiest questions to ask were the ones that related to her livelihood outside of the academy. She did have a parent to go back to, a couple younger siblings who were growing up too fast. But she didn't speak to them very often, didn't take up the school's payphone service that connected each building and the academy to the outside world.

And that didn't consider where she would complete the last three quarters of senior year. If she could even jump ship that easily and continue where she left off.

In these walls, it was easy to forget everything else outside, and easy to remain attached to everything that Adraredon Academy had to give.

"Of course, all three of us. Adair's my sibling, yes—but you're my best friend, Ve." He smiled but his eyes were swirling with conflict. Veaer instinctively glanced downwards and regretted it. She didn't realise Haiwrin saw her so importantly in his life. "I didn't—I haven't thought about that yet. But we can go somewhere together. We could... could rent a nice apartment in the town and then work on applications to a great program somewhere else in Syriphia."

Her heart clenched with the desperation yet hope in his voice, the ideas flashing in his mind, a dream surrounded by fluffy clouds and butterflies.

"I don't have the money for—I can't, I mean my family... we're so close to—?" The sentence tapered off with a whine and she squeezed her eyes shut. She was yet to mention the most important question. "Why do you want to leave?"

Haiwrin turned around and silently climbed back up the stage. He sat on the edge and hoisted Veaer up after him. "I've had a lot of time to think about life recently."

"Life?" She couldn't help the chuckle in the back of her throat. Life was so vague.

"And death. I guess the rumours going around have caught up to me. Maybe he really is gone." Haiwrin didn't need to mention Tychon, for he lingered by the stage curtains, and kept getting closer. "I know these things aren't common and maybe we don't have anything to worry about. But I don't want to spend the rest of the year looking over my shoulder, wondering if something will happen to Addie, or you, or me, at any moment. Tychon disappeared and no one knew."

Specks of dirt fell onto Haiwrin's shoulder, and she reached out without a second thought, only to realise nothing was there and she was just holding his shoulder for what she imagined was Tychon's doing. She squeezed to make up for it and Haiwrin gave her a look of appreciation.

He took another deliberate breath. "I think I'm scared, Veaer. I'm scared to leave you and everyone behind."

Me too.

She pulled him closer and hugged him tight.

The double doors slammed open, a flurry of footsteps rushing towards them and a familiar heave of breath permeating the hall. Veaer released her arms.

"Haiwrin! Ve!" Adair's hair was a mess, and she was still wearing her uniform, so she either didn't change from yesterday or decided to dress this way for a Saturday. She picked at her lips as she slowed her approach and glanced between them. Something was clearly wrong. "I'm so sorry for being late."

She shuffled over to Veaer and grabbed her palms, kissing the back of her hands. Then she hopped over to Haiwrin and laid a hand on his knee.

"Did I miss very much?" she asked when no one said anything.

Haiwrin continued to look elsewhere, and then met Veaer's eyes. *Help.*

Veaer nodded slowly. "Not too much. But I think this is a difficult topic for Hai to share... take a seat?" At first, she gestured to her own lap and when the twins broke into chuckles, she shifted over to allow her a space between Haiwrin and herself.

Just as Adair was getting into her spot, Haiwrin blurted out, "We're leaving the academy." A beat of silence. "Wait—"

"I think that came out wrong," Veaer immediately noted and stared at the side of Adair's head, as if she could go into the caemi's mind and hold the gears in place so Haiwrin had enough time to recover.

Adair lifted her hands to fix her hair but dropped them as soon as the words processed.

"I didn't mean it that way," Haiwrin added. "This is supposed to be a discussion, not an announcement."

Adair narrowed her eyes. "Then discuss," she said carefully.

He explained again the same as to Veaer, with more composure. About life and death, about renting an apartment in the next town over, about applying to new programs, and being safe. About love and being scared.

"I'm not leaving." Adair's expression was hard and set into a small, straight lipped smile and her eyes still trying to read her brother and Veaer like they were really joking, and she was meant to figure it out.

"And?" Haiwrin noticed words unsaid. His fingers climbed his arm in anticipation.

Adair jumped off the stage and turned to Haiwrin with her fists on her hips. "Are you serious? We're almost done with our studies, what's another few months?"

Flashes of blue and orange hair, Veaer's head flicking from side to side. The theatre became their grounds for debate and Veaer was nothing but a potted plant in the corner, listening but without a mind for a say.

Haiwrin: "A few months? And in those few months I might never see you again."

Adair: "I can't believe we're having this conversation. You really think we're just going to leave everything behind? *C'est n'importe quoi!* I thought a performance student like you would be better at looking at the bigger picture of things."

Haiwrin: "You don't understand—"

Adair: "I do understand."

Haiwrin: "And don't you dare bring our majors into this. What if I were to say you focus on the details way too much with blue curtains and yellow wallpaper? Literature students make me laugh sometimes."

Adair: "Okay, you're telling me not to bring it into the discussion, and then you bring it in? Much of a hypocrite."

Haiwrin: "Adair, I don't think you're taking Tychon's disappearance serious enough."

Adair: "Haiwrin, you're telling all of us—not just you, but all three of us—to just leave everything behind?"

Haiwrin: "What even is everything? The tests, the essays, your books, this hall, Veaer's portfolios, which are portable, actually, and the trail of imminent death?"

Adair: "*Mes dieux!* You're being dramatic."

Haiwrin: "You're being difficult!"

Adair and Haiwrin: "Veaer! What do you think?"

Two sets of eyes stared at her, pleading in their own senses. Adair's cheeks flared red, the tip of her ears bright as well. Haiwrin's gaze was glassy, and his hands shook in his lap.

Veaer inhaled loudly, like she had just broken the water tension of an incredibly still pool. She couldn't bear to continue looking into their souls and instead stared at her empty palms. Her arms began to numb.

"I think that..." The tension surrounding her was palpable—her lungs constricted and her breaths sounded raspy in her lungs.

There are only a few months left, but what happened to Tychon happened so fast.

Everything I need is here, but maybe there's more for me elsewhere.

The reason this happened has a name and its Elise.

Elise is why I want to stay, she promised we can't get hurt if we're together. I don't want her to get hurt.

Tychon's disappearance is only a one-off, but what if it does happen again?—it always does.

It's not so easy to just leave.

It was hard enough to get here in the first place.

You're both being dramatic and difficult.

Don't ask me what I think.

"I can't help." Her voice came out in pieces. "It's just too much. I love you both." She watched the double doors in the distance and wondered if anyone would walk in on them and solve this issue, just so she didn't have to hold it all. But when no one did, she moved closer to Haiwrin and gestured for Adair to come forward. She held them both in her arms.

"You don't have to help us. We can deal with our own feelings," Haiwrin said into Veaer's shoulder.

"I know this is hard, Ve," Adair added. It's hard. So hard. "But tell us what you want to do. This isn't only about us."

As Haiwrin wiped his tears with Veaer's jacket, Adair continued to stare. Those orange eyes that shone like gems, a beautiful face that she loved to run her fingers across. Coconut and strawberries, a refreshing feast of her own for the last couple of years that made existing less lonely. She didn't know how to describe the feeling that came with spending time with Adair. If there was a word for wanting to be with someone forever, and trying new things with them, and having them know they meant so much—without what a romantic relationship was. Because she knew there was someone else out there for Adair, and that she didn't deserve Adair.

Maybe *philia, storge, and ludus* was what she wanted to say.

Haiwrin looked up and he must have known Veaer's answer.

Hurt flickered over his features. He pulled back and stood up, shaking his head.

Veaer reached an arm out, but he was already walking to backstage. "Haiwrin—"

"Don't worry about it." He turned around with a smile that hardly reached his eyes. "Maybe... think about it, I suppose."

"Haiwrin!" Adair tried but made no effort to go after him.

When he left, silence consumed them, and they continued sitting in silence until the lights turned off on their own.

CHAPTER 30

A CONTINUOUS SEARCH FOR BEAUTY

By Saturday evening, Veaer hadn't completed anything productive.

She missed Elise, but she didn't want to think too hard about what happened the last time they were in the crypt. At least, the bad parts. She brought her fingers to her lips and an overwhelming desire and longing for that moment to happen again caught her heart. But would Elise really want that again? *She meant it.*

She didn't forget to take her antidote on Sunday morning—the reminder kept her up until after midnight and then she forced herself to sleep in case remaining awake for too long would summon the pain and spasms.

After she took the shot, frustration overtook every thought. She had two papers due next week and a folio to complete before the Friday after next. When she took out her sketchbook and laid in her bed, she did anything but draw. Counting the symbols in the wallpaper, taking her sheets off the bed and then putting them back on, rearranging her closet, and tidying her desk. She picked up the book on angels and Tychon's tarot journal and they would've been a productive way to procrastinate, but she convinced herself that picking them up would be too much of a commitment and, instead, wrapped a spare jacket around both books and pushed them to the back of her closet.

It was only midday. She decided to take another trip to get water from the kitchen, but when she returned, she noticed that her door was left ajar. She knew the locks worked well so it wouldn't have opened on its own.

Caution was her priority when she stepped back into her room and the first thing she noticed was her chair lying on the floor and pushed almost entirely under the desk. She didn't want to admit that the peculiar placement frightened her.

When she bent down to retrieve it, checking under the bed at the same time, something hanging from the desk's underside brushed the back of her neck. Her head hit the table at the same time as she whipped around. A spider, a piece of string, Tychon's ghost, or something else entirely—it didn't matter, and she scrambled towards her bed while slapping her hands on her neck.

A glance back revealed a folded piece of paper attached to under her desk.

She pulled it out and unfolded it.

Veaer ROSELL of SYRIPHIA. RED WOLF CAEMI is cordially invited to her initiation rites.

DRESS LIGHTLY. Preparation items and offerings will be provided.

Only bring yourself.

```
M T O C R T F E
E P T T A H O S
E R E O T E R T
2/0/0/0
```

More encoded text. She thought back to Elise finding that piece of paper and immediately going for the cathedral. This information had to lend itself to a location then. She wasn't provided an instruction for the initiation except to 'return', and perhaps the gallery lift wasn't the best method to try again.

The only numbers that would relate to the four provided was a time, and she quickly attributed it to twenty-four-hour time indicating eight pm, as instructed on Friday.

But the slashes between each number confused her. They weren't required to tell the time, and the numbers didn't seem to relate to any letters in the grid.

If Tychon was their original leader, then perhaps his journal's encoding style was the same.

> a b c d e f g h i j k l m
> n o p q r s t u v w x y z

She didn't have to do the third line to realise that wouldn't work. If anything, she knew by the middle of the first line that things weren't right but wanted to make sure. Her next idea was backwards:

> t r e t o e r e s o
> h a t t p e e f t r
> c o t m

She could see the words 'to', 'so', 'hat', 'at', 'pee', 'cot' but none of those seemed all that interesting. But she did like the idea of finding words in the puzzle.

'TFE' in the first line almost spelt 'THE', until she hooked onto the 'T' and traced downwards to find the word instead. A gasp escaped her at the realisation that this cipher could've been made with the columns, which made sense if the slashes on the numbers were meant to hint at such.

meetprotectorattheforest

meet protector at the forest

A burst of adrenaline rushed through her, and she cheered while hopping on her feet.

And then the fun and warmth disappeared, and she sat in bed until the evening, tracing triangles on a page.

A hooded protector led Veaer through the tunnels again, and this time they arrived at the door she recognised faster than the trip to the forest last time. The protector opened the door and then stepped back with the rest of the protectors, around six of them, waiting for Veaer to go forward.

She looked back to see if they would offer any information, but they all looked the same and did the same. Masks full of eyes, dark cloaks, and standing still.

When she did step in, Elise was already standing by the table at the back of the room, wearing a beautifully short and silky black dress that hugged her curves. Veaer covered her mouth, part feeling under-dressed for track-pants and a t-shirt as her version of dressing lightly, and part to hide the rising blush on her cheeks. *I could run my palms down from your shoulders, down, down, down to the hem of the silk and then pull it all the way up, revealing every surface that I can claim—*

If she thought the room was dim last time, now even more lanterns were put out. Every piece of furniture was pushed against the walls and the floor looked incredibly bare. She briefly remembered there being a rug last time.

"You're here!" Elise smiled brightly and darted towards her. "I'm glad we can do this together."

Veaer smiled back as best she could, noticing that the red-haired angel was crouching to the floor with a piece of chalk. Magical circles and ritual items. All a recipe for the death of Tychon Alastor Galacia.

"Me too, Elise." Her hands landed on Elise's hips, and she gently tugged her forward without a second thought. The material felt so nice, so easy to mold. Then she watched Elise close her eyes, and her heart began beating out of her chest. She leaned forward to meet lips and any regrets or worries dissipated effortlessly.

"Welcome, new initiates," a voice drew closer, and the leader appeared beside them in the same outfit as the last time they met. She didn't miss the white clothing and crystal jewellery that sat in two piles near the door to the next room. "Please get dressed while we set up. We're very excited for you to join us." She had to trust the smiling voice behind the mask.

Elise left her hold and scooped up the clothing laid out for her, then entered the other room to change. But wasn't Tychon in there? What was that room for? Would they be attacked by the smell of a rotting corpse when they least expected it, another punishment for really thinking this secret society would let them in? But Tychon's ghost sat in a chair to the side and reminded her that this was okay and what he wanted.

No screams or crying came from the other side of the door when it shut, and she only noted the rustling of fabric.

Someone placed a hand on her arm and she jumped, backing up into the table and frantically spinning around in fear of knocking anything to the floor. No broken goblets today, no shards of glass. They would have replacements but that didn't matter.

"Sorry, oh I'm so sorry." This voice belonged to the red hair angel, and upon closer inspection she noticed a small braid just to the side of their fringe. "I—uh, hello. Nice to meet you."

Their voice still didn't have a distinctive quality to it, and it made Veaer wonder how much of this place was fueled by magic. She couldn't exactly tell what spell it was, but she could feel it. Like hiding one's ears and tail, but for a voice. Her hands flew to the top of her head and as expected, she found her caemi ears.

The angel didn't have any visible caemi features, but through everything she still felt an aura. It was stronger than last time. Something in her knew for certain that this was the same angel as the one in Tychon's room.

"Nice to meet you too..." Veaer looked behind them to see if Elise had come out yet, but she was stuck speaking to the mysterious person. They were standing very close. "Did you need something?"

The angel shook their head and seemed to get the idea, taking a step back. "Everything is fine. Well, I wanted to check... if you're okay."

"With what?" Too vague, and there were a lot of ways to answer if she was okay.

"You should know what I mean." The irritated tone in their voice only set Veaer on edge. "You've been poisoned."

"Then you should know my answer to that!" Veaer shot back and she felt the leader turn to her from behind. Her shoulders shrunk into herself, and she sighed. "Fine, yes. I take the antidote each day and it fixes the problem. It's quite nice if I don't think about the poison part. How a little glass of liquid can cure all that..." She didn't know what to call it.

"Okay, uh. Drink water. Lots of water, when you take the antidote."

"...why?" Veaer crossed her arms and took another step back, but the angel closed the space this time.

"Alcohol. You can't take it well. You don't have the tolerance."

Veaer blinked a few times and her arms dropped to her sides. This angel knew her name, wanted to know if she was *okay* after poisoning her and now was offering advice based on her alcohol tolerance. Why was alcohol even relevant?

The angel answered as if they read her mind, "The antidote is there, but it's mixed in with rum or something. You shouldn't have more than a bit, and again, drink water."

She frowned and looked away from the expressionless mask. She didn't need to take advice from this person, but the urgency in the suggestion had her considering it.

"Thanks." She touched the tunic and linen robes on the table to do something with her hands.

"Fraternising with the initiate?" The leader had joined them, and Veaer noticed that they never mentioned each other's names. She could understand the anonymity while they weren't initiated yet, but had everyone else here seen their faces or heard their names? "You know you mustn't, yet."

"It's a courtesy," the red angel said in a clipped tone and then went back to finishing the magic circle.

"Hmm, and you, Veaer." He leaned forward and she almost saw the smirk behind his mask. "I hadn't realised you were the type to have more than one partner."

Her brows furrowed. She didn't appreciate these angels making assumptions or suggestions about her when she didn't know anything about them. "You make it strange by mentioning it. With no context at that."

"You and Adair, you and Elise. It's so entertaining." He laughed and Veaer forced one hand into a fist as the other counted fours. *1, 2, 3, 4.*

"What in the name of the patrons are you talking about? How do you know anything about me and Adair?" She turned her body away, but it only made her face the completed circle and the candles that were being placed along the edge. Memories crept up the walls of her mind and she shivered in anticipation of what would come next.

"Thursdays," was all he said with a shrug and then he walked past her to light a stick of incense by the vent.

The first name that came to mind was Izot Excava and that alone made her narrow her eyes to the back of the leader's head. But Izot didn't have dark skin and braided hair. At the same time, could she even trust her own eyes?

The door next to her opened and in the doorway stood a redressed Elise.

Elise's beauty and elegance instantly enamoured Veaer, now seeing the white cloth with embroidered purple, orange and blue hems in detail—on someone she really did want to lay her gaze on until she learnt every bit of her body inside out. Each earring twinkled when they managed to grasp a flicker of candlelight. Her necklace created an alluring line across her chest. *Beautiful, beautiful, so beautiful.*

They would be beautiful together.

CHAPTER 31
RITUAL

The ritual began with guided prayer by the leader, hang drum music playing through the gaps in the walls.

"Thank you, Angelus Caelum, for joining us. May the tower of air guide you safely and swiftly to our protection this circle today where we shall initiate Veaer Rosell and Elise Excava to the Ascension Order.

"Thank you, Angelus Cetus, for joining us. May the tower of water guide..."

His voice carried on in a repetitive fashion, but Veaer couldn't peel her eyes away. He didn't need to refer to any papers or books, and each word was smooth, like practised many, many times.

She inhaled the earthy scent of the incense and the walls around her started to breathe. They must have loved the smoke as well, an intoxicating quality that made her wonder if a candle was made in this flavour so she could keep it in her room forever. There was also something metallic that she wouldn't quite place, whiffs of something like burning sulphur.

"Angelus Caelum, Angelus Cetus, Angelus Orion, Angelus Pavo. The power of the past, the vision of the future." The leader clapped twice, and then bowed his head. His voice echoed through the vast and cavernous space that seemed to expand by the hundreds in seconds. "We also meet today in memory of Tychon Alastor Galacia, descendant of Iris Galacia, spirit of Angelus Caelum. His service will not be forgotten, and his legacy will survive for lines to come."

Veaer bowed her head too, and she wished to have been on her knees in order to bring her forehead to the chalk lines and stain it to show something of her guilt. But for now, she was weightless and floating above the circle, unbothered and tingling. Her limbs stretched and shrunk.

The leader continued, "We and our initiates have brought offerings for your favour." The four of them sat at each quarter of the circle, surrounded by a selection of items. The items spun and their colours became brighter and more intense. The spheres became pyramids, and the discs became bowls and then flat again. "The candles that behold this circle are for you. We present a selection of fruits for you to feast on with us."

Veaer grabbed the plate of ripe red apples next to her and the red angel lifted their chin in approval. The plate was soft and pliable under her touch, as if it would fall through her fingers at any moment. She placed the apples as close to the middle of the circle as she could. Elise did the same with a pile of green grapes.

"We also offer our ritual actions in initiation."

Her heart pumped to the beat of the music as they all picked up a small blade. The euphoria consumed her, and terror devoured her, and she felt truly happy to be here when she set her eyes directly across from her and saw Elise laughing. More laughter joined in from inside her own head.

Blood rushed through her veins as they all set a goblet of wine in front of them and held their fingers over the rim. The blade pierced her skin and a drop of red trailed down her thumb and into the liquid. Veaer stared at the ripples and smiled at the crystal butterflies dangling from her ears.

She followed the others in tracing her nicked thumb along the edge of the cup and then her other hand grabbed a pinch of cinnamon to sprinkle on top.

A flame burst from the wine and Veaer laughed before she blew on the fire. Her vision exploded into a kaleidoscope behind her eyelids as she brought the cup to her lips and drank.

When she lowered the cup, the walls had turned from brown to yellow, the circle wider and a strong draft almost tripping her. She remembered the sound of dripping crypt water and now it was loud and rushing in her ears. She looked down and the floor dropped into a pool of beautiful crystal water. So refreshing, so clear.

Elise was standing next to her and held her hand, tightly. Her lips moved but nothing came out, just rushing, rushing water. She looked divine, like a guardian spirit who had descended from the heavens, basking in a holy, holy, holy light that only she could see because she was worthy enough to see, but not worthy enough for what wisdom Elise was bestowing upon her.

A voice slithered through the cracks. "Our new angels have taken their blood oath to the Ascension Order." For a moment she remembered who the voice belonged to, someone she knew in school but didn't see very often. Someone important. "Now we ask for you to cleanse their souls in our waters. They will take the leap of faith in order to join us in mind, body and soul."

A pomegranate appeared in her hand, and she noticed one in Elise's hand too. They turned to each other and hooked their arms, bringing their fruits to each other's mouths and taking a bite into the sweet, sweet juice, seeds breaking between their teeth. Pink and red dripped down their chins and stained their robes but the angels assured them that the water would wash it all out.

The red angel pushed her, two solid hands against the small of her back, and she fell and closed her eyes and braced for the salty water to overtake her and cleanse her.

Wash away my sins. Take away my guilt, I can't hold it anymore. It's too much, it's too much, it's too much. So much to gain, so much to lose. Wash away my sins.

The salt stung her cuts and scars, especially the ones she couldn't see, and she screamed under the water until someone pulled her out and wrapped a towel around her.

When she opened her eyes again, she was back in the warm, ritual room facing Elise. Her pretty little mouth moved again and this time she heard *I love you, Veaer.*

I love you too, Elise.

The leader said more words that bounced off the walls which were covered in strange symbols and sigils. The red angel danced around them, throwing herbs at their feet. She wanted the red angel to take her to dance too.

Instead, she giggled and took Elise's hands as the leader anointed them with oil.

She watched the oil drip down her forehead and onto her nose and down to her lips.

The music grew louder, and the leader chanted wondrous words that she didn't understand. The spirits of the angels were upon her and now she knew she could dance as she pleased. Their spirits were so familiar, lifelong. They were friends and they knew each other. When she stared into the smokey forms of the four heroes, she knew their names, their real names. *Iris, Marin, Myst and Kalaya, is this all that you ever wanted from me? When you sought the help of a Rosell, was this it?*

An overwhelming amount of silk surrounded her, and she grasped for something to hold onto, until she found Elise in her palms and the princess was smiling down at her. It was only when she looked for where the breeze was coming from that she looked upon a balcony she knew very well. Framed butterflies scattered across the room, so many specimen frames. Butterflies of all colours and they kept changing shapes and sizes.

The walls bent and broke and a grassy field fell upon her, sunny even though it was night. Cold even though she was hot. She was so little, and the trees touched the stars. Then her entire being filled to the brim with dread. She knew what happened here. She watched a young girl running away from her. Veaer held her arms out and tried to run too but her legs were too short, and everything was so far away. The young girl fell to the ground, her brown hair pooling around her like blood and an angel appeared above her. *Kalaya Thawan, Angelus Pavo.* And the angel cried.

Veaer, I love you. I love you.

Elise was still wearing her robes, stained with fruit juice and blood, and she laughed while bending down to kiss Veaer like she wanted to suck her soul away. And Veaer kissed back and let her hands roam and pulled Elise into her because she wasn't allowed to leave.

Don't leave, don't leave, don't leave. They can't hurt us if we're together. They can't hurt us.

CHAPTER 32
HARQ CARRASH

Year 3, Semester 1, Week 10

Veaer spent her Monday morning with her head in Elise's toilet.

When she finally felt entirely empty inside, she flushed and washed her face and mouth, and Elise offered for her to take a shower from the other side of the door.

"What about my uniform?"

Her voice was dry and quiet, but Elise seemed to understand as she answered, "I'll have someone bring it up, don't worry." And she didn't worry.

She let the warm water thread her skin back together as she slid the bar of soap across her body. She hated feeling sick and nauseous so when she woke up this morning with a headache that rivalled every headache she'd ever had and saliva pooling in her mouth, she only wanted to cry. She preempted what would come next and locked herself in the bathroom. The words of the red angel played in her head, on drinking water when it came to alcohol, and her experience only worsened when her body started to convulse in need of the antidote.

As soon as she stepped out of the shower, tremors overtook her system and she rushed into the main area with just a towel in hopes of finding her uniform somewhere in the room. She was pleased to spot it on a chair next to the tea table, a shot of the antidote poured out for her already with two pills and a note reading 'medicine'.

At first, she was hesitant to take it, unsure if this was for Elise instead. But then she saw an identical bottle next to the bed and threw her head back for the sweet and spicy liquid, the pills being strange lumps that moved through her throat.

The bedroom door opened just as she fastened her loafers and Elise walked in holding a folded piece of paper, already dressed for the school day. It appeared to be a new message by the frown that settled on the princess' lips.

"What's it say?" Veaer pushed the chair back under the table and then pocketed the amber bottle.

"Tomorrow night is the next ritual."

"So soon?" She walked over to the large bed by the balcony, finding her satchel of sketchbooks and paper. A well of appreciation rose in her chest and she looked back at Elise with a smile.

"Yes," Elise replied but her eyes said something more in the way they darted away from Veaer. "We must fast as well. A sort of abstinence as part of the ritual's offering."

"Okay, though I'm still wondering why so soon. One or two days doesn't seem like enough time to recover." Veaer monitored Elise's reactions and found something suspicious in the way she took a step back and wrapped her arms across her chest. "Did something happen?"

"They want to capitalise," Elise started, a vacant look in her eyes as she stared out her glass balcony doors. Maybe the trees knew something she didn't. "I remember conversing with the leader last night... about visions." Grass blades and a waterfall of brown. A crying angel. Pomegranate. Visions may have been the correct label for her too. "I saw Tychon, and he was with us, dancing and singing. He wore the same robes with pink and blue gems, clear quartz around his wrists."

Veaer didn't want to admit that she'd been seeing Tychon this whole time and also met the four heroes last night. But maybe they weren't even there—she could hardly remember anything else that happened, or how she ended up in Elise's room, but Elise didn't appear to have a problem with this development.

"Is it... the grief?" Veaer asked. What she really meant was *is it the love left behind that's coming back for you now?*

"I think about him sometimes. But not enough that he would... seem so happy to be around me again. Like we used to be." Elise busied her hands with preparing her own satchel for the day.

Before he passed, Elise and Tychon didn't leave each other's side. If Elise sat down, most knew not to take the next seat over. When Veaer looked at Elise's assignments that required a partner, Tychon's name was always right next to hers. When they wanted the world to know them and what they had, they sat on the balcony and spoke to the moon. Veaer wasn't meant to know, but she did anyway.

"Had they not seen Tychon before you?" Despite how strange it sounded, it seemed to be the easiest question. Rather than 'what made your experience so special?' or 'so we're meant to break the rules for this?'. They were already breaking many rules.

"No. They considered it a sign to keep trying, because if we can contact Tychon and learn more about what happened when he..."—*you really do want to know what he was doing, don't you?*—"And if he can tell us what to do next, it would provide proper direction to the order, more than Q can provide."

That was true. She had never made an effort to have a constructive conversation to Tychon to see if he would lend anything useful past his death. Perhaps that would've been a useful avenue when she wanted to know more about Elise initially, but she was making her own progress in that sense.

Veaer strode across the room with a glance at the clock. She had plenty of time to get to homeroom—

She stopped in the doorway, her fingers letting go of the handle as the door remained open.

"Q? Who's that?" She turned around and found Elise closer than she anticipated. The princess placed a hand against the door frame and Veaer took that as a sign that she wasn't allowed back in.

"Oh, it's what the leader told me to call him. Q." Elise waved her hand dismissively and then went to step forward, forcing Veaer to move away from the door and let Elise lock up behind her. "Just like the other angel. R."

R for Red? "But why did he only tell you, not me?" Veaer said quickly, wanting to catch Elise's hand as she darted towards the staircase, but she was just too late, and her palms were left cold and empty.

Elise didn't get a chance to reply when the other door opened. Izot walked out first, chatting away about something with no regard for the others in the hallway. Harq stepped out after him, then balancing on his cane as he took a key out and locked Izot's room.

"Ah, Elise." Izot paused to take a moment to stare. His lips smiled but his eyes did not. "And Veaer. Happy Monday morning, yes?"

A thread had been tugged tight between the Excava siblings and Veaer wanted to be anywhere else, but Izot had blocked the way back, there was nowhere to go when both rooms were locked, and Elise was still standing at the top of the staircase.

Harq was the one to push past the prince and smile, gently and kindly, at Veaer. "Apologies, Veaer. The way these two act when no one is around... it's appalling, really!" He laughed and she found herself joining. That was true if she considered herself part of this 'no one' collective. He pressed his glasses up the bridge of his nose and a corner of his lips twitched upwards. "You've taken a liking to Elise?"

Veaer's cheeks flushed red, and she turned to gain Elise's opinion on the question, but only caught a glimpse of an underclassman climbing the stairs to escort Elise to class, leaving Veaer to stand with the prince and Harq in a space she entirely didn't belong in.

She shuffled against the wall, watching Izot walk past her like she was nothing. Harq shook his head, turning his feet towards the staircase as if he wanted to escape this manor as soon as he could, though remained still.

"Shouldn't you follow?" Veaer prompted quietly. She didn't want to be scrutinised any longer under his gaze.

"Those Excavas, always testing us," Harq mumbled for Veaer to hear only. At this, she perked up and wondered where this was coming from or where this was going. "Perhaps you and I are not so different. Wouldn't you do anything for Elise Excava?"

Somehow, when he turned away for a breath, his glasses didn't reflect against the light at all. As if there were no lenses in those frames. Why would he wear broken glasses?

"Yes," she whispered, trying to shake off any paranoia. "I would." Just as she made an oath to the Ascension Order, she made one in heart to Elise.

Harq picked up his cane and held it in two hands behind his back. Veaer's gaze instantly flicked to his bad leg, but it stood like the other, no telling sign for which had been injured. She knew nothing except for her racing heartbeat and melded even closer to the wall when Harq leaned towards her ear.

"I would do anything for Izot Excava."

∼

Veaer stayed on the fifth floor for a very long time, staring at the patterns on the wall. Her thoughts were quiet.

I wonder why Q only revealed his code name to Elise and not me. Did I simply forget about it?

It would've been so easy for him to come up to me and say, "Hello there, Veaer, my other new initiate. It slipped my mind to introduce myself! How rude. I'm Q."

Oh, thank you, Q. I'm so glad you were able to share this necessity of an answer with me and not just the princess. I did the same ritual as her. I'm as deserving as her.

Then they grew louder.

Elise, why did you just walk away? We have something special, and we need to stay together. You said it yourself, and now you've turned your back on your own words?

"Everything we have. Everything that is ours."

You are everything I have. Is that not enough?

And louder.

"We're leaving the academy."

"I'm not leaving."

"Veaer, help us. Tell us what to do. You're important, you can tell us."

I don't know the answer, I don't know the answer.

And louder.

"I would do anything for Izot Excava."

What the fuck did that mean?

We aren't friends. Do non-friends speak to each other in this way? We have only spoken on rare, polite occasions. Does he plan to hurt Elise? Do something to her for his loverboy?

Patrons above, why have you done this to me?

It pained her to no end, a cramp setting in her jaw from clenching too hard, and when she finally moved, it was to turn around and hit the wall over and over again. For too many days she was left with questions and questions and more questions. Why were answers so scarce? In an academy dedicated to learning and gaining information, why was she so useless?

She could only hide behind the affections of Elise and the familiarity of the twins for so long. The desire for knowledge that burrowed deep in her heart and bones laid dormant when she pleased it through dopamine and thrill. But when it woke, it woke up frustrated and overstimulated and in need of a buffet.

What she had learnt in the last week wasn't enough to feed the beast.

Consequence and penance for what happened to Tychon wasn't enough.

Could this be a different feeling entirely? Perhaps she hadn't really awakened it.

Was this jealousy? She didn't like to feel jealous because it meant she wasn't grateful for what she had. It was a sick feeling that stuck to her like mud on her face. For everyone to see, to show how out of touch she was. The world didn't revolve around her.

Her body heated up and her hand flew to her face, glad for her cold palm against red cheek. Something vague about water echoed in her mind but she didn't have time for that. The wallpaper merged into dancing patterns and Tychon was at the bottom of the staircase, throwing petals and herbs on the carpet to a song she almost didn't hear until it started playing in her head.

Light bulbs appeared in the wallpaper until they exploded and became replaced by little feathered angels.

More answers. If she could answer her own questions, the beast would go away, Elise would come back, and Harq wouldn't hurt them.

She rushed down to the fourth floor, crashing through the ghost of Tychon and leaving him in pieces. He cried and cried but the sound disappeared with each floor she descended. Gold and red wrapped around her, flowers flying out of vases to run along with her. The paintings came alive and danced as she spotted her dorm room and burst through the door. An explosion came from somewhere behind her and she dove for the closet, digging out the books she had wrapped in a jacket and tossing them on the table.

She opened the cover with a smiling angel, but the words wouldn't cooperate and hid among blades of grass. Every page she turned revealed a little girl that bled hair, then blood, then crystals, then wings, and then blood again. That day continued to elude her. She shut the book and slid it across the desk until it fell on the floor with a satisfying thump.

Her fingers tried to find the tarot journal, but it started sinking into the table and didn't come out underneath. She sighed and rubbed her eyes, and it was on the floor now too.

Before she knew it, she was in front of Adair's bedroom door. Uncertainty coated her as she wondered how she managed to get up here with no permission. She knocked, despite knowing Adair was going to be at class already. When no one replied, she tried the doorknob and found it unlocked.

Adair's room was just as she remembered, warm autumn colours and incredibly neat. A bookshelf and a desk combination, the books alphabetised and Veaer remembering every time she was invited here and would swap some of the books around to see if Adair noticed. She always did.

Veaer walked over to the desk and opened the drawers, pressing at the bottom of each until the third one budged and moved to reveal a key.

A master key to Miriam Manor; she could get into any dorm room she wanted.

When she exited and closed the door, she was in front of Tychon's room. A clock ticked nearby. *Tick, tick, tick.* Oh, she was late for class.

A sign that read 'under investigation' hung from Tychon's door-knob, covering the keyhole. She moved it out of the way and stuffed the key in, backwards at first, and then correct. The door unlocked under her command.

"I'll find you," she said to the void. A black hole sucking her into Tychon's desolate, abandoned room. So quiet, it was so quiet. Perfect for thinking, perfect to create a masterpiece.

Her vision rifled through shards of images and symbols that felt familiar enough that it may have been a memory but strange enough that it could've been one of her projects, but also what if it was all a dream? She always believed dreams were a way to access parallel universes. Just as she could rewrite memories whenever she wanted, she just had to remember. Memories weren't real, they were recollections of the last time they remembered something.

The tears of Angelus Pavo channelled through Veaer, and her cheeks soaked in sorrow and regret, into the carpet, into the dirt.

"Who did this to you?" Veaer sobbed as she clutched Tychon's bed sheets. A kaleidoscope of butterflies sat in the criss-cross pattern of the donna, open and without concern for prey. "You were always so kind. You gave me a flower. You told me that I could make a wish."

The flower was so pretty. It matched the little girl's purple cat ears and tail.

Kitt. Kitt Kitt Kitt. What a pretty name.

"You believed the world could be better. We were only little.

Only ten. Why did they take you from me? Why did they prove you wrong?"

A name echoed in her mind, but it was too far away to remember.

The murmurs coming from the doorway, spilling blinding light, only made it harder to remember.

Then a shadow of a girl blocked the light and stood above her.

"Kitt?" Veaer asked the shadow.

"Veaer." The voice was too familiar to be Kitt. It must have been—

"Elise?" Veaer choked on smoke and dust. "Oh, Elise."

CHAPTER 33

CONSIDERATIONS FROM A YOUNGER TIME

First the physician asked her to walk in a line while touching her nose.

Then she had to state her name and birthday.

Then he shone a light into her eyes and asked her to follow his finger.

Headmaster Doallan Excava wasn't happy that she failed all three tests.

"Miss Rosell, being under the influence—not only as a minor, but during school hours—is a great offence to the academy."

Veaer frowned at the colours that dulled around her. The browns and greys in the headmaster's office were just as they seemed the day she stole that folder of maps

The big leather chair behind the headmaster only made him look bigger and the light that dangled above them made everything so close and tight. The shut door and windows suffocated her lungs and as much as she wanted to watch the wallpaper again, the headmaster's eyes burned flames through her for seeming the least bit distracted.

She didn't remember when she sat down or how she had arrived in the admin building. She didn't exactly know what she had done wrong.

I remember... I remember Kitt.

And another big leather chair in a different room. The wallpaper wasn't as fancy, and the desk wasn't polished, expensive wood. This headmaster was a principal, with cheap landscape paintings on either side of his office to make it seem peaceful. It was not.

"And what else can you remember, Veaer?"

I don't... I only see...

"How did you feel?" He folded his hands with a sad smile. "Did you get... angry? Frustrated?"

"I didn't do anything!" Veaer snapped and clutched the arms of her chair, the leather squeaking beneath her fingers.

She took enormous breaths as if the room didn't have enough oxygen. She only heard the snapping of fingers and the physician returned to her side, placing hands on her shoulders, and then gesturing to the glass on the table.

"Have a drink. We have time to discuss this, Veaer," the physician prompted. She hated it when they kept using her name.

She took the tall, beautiful glass of water with two hands and gulped down half. The liquid moved through her throat, her chest, and her body.

"I didn't... do anything," Veaer repeated, slowly, deliberately like it mattered in this situation. She hadn't taken anything that would be considered 'influencing', and the daily antidote was so small, barely anything. It wouldn't have forced her into the headmaster's office.

"I'm not here to berate you, young Rosell." The headmaster smiled, his trimmed beard moving with his lips. She couldn't bear to look at his eyes again, and so she didn't know what he really meant. "I'm protecting the school, the students, and you."

From me?

"Yes, we need to keep the other children in another room. Just for a little while."

They're not in another room, I am.

"And you'll have special activities with the doctor to make sure you're okay."

But I am okay.

"There are big feelings that come with losing a friend."
Losing a friend.

"I don't understand," Veaer spoke to the gap between the headmaster's eyebrows. At least she would look like she was making eye contact. "What happens now?"

"Typically, something like this would be grounds for expulsion. It promotes ill behaviour, damages your education, and it may come to harm others."

The ceiling may as well have collapsed upon her and crushed her little bones and brains. Expulsion. She couldn't afford that in more ways than one. She had to stay with Adair and Haiwrin, had to complete her education. She couldn't have something so dastardly on her record—expulsion from an elite academy for being under the influence. Even if the three of them did move into an apartment in another town and wrote up applications to send in, she would only get a big red stamp in response. Rejected.

"I must add," Headmaster Excava continued, "You were reportedly found in Tychon Alastor Galacia's room. After recent events and the ongoing investigation, that was in very poor taste, Miss Rosell. I will not ask why you were there; I'm sure there were reasons." Veaer considered the headmaster's own mistakes in this situation. When she flitted her gaze across his face, she noticed the slight nod he made towards the physician. "But it is still unacceptable."

Because the Galacia family would sue? Be willing to cut their founding ties to the academy as one of their own met their demise right on this land? But she didn't feel her addition was appropriate.

The headmaster reached over to a drawer and pulled out a stapled booklet of papers. He placed it in front of Veaer, and then grabbed a pen to set on top.

She didn't make a move, trying her best to not even look at the papers.

"I'll need you to sign and initial in a few places."

"I didn't do anything," she repeated and stayed still. The headmaster also remained still except for an arch of an eyebrow.

"I'm not finished, Miss Rosell."

She stuffed her hands under her thighs and counted her fingers with each dip into the leather cushion. What else did he have to say?

"These papers are not for your termination." He gestured an open hand towards them. She didn't like the word termination. "As mentioned, you are also under my protection. Excava protection."

A knock sounded at the door and Veaer whipped around to look, fast enough that something cracked in her neck, and she winced as she settled back down. She didn't have to get excited for a secretary or receptionist wanting to speak to the headmaster.

He jutted his chin up and called, "Come in!"

Two sets of footsteps, often heard together at the start and end of the day, upstairs on the fifth floor, but never—hardly—during the day. One confident and strong, the other light and like a ghost.

This time she did turn around, and she was a mess of feelings at seeing Izot and Elise walking in and standing side by side to the left of the headmaster's desk.

"My lovely son and daughter were kind enough to vouch for you." *Vouch?* "My boy—" The headmaster reached up to Izot's shoulder and shook it heartily. "I trust him and his judgement on the students. He says you're dedicated, a gem among rocks—his words, not mine—and deserve to complete your capstone year."

Veaer couldn't help but narrow her eyes at the golden boy. He didn't smile like he had said those words genuinely and was reliving that conversation. But he didn't frown or have a strange look on his face. He simply stood there like he was a soldier, waiting for a command. The only bit of movement was his eyes darting to her and then away.

"And my dear, Elise. She has so much to say about you." *So much?* "That you belong here. That she quite appreciates your insight in the studies of the art stream. She would be saddened for me to expel you for this." He didn't grab Elise's shoulder or gesture for her to come closer, but he did look over at his daughter with a fountain of affection.

Elise wasn't like her brother. She stared at Veaer with a smile.

Like *come here, you're protected.* Just like the headmaster said. Excava protection. And each word was real and valuable like gold. Like crystal earrings and white linen robes.

"For a stunning record, apart from this occasion, I have, instead, decided to assign community or voluntary work to make up for the misconduct. You are to report to an experience leader anytime you have a study period, until the end of the year."

That wasn't so bad. It was perfect. Anything other than being expelled from her dream academy was perfect. She only had to miss her sessions with Adair, but perhaps she would understand.

She wanted to run into Elise's arms and hold her tight enough to express how happy she felt.

"Thank you for your generosity, headmaster." Veaer would've kneeled and prayed but instead she bowed her head politely and signed where required so that she could be admitted into the community work program. "I won't forget this."

"I hope not!" The headmaster laughed and clapped Izot's back.

The prince and princess laughed too.

Veaer connected invisible threads between Elise's black academy standard blazer and Izot's special red and gold student council blazer as she walked behind them.

They were silent as they strode, side by side, through the admin building lobby. When the autumn-turning-winter breeze hit them from the open door, she only heard soft grunts from both siblings.

Then they stepped outside and shut the door behind them, and Izot practically leapt away from his sister, down the stairs and already looking for the next place to be.

"You're welcome. I hope you're happy," Izot grumbled into his hands as he brought them to his mouth and blew hot breath.

Veaer furrowed her eyebrows and turned to Elise for answers. The young woman was staring off into the distance, like she had already left for her next place internally.

"Thank you, dear brother." She faced Izot and smiled with all teeth. "Your performance was stiff, but believable."

"I'm an international studies student, not music and performance. Do not even compare." Izot returned the same striking smile, and Veaer wondered if a snake would fall from both of their mouths and start fighting before eating their own tails. "Goodbye."

The prince walked away, turning around only once more to look at Veaer, and then continued onwards to the learning centre.

"Do you have somewhere to be?" Elise asked as Veaer stared at the sky.

"I don't even know what time it is."

Elise shook her head and then held out her hand. Veaer took it and was happy to be led, even if she didn't know where.

They walked the neat stone paths that gave the courtyard meaning. Each tile was perfectly imperfect, like they were designed, with slants and chips, to carry lost students to unknown revelations.

Sweet air filled her lungs, and she was never more ready to take on life. She wondered if someone had moved the buildings back by several metres, rearranged them just to have a go. A giant hand from the sky replacing every brick with fresh plaster. The flow of magic, even if restricted, suddenly able to touch their faces, hands, hearts, and mind.

"I should make you my muse for the final portfolio," Veaer whispered so she wouldn't disturb the birds in the trees and bugs in the grass.

"Why would you do that?" Elise said from somewhere behind her.

Veaer paused and looked back. They stood at the centre of the universe. The grand sculpture in the middle of the courtyard where all four heroes watched over their creation for eternity.

Because I love you. "You saved me."

"I know what my father is like, that's all."

Veaer joined her side and glanced into Iris Galacia's eyes, full of stars, at Iris Galacia's hands, full of cards.

"I think it's fate that brought us together," Veaer said, the profound thought dropping upon her from the heavens. She hadn't considered the idea before but felt sure more than anything. "If I am only left with my art of you, then we will still be together."

Soft touch caressed her right hand. She filled the space between them and connected their fingers, palm against palm. Each line that told Elise's story was a line pinned on hers. She would need to learn palmistry one day but that wouldn't be hard. Not if it was for Elise.

"Even after everything? Even after today?"

"It wasn't your fault." Her gaze ripped away from the statue, replaced with silky black hair, deep brown eyes, dark painted lips— rose-gold cheeks that fit perfectly in her hands. She elected to test that theory again, stepping in front of Elise and holding a hand to her cheek.

Elise smiled up at her and when Veaer looked through the windows of the soul, she saw peace, power, and angels. Angels clad in white and purple and blue and orange robes, winged, with jewels hanging from their ears and necks.

She let go of Elise's hand and instead held her waist, pulling her closer so that their breath warmed their faces.

"Tychon always said there was a reason for everything." Elise's words hovered over Veaer's lips.

And Veaer closed the gap, leaning in, and pressed their lips together.

The angels sung above and Tychon danced in circles throwing lavender and foxglove.

Elise's hands flew to her shoulders and held them tight.

They smiled and giggled like little kids and then waltzed to a song floating through the air.

They made it through another day.

CHAPTER 34
THE SECRETS OF AN ANGEL

Essays to write, folios to work on, community work journal to maintain. Time seemed to run from her, as opposed to her ability to complete work in advance just weeks ago. The cogs in her mind pumped harder than they had for a while and she was glad of it, for the structure and direction it brought to her derailed days. But when she looked down and among messy papers and half-done art pieces was the tarot journal open to a random page and the book on angels on top of a pile of art theory books, everything stopped. She knew, or at least she thought she knew, that she wasn't the one who did this, and she hadn't known anyone to come into her room without permission. Adair and Haiwrin were always respectful of her space.

Had another student walked in and touched her things?

She reached over to a small box that sat against the wall and opened it; the gem necklace was still in there. So not a valuable robbery. Her art was clearly still sitting here, waiting to be done. So not an academic robbery.

Perhaps it was no robbery at all, as she looked through her closet and found all her clothes. And her library books were all accounted for, so no one had taken the task of returning them for her.

She returned to the desk and sat down. Her finger touched the open page, and nothing happened. Then she flicked to the next.

"I tell you the things that I care about you knowing."

Her name was repeated several times among paragraphs over the spread of pages.

Curiosity ached in her limbs and folded her mind.

The cover still had a sigil drawn upon it, even if faded, and the title page wasn't encoded this time, Tychon's name clearly written in the top right corner.

She pulled the book closer and brought her finger to the first thing she saw.

She hurried to the previous notes and scanned each card.

> Ten of Pentacles
> Forms of inheritance, not only in monetary form. The ten, like a circle, like a cycle. Though I'm not reading the end of a cycle, in the sense where it completes, but that it is reaching a point that marks an end, only for it to start again. I haven't read her enough to understand what this cycle end entails but in conjunction with the previous pull

Her tongue was heavy in her mouth and her hands grew numb as they held the leather journal cover.

> Six of Cups.
> Wheel of Fortune.
> Two of Wands.
> ...young intervention.
> ...past lives.
> ...destiny.
> Veaer Rosell and Elise, destined to cross paths. Together bringing something anew, for better or for worse.

She looked at the start of the entry. Recorded more than a year ago.

Had Elise known this whole time?

When Veaer donned her full-face angel mask, she felt invincible.

That incredible earthy scent returned, and the walls woke up again. She looked around to find Q and R's heads turning into blue triangles, then yellow circles, then red squares. Then they went back to normal, with their million eyes and no mouths.

"Thank you Angelus Orion for joining us. May the tower of fire guide... Thank you Angelus Pavo for joining us. May the tower of earth..."

Chanting filled the room that suddenly went from dark and cold to sunny and warm, dirt and grass beneath her bare feet, butterflies dipping between red roses and then flying away. She found a bush of lavender by a tree and pulled the flowers away, bunching them in her hands and then tossing them in the air.

Please accept my offering angels! And she spun, linking arms with Elise and pressing their masks together. A kiss in spirit, in a higher place. *Please don't hurt me, Angelus Pavo!*

The Order read poetry and excerpts about love and adventure and hurt and dying. They sang a song she didn't know but learnt from reading Elise's lips after they took off their masks to embrace pomegranate once again. They read what were considered myths of the four heroes, but they knew them to be true when the angels told them so.

"They're telling me things," Elise whispered, and Q and R gathered around her. "They told me..." Elise gasped and clutched her heart. *What did they tell you?*

"They told her to do it. To get rid of her."

Who, Tychon? Who? Tell me please. Don't hurt me.

"She had to get rid of her. She had to do it. And then it was me. And the others are next." Tychon cried as he bit into a slice of apple, mushy and decaying like his arms, turning black. "It's in her blood, in her name, in her nature."

Tychon, on all fours, his face made of teeth and his eyes stuck in his hands, bolted up to her and grabbed her collar, throwing her backwards into a table. Air escaped her and she cried to get it back. Something snapped and she didn't know if it was the table or her bones, but she clutched the wood and screamed.

"Veaer!" A voice broke through layers of mud and petals and for a moment her head flung back and forth, unsure of where the voices started and ended. It sounded familiar. Like a Thursday afternoon. Like strands of orange hair. Like a beautiful girl who deserved so much more. She should've been with Adair right now, comforting her as her brother wanted to send them away. "Veaer, what happened?"

R crouched in front of her and helped her to her feet. They patted her robes down and guided her to a chair to sit. Then they poured a glass of water and held it out.

The music still played its tune with Elise's droning voice in the background, as if reading scripture from a book only she could see. A whine rose from Veaer's throat.

"You need water."

"Why do you keep telling me I need water!" Veaer forced the glass out of R's hand and threw it to the ground. The shards of glass burned into the ground. Then, when she blinked, a broom leaned against the wall with a small pile of glass behind it. "Patrons above, please. I just—I don't...."

The voices, the smells, Elise, the grass, the butterflies, and angels. She couldn't understand, no matter how hard she tried. She needed answers to something, and she had failed on all accounts today as well.

R took a seat next to her, their short red hair appearing so fluffy. She confirmed her thought by bringing her hand to their head and stroking. The angel flinched but didn't make an effort to move away, their mask staring back at Veaer.

"I want to make sure you're okay," they said, voice cracking in a strange way. Like a chick trying to get out of an egg so it wouldn't be forcefully broken by large, fleshy hands. A light like a fire, full of red, orange and yellow, pulsed from the outline of R's being. It was nice.

"Well, I wish I could be more okay," Veaer managed as she closed and opened her hands. She also wished for that glass of water to come back.

Then it appeared again in R's hand. "Here you go."

They must have heard, or the angelus told them.

"Can I ask you a question, Veaer? It's very off-topic."

Veaer looked through the bottom of her empty glass and towards R's face. Sort of face.

"Maybe off-topic is good."

She watched R's mask move up and down, but with no mouth to see, there were no words to put together. After a few moments, R was completely still. Then they placed a hand on her shoulder and shook her back to reality.

"Were you listening? What do you think of what I said?"

She could've cried then, knowing that she hated it when others didn't pay attention to her words as if they didn't matter. How could she have done it to someone else? And with every second that ticked by, she was getting further and further away from a sincere apology. Even as she thought this, she watched R move their hands back to their lap, their back turning ridged, distant.

Veaer reached a hand out to R's knee. It was half covered in robes, half revealing light smooth skin.

"Please repeat... maybe you can take your mask off?" Veaer asked, but she had a feeling that was a futile request.

"The mask will stay on." The expected answer. "Until... it's safe." The unexpected addition. Yet they continued with no elaboration, "I have a friend, someone I'm close to and really care about. I've only known them for so long, yet I know them in many ways." Somehow this sounded like a riddle more than a question. "And they know me in many ways. But there is something I haven't been able to reveal, in that... not that I'm embarrassed at all about this but it's new and my friend hasn't known me as anything else. What do I do?"

Veaer's mind drifted to eight years ago, a time when she considered Kitt to be that person. They hadn't known each other long but knew there was a future that would change that. Going to school, walking home, asking her mother if she could have her friend over and when her mother said no, she asked her father. They made plans and she remembered something about a Tuesday and two weeks. She knew Kitt as the girl who sat behind her in the classroom. She would twist herself around to say hi, but only after she threw a pencil at the girl for kicking her chair too many times. She also wondered about a specific memory, where she watched Kitt hold her hands together and a small glowing creature emerged from the depths of her palms. Magic, but different. They were both caemi, Veaer: a red wolf, Kitt: a purple cat, but what Kitt did that day was supposed to be something wonderful for the present.

"It sounds like you have a nice person in your life." What was known about their life, at least. "Does this person care about you in the same way you do for them?" Veaer leaned back in her chair and played with the glass in her hand, trying her best not to drop it.

"Sometimes it's hard to tell, because when we do spend time together, it's entirely thrilling and wonderful. I wouldn't want to be anywhere else, and it seems the same for her as well. But when we aren't together, there's an absence and I don't know if I want to get... whatever *it* is back to fill in the gaps. There's a lot in me to give, but I fear that she doesn't want to take. That she is afraid of taking as I am afraid to give, but I am willing to because that's how much it means to me."

Veaer held a hand to her chest and scrunched the material that bunched there. She related to the feeling so well that she wanted to run away from this conversation. She wasn't the right person to advise on this. But if it was for someone else then maybe it was okay. Maybe she could help R and their friend and that would be enough.

"How about you practise with me?" Veaer suggested.

"Tell you my secret?"

"Calling it a secret might make it scarier. Maybe you want your friend to get to know you even more because you care about each other." She straightened up and placed the glass on a nearby table. "I think I know how your friend feels. I'm scared to hurt someone, and so why should I take from them? They have better people to go to."

"I don't want to go to anyone else," R said with whole certainty. "It's her. I want it to be her."

Veaer nodded slowly and attempted a discreet look over at Elise. The princess and the leader laughed and danced together, and she could see colourful mist surrounding them, a sign of strong magic being manifested. A beautiful mix of orange and gold that reminded Veaer of home, where magic was convenient and not seen as a hindrance.

Her gaze followed the leader as he ran to the door and called out to the darkness. The protectors burst into the room and joined the dance and feast. Some of them rushed up to Elise and questioned her to no end, sitting at her feet and eagerly consuming what she had to say. Veaer couldn't tell what was being said, somehow the intangible magic and energy of the room prevented her from doing so. She tried to read her lips, but only got distracted in the thoughts of them against her skin again.

"For Elise, are you afraid of taking from her?" R asked. She hadn't hidden her longing look very well. "She has a lot that you may not. After all, she's an Excava. She is the daughter of the headmaster."

I know that. "She is beautiful." The protectors held Elise's arms and hands and spoke to her in hushed tones. Just like the past, when she would stand in the hallway and watch Elise and her court.

Girls like you have secrets. I'm going to peel you apart and reveal every part of you. I will consume you.

She swallowed and needed more water, again. "She makes me excited more than anything. The way she speaks and moves. The way she thinks. There's so much to learn, I feel like it will never end. She doesn't only land in my lap at my command, she is something to continue exploring. Like the quest for knowledge personified."

You're my blossom and I am the only one who can stroke your bud and become the creator of springtime.

She ran her tongue between her lips and sighed. "I think I love her."

Her gaze ripped away from the scene of draping arms, mixed

fabrics, pomegranate juice, and grapes brought to lips. She stared at the mask of R and listened to the silence that hung between them.

"Okay," R said after several moments, an edge to the word. "I'll tell you. It'll be good to get it out."

Veaer nodded though suddenly wanted to wear the mask once again. She sat naked as R inched closer to her and she had a feeling that they didn't register her confession about Elise too well. Maybe this was jealousy. That they were unable to feel or express their thoughts to the one they admired so much.

"Veaer," R began, taking her hands. The room shrunk away, and the walls became silent as they watched. "There's something I want to tell you." A pause, a breath. "But it requires some context, so please let me explain." Small winged angels flying in circles around their heads, soft bottoms on soft clouds. "Angels have always meant a lot to me, even though we haven't talked about it a lot. As caemi, we usually reserve our faith to the dragon saints, and they have served me well. But there's something else inside me that I can't describe in an easy way. Like a bundle of wings flapping in my chest because they don't have a name and without a name, they just exist in limbo." They tilted to the side but then quickly straightened up, not allowing their words to teeter away from them. "Angels are more than winged creatures. They are divine creations. Ter and Mian moulded them without a template. They are more energy than they are formed, yet they still chose to create many images for themselves. Like... a piece of art. Where you must trust the process and while your piece may begin as strange shapes on a canvas, they eventually form something. Sometimes we are born knowing what shapes we become, but I've always known that I wasn't one of those people. Just as an angel would be unsure of appearing in one way forever."

Compassion lined their words and Veaer had the urge to be sucked away into the void R produced with their gentle words, revealing something so dear to them as if they were slicing themself through the middle for her to crawl into and make a home. She was enlightened with flashes and visions of angels appearing as blinding light to caemi-like figures to dragons to animals to leaves to butterflies to something impossible for her to comprehend but she knew it was beautiful.

"When I found Tychon," R continued, squeezing Veaer's hands tighter. "He showed me something that gave a name to the feathers. The privilege of self-creation. *To create is to be alive. We love art. We are art. Why shouldn't we go further?* Those were his words. That's why I am here."

Feathers sprouted on Veaer's tongue and she lurched forward as if to expel them from her body, but nothing happened. She kept still in the position she ended up in with R's voice wrapping around her and the fiery glow grew stronger and warmer. She whined against the thorns at the back of her throat and grasped R tighter. The glow felt so nice, so familiar.

"He cut his hair, scarred his chest, took supplements concocted by some of the best alchemists and herbalists in Syriphia. He took what Ter and Mian made of him and changed it, created himself so that he was the same outside as he was inside. In a sense, he had become an angel, just without the magic his ancestors held. And I am to follow a similar path."

Tychon was transgender. The words echoed in and around her. She had known it to be so; Tychon was happy to share the fact and welcome a safer world for others like him. She just hadn't realised to this extent.

Their bodies grew apart from the circular ritual room, leaving them in a new abyss. Their robes provided sufficient hope and light. The trust and care R exhibited was heavy and full of promise, to have shared this intimate discovery with her. But now more than ever did she feel like an intruder. As if R's friend should've taken her place instead so that she didn't end up the primary holder of this holy revelation. She was not R's *her*.

"I'm non-binary, Veaer. And I've been afraid to tell you because you've only known me as something else that was only a small part of me. And I'm afraid that this will undo everything between us. I didn't know if you—"

"It's okay, R." Veaer swallowed the feathers and flowers—dry and prickly down her throat and into her blood—and reached her hand out to hold the side of their cold mask. "Tell me more."

"I— are you sure?" Their voice cracked again, and she sensed the cracks being sealed by tears. "I'm not neither, and I'm not both. Not both male and female. But I... it's different at different times. This doesn't make sense."

"It's like the angels, like you said," Veaer said quietly, leaning in and lifting her second hand to hold their face up. In a way she wanted to do her very best to understand, for the feathers that tickled the inside of her chest.

"Yes, like the angels. And I can be more of a boy one day, and a girl another day. And sometimes it *could* be neither or both. But my inability to choose, I fear that will betray me one day. That I may not be an angel like I wish."

"But you are an angel."

"How do you know that?"

"I can feel it, lovely. And you don't need to prove it to anyone."

"But I can't prove it to myself, and that matters to me."

Veaer pulled R towards her and wrapped her arms tight around their torso. She pressed her hands into their shoulder blades and tucked her face into the crook of R's neck.

"Maybe you can't now, but you will. You will keep going and sharpen your edges and trace your outlines and shade in the light and dark that makes you. Just like Tychon and the rest of the angels. You have Q, and Elise, and me, and your friend. We can help you."

R exhaled deeply and slowly against Veaer's hair and tightened their grip on her back, balling fabric between their fingers. They hiccuped against their own words that came out in a mess of mumbles and pleas.

"I love you," Veaer whispered. She couldn't help the words tumbling out, familiar in her mind and bursting to be said, as if the angels moved every muscle in her mouth and tongue.

"Don't say that. Don't say what you don't mean."

"I mean it."

"But you love Elise."

"And I can love you too."

They basked in the fire and let it play along their skin and robes. They spoke to each other with hesitant touches and meaningful looks. Veaer knew this to be something like habit but was unable to fathom how that could be so.

The next morning, Veaer woke up in her dorm dressed in clean pyjamas and without the warm body she spent the night next to.

CHAPTER 35
ATTUNEMENT

"I t's been four days since we spoke."

Veaer had opened her dorm room door, reluctantly dressed for the school day and just about to leave, to Adair pacing in front of her room with hands in hair.

Her friend wasn't even dressed in uniform which only brought concern to the forefront. If Veaer had been able to get out of bed after the night she had to go to class, Adair surely should've been able to as any other student.

"What? You and Hai?" Veaer stepped out of the doorway and locked the door behind her, slipping the key into her skirt pocket. It clinked against something else and Veaer paused with her hand on her satchel's handle before she remembered the master key she took from Adair. This didn't seem like the best time to return it.

"Yes. He's been holed up in his dorm room and isn't even attending class. I haven't seen him in homeroom and his director caught me between classes yesterday to ask about it. I tried talking to him last night, but he didn't answer. I tried this morning and—"

Adair pounded her fists against the side of her head and Veaer reached out to stop it. Patrons above, she hadn't realised Haiwrin's absence, and it made her want to run her head against the wall too.

Adair shivered from a breeze that caught them from down the

hall and wrapped her arms around herself. Veaer slid her blazer off and brought it to Adair's shoulders.

"Okay, okay. Let's go up together and see?" Veaer played with her lip between her teeth. She hoped that Adair and herself only missed when Haiwrin left his room. Otherwise, he wouldn't have had water or food for days—and with how well the academy looked after students, no one would feel good after that. She knew just as well from fasting for just more than a day.

Adair gave her a silent nod and started leading the way. The students who liked to guard the staircase to floor two, three and four must have already gone to class, so they only needed permission by intention to get Veaer through the invisible field. She still remained cautious while crossing the threshold in the carpet, remembering the times in her first year when she learnt her lesson about trying to brute through the fields. She found it highly contradictory for faculty to use magic to keep students out of the floors of their own dorm building, while students had to wait until graduation to cast again. If there was ever a reason to change schools, if she did follow Haiwrin's plan considering his condition now, it'd be to a school that loved to expand on caemi magic instead of restricting it.

They arrived in front of Haiwrin's room, a foreboding atmosphere prickling Veaer's arms. Shadows stretched from under his door, and everything was awfully quiet.

With a quick glance at Adair that didn't offer much of a suggestion, Veaer stepped forward and knocked in the way she established as unique to her when they first met. When nothing came of it, she tried the doorknob which confirmed what was most reasonable; the door was locked.

"Haiwrin, hey!" She knocked again. "It's me, Ve. I wanted to—I just hope you're... I haven't seen you in class. Do you want to talk?"

Not even a snore came through which would've reassured them of something, anything.

"I don't know what to do." Adair's words quivered. She backed up against the wall next to the door and sat on the carpet. "I don't have a way to get through to him."

The master key weighed heavy in Veaer's pocket. "Like, actually... physically? Or, in a twin-sibling sort of sense?" She opened and closed her hands behind her so that Adair wouldn't see and so she wasn't tempted to take the key from her pocket.

"Both? I've been distracted with other things."

"Like what?" She dropped next to Adair and placed a hand on her thigh. She also let her gaze wander across the walls, searching for a clock. She didn't know how long she had before class.

Suddenly a click resounded through the relatively empty hall and both of them snapped towards the door that opened ever so slightly. In the darkness that slipped through, nothing made itself known.

Adair rushed up and tried to push on the door, only to be met with resistance from the other side. Haiwrin must have been standing against it, listening to them speak.

The orange caemi laid her palms on the wooden door. "Hai? Hai, is that you? Oh, who else would it be? Please let me in, please?"

"Veaer," Haiwrin said, his voice fragile like frayed rope, and sent a spark of lightning up Veaer's neck that had her standing next to Adair too. "Just Veaer."

Adair's hands slipped from the door and landed weakly by her sides. Her cheeks puffed up with air and the tips of her ears turned red. "Why not me?"

"I will close this door if you don't leave."

Veaer stared through the gap and now caught the glint of blue that reflected against Haiwrin's eyes. She pursed her lips, words escaping her and unable to understand why he wasn't opening up to Adair either. They were perfect twins to everyone else, complementing and two halves. Good looking and well educated. Blue and orange. She had witnessed a few disagreements here and there for silly reasons that she had no problem being the tie breaker of, but this situation was entirely different.

"Don't do this, Hai. You can't do this, not now." Adair faltered between reaching up to push the door again and keeping her hands to herself. "Class is starting soon."

"Then get out of your pyjamas and go." He shut the door with as much of a slam as a slightly open door could—not much of one, but enough to force Adair to step back.

Veaer met Adair's step but kept staring at the door. After a moment, she leaned back in and said, "Haiwrin, I'll be back later with some water and food, okay? Please don't do anything stupid."

A small grumble came through, "Fine." Then shuffling, and silence.

"Argh!" Adair flung her hands in the air and stalked down the hall, grabbing Veaer's blazer from around her shoulders and holding it in the crook of her arm as she stomped around. "I can't believe him!"

"Adair, what's going on?" She approached slowly and took the blazer to slip back on. They were heading to Adair's room, supposedly to action Haiwrin's request. "There's something else."

"There's nothing."

"You said something was distracting you."

Adair unlocked her door and waited for Veaer to step in before shutting it behind them. "Yeah, school and stuff... assignments. Essays."

"You're not that great at lying, sorry." Veaer punctuated her words with a chuckle in an attempt to lighten the mood, but Adair only froze. "Addie... sorry. I didn't mean anything—"

The orange caemi then mumbled something over and over to herself, so quietly that Veaer couldn't hear, and when she leaned in to try and get a better listen, her arms were grabbed, and she was forced to sit on the bed with Adair dragging her desk chair over to sit across from her.

Adair carefully took Veaer's hands in her own. "Veaer," she began, "There's something I want to tell you."

The air was suddenly sucked from Veaer's lungs as her vision flashed between Adair's soft face and a mask of a million eyes. She returned to last night when the walls grew and shrunk and danced to the music. Smashed glass played over and over again, and she blinked hard to bring herself back to the present.

"A... A secret?" Veaer blinked again and tried to pluck her thoughts from the sky.

"No, not a secret. That makes it... more than it is. I want you to get to know me more, because I care about you."

Blood pumped against her ear drums and her shoulders stiffened. Her hands were searing hot compared to the rest of her body and she didn't realise what was happening until she looked down and watched fire engulf both of their hands and climb their arms.

She screamed and tried to scramble back, finding herself stuck in place and only feeling hot, hot, hot from whatever was happening.

"Addie... Adair, what are you doing? Is this... magic? It's..."

Everything flicked from light to dark as she pictured the glowing outline of R and the fire that flowed from Adair's hands and into hers. Caemi magic, right in their hands, within the limits of barriers that restricted magic and caemikind.

"This isn't possible..." Veaer gasped and settled down, the fire cooling off, yet it only climbed onto her even more. At some point, the fire turned completely red and fought against the orange of Adair. Power coursed through her veins, and she had never felt more alive and rejuvenated.

"I think I'm better at hiding things than you know, Ve," Adair said in a voice that was hers but not at the same time. It sounded like R, the short redhead, in an order of angels that pulled her in and wouldn't let her go. Not that she wanted to leave, not after everything she had done within the circle. Not if it was her penance for her sins. "Yes, this is magic. My aura attuning to yours."

"But the anti—"

"Is for students. The anti-magic field is for *student level magic*. You know that the faculty is using their own magic to keep us in place. To keep you in place."

"But you're a student." Caemi couldn't attune to each other's auras here.

"In Adraredon Academy, yes. In the Ascension Order, I am more than that. I'm an angel."

In a burst of light, the orange and red came together to form two large, beautiful wings behind Adair, taking up the height of the ceiling and length of the room. They flapped in a slow rhythm, sparkling and so bright yet Veaer could not rip her eyes away until Adair took her chin to face them.

"You said so yourself, Veaer." Their voice crackled in and out from a voice she knew to the one she recently made acquaintance with. Their hair morphed into something between long orange hair and short red hair. "You remember what we talked about last night, don't you?"

Veaer nodded frantically, afraid that any other response would earn something even worse than what was happening. Adair was R. R was Adair. One in the same.

"This whole time... you were telling me..."

"It's really happening, Veaer! We're going to be angels!" Adair laughed and the sound was so loud yet contained in her own head. "Look at how powerful I am, stronger than I've ever been. This is what Tychon intended, and Q and I are going to keep going." Adair's feet lifted from the carpet until their entire body was horizontal in the air, their wings forming a ceiling above Veaer. Their hands lifted Veaer's cheeks. "Oh, it's just been so much, Veaer. To keep it all inside, to wait for each ritual, to watch you from under a mask. I am but another student among others, magic simmering under my fingertips but following the academy rules. And then my brother... he's so troublesome. He wants to leave but we can't. Not now. We haven't reached our full transformation. Our highest ascendance. And it'll be okay because I have you now."

Veaer blinked and her mouth opened and closed. Adair was so incredibly beautiful yet terrifying at the same time. Their clothes burned in the auratic flames, and it was fortunate that they weren't wearing their uniform. Embers dropped from each golden feather but vanished before they hit the carpet. The body she had gotten to know shifted between curves to hard edges, to both at the same time which had blood rushing to Veaer's cheeks. She had the incredible urge to reach out and run her hand through Adair's wings and across their divine body—and then stopped herself.

Her chest tightened and it was as if Adair's form was taking the oxygen from the room. She stood up and spun towards the window, grabbing onto the bottom and trying to force it up, but it just wouldn't move. Then she ran for the door before Adair grabbed her and turned her around. Veaer floated from the floor into Adair's arms, raspy for air.

"You—you tried to kill me." Veaer brought her hands up to push Adair away, but it was no use. There was nothing to push away.

"Oh, the air? It's a little thin but all the better for you to become like me."

"No... No!" Veaer wriggled and turned her head towards the bed, aiming for it if she were to drop suddenly, but nothing went her way. She was only brought closer to Adair's face, more wings sprouting from their back to hold Veaer in place. Two eyes turned to four turned to eight turned to sixteen and kept going. Rings of gold situated themselves around Adair's head until they were unrecognisable except for the jewels in their many, many eyes and the touch of their many, many hands. "You poisoned me! You were going to kill me even though you knew who I was!"

"That wasn't my idea!" they screamed, like Veaer imagined an angel would. Horrifyingly and raw. Scratching her ears in the completely wrong way. "That was Q. He was making sure no one could take our power away. No one can hurt us like they did Tychon."

Where was Tychon when she needed him? He was never as forward as this, except for last night when he just had a moment. He always stood on the sidelines and watched, careful and quiet. That was better than this.

"You fucked me over, Adair. And you know that. You know what you did. I wake up every day with that stupid poison in me and I have to drink that stupid antidote."

"It's for our own good. It's to protect us," R hissed into her ear. "And it's a reminder of the sacrifice we must make to create ourselves. We must abstain from our material needs and only then do we become more like the angels."

"Get away from me!" Veaer thrashed around again and this time she dropped, onto the floor and onto her back.

"You're no different than me." The angel floated downwards until their feet met reality. The wings dissipated as did the eyes and extra arms. Their hair returned to what Veaer knew, orange and reaching the middle of Adair's back. If Veaer didn't know better, she may have imagined the entire thing as her friend smiled sweetly while looking into her eyes. "You have a thirst that cannot be sated. What did you say, again? The quest for knowledge?"

"That's..." Veaer crawled towards the door and hoisted herself up in a hurry. Her back hit the door when Adair got closer. The pain in her head pulsed and the wood didn't help one bit. "That's different."

"Tell me how. Tell me, how far would you go? To know, to understand. You've always been this way, ever since we met. You couldn't get enough."

People like her have secrets, secrets only people like me can find— can pull out from between petals and thorns.

I'll keep her secret. I'll do what she says. I'll follow her steps. I'll join the order. I'll dance to the music. I'll listen to the angels. I'll pray to them too. Don't hurt me, Angelus Pavo. Don't hurt me Kitt. Don't hurt me Elise. Don't hurt me Adair.

I'll love you. I'll love as much as I can until I know.

"I—" Veaer stared at Adair's lips and then eyes. They were so... normal.

"Exactly," Adair answered with high reverence skimming the edges of their voice. "So far."

"I don't understand—" The words tumbled from her lips before she could stop, and it only fed into Adair's smile.

"Yes, so you will want more. You'll figure it out, lovely." Adair pushed forward and every passing second had Veaer attempting to climb the wall in any way she could. As they stopped, they hovered their palm under Veaer's chin. "Please, make sure Haiwrin is okay?"

❧

Veaer juggled two cups of water, an apple, and two sandwiches in her arms as she weakly knocked on Haiwrin's door to avoid spilling anything. It only took a few moments for Haiwrin to open up and let Veaer in.

She kept a close eye on Haiwrin until she got to the desk to put everything down, lest he also turned into an angel in front of her too. But he seemed fine, if a little wary himself, as he closed the door. His hair was sticking out in random places and his bed was unmade. Snack packaging and paper cups littered the floor around the bed frame. The window was shut, and the curtains were drawn.

He was at least dressed in his school uniform, so there seemed to be an intention to attend class.

She drew the curtains back and slid the window open, glad for the fresh air she wasn't able to manage from the other twin. She opted to distract herself by picking up the rubbish and pulling a trash bag from her pocket, aware of how staying in the same room for a few days would turn out.

Haiwrin moved somewhere behind her, grabbing one of the ceramic cups from the table and taking a long drink. He mumbled a small thank-you before asking, "How you doing?"

Veaer paused mid chip pack pick-up and turned to Haiwrin. "What do you mean? I'm not the one who stayed in my room for four days." She shook her head and tossed the pack with the rest. "We're not here for me, I'm here for you."

He shrugged and took a seat at his desk, also taking a breath of the light breeze. "It was the easiest way for me to start the conversation."

"Okay well, I'm doing okay. I think." Two laughs echoed in her ears, the laughs of angels. "Learning a lot."

"Me too."

"Oh yeah?" She tied up the rubbish bag and tossed it by the door. "Take that out when you go to class."

"Alright, and yes. I've had time to think. It's hard sometimes, when we're in proximity in this manor." He waved his hand vaguely in the direction of the hallway. "I don't feel great about skipping classes and leaving you hanging. It was just so..."

Veaer leaned against the wall next to the window and pointed towards the other cup on the table. Haiwrin passed it over before he continued, "I was so frustrated. I know you were listening, but Adair didn't get it. She didn't even try to understand. The moment I said we were leaving, she already knew she wasn't."

"How are you feeling now?" Veaer asked carefully and then sipped from her cup to fill the silence, so that Haiwrin had a moment to think.

"Better, kind of. I don't really want to go to class. But I'm happy that I got out of bed and got dressed. Those shirts and pants need a wash." He nodded towards a pile of laundry in front of his closet. "Thank you for coming, Ve."

The corners of her lips tugged up and she stepped over to the desk to place her cup down. "You need to eat something." She pushed the sandwich closer to Haiwrin. "Your sibling put me up to this. Wanted me to make sure you were okay."

"Of course." He sighed and stared at the sandwich. "Apart from my relief about seeing you and getting dressed, this other feeling is here to stay. Like... I feel it inside, under my heart. It's heavy and numb at the same time. It makes me sad and want to close everything away. Maybe it's safer this way, in here. Until they force me to go home."

Veaer pressed her hand to her chest and tried to channel her own feelings in order to understand. Something sat under her heart as well, but she didn't know how to describe it. It was something that continued to expand and shrink, sometimes racing, sometimes so still. It wasn't the same as Haiwrin, though she could tell there wasn't an easy solution to this.

He unwrapped the sandwich and took one bite, then put it back down. "It's a lot. Rehearsals, new scripts. Doing drama brings drama. The new lead's understudy isn't happy about their casting and there are some first years that don't know how to conduct an act change—I get it, they're new. But why did they choose music and

performance if they didn't have any experience before Adraredon?"
She nodded. There were plenty of art students who chose art because
they thought it was easy. Their acceptance to Adraredon was based
on the riches their family provided. "And then Tychon... and you,
you've been doing other things so you're around less. And Adair is
getting annoyed at me. It makes me realise I don't have that many
people to rely on here—maybe that's why I feel so adamant about
going."

Veaer sniffed and swung an arm around Haiwrin, bringing his
head closer to her chest. They remained there with a heartbeat
between them.

She wasn't one to project herself too much into the future
anymore, because she had done it so much as a little girl. There was
no use when the world didn't open itself up to her. She didn't want
to think about what would happen after graduation.

"I'm not much better than those first years, but is there anything
I can do to help?"

Haiwrin took a deep breath and ran a hand through his hair,
allowing some of the pesky strands to blend with the rest. "Walk with
me to class?"

CHAPTER 36
WHEN THE PAST MEETS THE PRESENT

Veaer's professor walked past her desk and dropped a folded piece of paper in front of her. A shiver struck her shoulders and her gaze hovered until she spotted a pencil she didn't mind disposing. She nudged it with her arm until it clattered on the floor and she bent down to double check underneath her desk, just to find it empty. She exhaled a sigh of relief and opened her feedback form.

> *Appreciated your effort in describing how choice of art form can reflect an artists's mind palace. Would be interested in hearing more personal experiences and applications rather than gathering from textbooks. Self-reflection is required for at least 10%. Make sure to reference in the academy style. This assignment requires no re-submission. Take note for future reference.*

She grumbled at the words, and a fleeting insult crossed her mind. Part of her wanted to walk up to the teacher and rip her head open to show how little room there was for this self-reflection in essays. She preferred the practical assignments over the theory ones. But she usually didn't have issues with referencing, and self-reflection only came into play in Art 5. Maybe her idea of cruising through the last year wouldn't suffice.

She tapped her pen on her desk, not realising that it was clicked open and leaving unsavoury marks all over her fresh sheet of paper. A noise of frustration remained stuck in her throat.

The supply cart was unoccupied now that everyone was getting into their own work, and so she made her walk of shame to grab another paper. Just as she reached for it, another hand landed under hers.

"Veaer Rosell." A sweet voice caressed her ears, sending blood rushing to her face.

She held one hand up to her cheek in an attempt to manage the heat, before meeting eye to eye with Elise. A new perfume lingered around her and there seemed to be something different about her make-up. Maybe she had cut her hair too?

Veaer blinked. Had she been intentionally ignoring Elise? They saw each other last night but they hardly spoke, it was like she wasn't even there. She remembered Elise being surrounded and fed fruit, many hands gently bringing damp cloth to Elise's lips to clear away the sticky liquid.

Elise laughed under her breath and smiled, even when Veaer didn't say anything. "How nice for us to meet here, at the supply cart."

"Yes—yes, very nice." Veaer couldn't help the smile that stretched across her lips. A sense of comfort washed over her. She liked moments like this and sharing them with Elise. Two girls, growing up and falling in love. "Hey, do you... are you doing anything later?"

The princess picked up a couple pieces of paper and handed one to Veaer. "Yes, actually."

"Ahh..." Veaer avoided bringing the paper too close to her chest so as to not crinkle it.

"But you can come."

Veaer pursed her lips and occupied her fingers by randomly

picking out markers and pencils. She didn't want to stand on the outskirts while Elise's new friends followed her and asked her questions. "I wouldn't want to intrude."

"You wouldn't be, considering it's just me."

"Oh, but what about your new friends?" Veaer leaned in after glancing around them. "The protectors?"

Elise shook her head, with the kind of look that made Veaer feel young and small. "No, no. They're not my friends. They're like, my students. They love to listen to what I have to say, what the angels tell me to tell them. The angels have granted me a gift." The princess' eyes glazed over with a distant look, like her mind and spirit was transported back to the heavens from which she came. "It's wonderful. They all love me. So sweet and kind."

I'm sweet and kind. I love you too. "So, what you're doing later isn't related to...?"

"It quite is. But it isn't for them. They're all too young. Fresh minds that won't be able to handle the task that has been set out for me."

Veaer could just imagine Elise dressed in those beautiful robes again. A school uniform seemed so restricting now that she had seen what a true form really was. Was this the fate of Elise in all her angelic channelling?

"Will I see you then? Courtyard after classes end." Elise tilted her head and her hair fell beautifully over her shoulder. Veaer really wanted to move the fabric aside and take a bite.

"I'll be there, of course. Yes." She nodded in case her words weren't enough.

"Veaer!" Elise called as she rushed up to Veaer who was already by the statue with her hands on her knees, heavily panting but glad to see she wasn't late.

"Here I am!" she called in return with a laugh. She admired the beaming smile that the princess wore, and noticed the jewelled earrings and necklace adorned upon her. They sparkled in the afternoon sun though she was concerned for the students who may notice.

Elise also carried a satchel that she looped over Veaer's head and fastened across her chest. "Supplies, for a ritual."

"A ritual, at this time? And without the others?" Veaer clipped open the satchel and inspected the items. "There's just some chalk and a ritual knife in here—" She carefully ran a finger over the leather cover that protected the blade, and when she looked up again, Tychon was hovering beside them, watching. "Don't we need anything else?"

"Q has prepared the rest." Elise slipped her hand into Veaer's and began to make way on a path. "This ritual is special. The order has seen my wonderful gift and they will reward me with more."

"How so?" Veaer played with her lip between her teeth as she looked up and shielded her eyes from the blaring sun with her free hand. The cathedral stood tall and proud ahead of them. Her palms grew clammy. "This seems very different from what they promised when we joined."

"That's because they didn't expect such potent results," Elise whispered into Veaer's ear, the warm breath causing her to shudder. "They're doing something even more special within, but I am yet to find out. Our dances and meditations, it's only the beginning." The princess spoke with such knowledge and experience of the order, her open hand tracing mystical gestures in the air and her voice taking a breathy quality.

The two of them entered the cathedral hall, dim lights intact and no screaming feathered body laying with contorted limbs by the altar. Soft music played from somewhere that created a peaceful atmosphere against all Veaer's nerves lit aflame. They passed a couple people in pews, kneeling and praying, while a group of second years huddled together in one of the saint chapels, mumbling and giggling. It assured Veaer that a repeat of weeks ago wouldn't happen—the cathedral attendees serving as her safeguard. Each passing pillar brought them closer to the front and Veaer swore the scent of blood and iron remained in her nostrils.

She glanced next to the altar, but no glass shards. She looked down at her feet, but no blood stains. Then Elise led her to the side, towards the corner where a tower met the mass of the building, and a door was unlocked.

Inside was a winding staircase and they remained silent as they climbed. Their footsteps echoed and Veaer remembered finding the crypt and how they were led lower underground than she hoped to ever go. What secrets laid above them?—on a structure she admired from afar because she was too small in comparison.

As light shot through the exit at the top, Veaer breathed out and stared at Elise for further explanation. The cathedral was quite an important location for angels, though unfamiliar to the activities of the order. She kept her hands tucked behind her back, pondering her uncertainty about her aura being attuned earlier, for at least something—one thought, to grasp onto.

"This is my test," Elise said as she stepped into the sunlight, the rays creating a glow around her that had Veaer pausing. "When I complete this ritual, the order will know how strong I am and allow me to tap into my potential. And when I do, my students will want even more from me. They'll love me, praise me." Elise spun around, her skirt flying in the air and her hair following in a beautiful cascade. Her giggles carried with the wind and flew into Veaer's heart. "This is where I truly belong. Upon holy grounds, to complete a legacy and leave my own. Come see."

And she did. Every building and treetop could be looked down upon from here, and she could hardly make out the students below, who were ants when she climbed Miriam Manor, but now tiny particles at this height. The world tilted on its axis as Veaer clutched a nearby wall for balance. They stood at the top of a stone tower; a corner integrated into the design of the cathedral that one would never imagine standing upon one day. Those who created this divine place even put detail into the walls and buttresses that intersected with the tower and the main hall, and carved images ran along the inside of the stone that prevented them from falling to the ground if they wanted to lean over the edge.

Elise expressed a sound of excitement that inspired Veaer and she knew that this moment would change their lives forever. Sweet lips crashed into her, so quickly that Veaer grabbed Elise's perfect face in her hands to go for another. They remained forehead to forehead, chuckling between breaths.

"I don't think I deserve this," Veaer confessed. "I don't think I'm worthy to be here, for this."

Elise shook her head, gently to not break them apart. "That doesn't matter. Do you want this?"

She opened her mouth and closed it again, then decided to leave a peck on Elise's lips first. "Yes I want this," she answered after a moment.

A shadow moved by the corner of her eye and she broke contact, snapping to the side and staring at the pillar, waiting for the shadow to show itself. Nothing happened. It may have been Tychon's ghost, watching on but not wanting to interrupt the moment.

In her lapse of attention, Elise had started on drawing a ritual circle with the chalk. Masterful hand movements and straight lines, Veaer didn't expect any less from an arts student but wondered when Elise had the time to practise this. Soon a shape that looked similar to the circle used in the Ascension Order and the one Tychon drew by the altar came to fruition, though it had its own qualities to it as well. Instead of four distinct points of the cardinal directions being marked, everything seemed to direct itself into the centre.

Elise clapped her hands together, chalk dust flying away, and then pulled something out of her pocket.

"Here." She placed a small candy in Veaer's palm. "For the nerves."

The candy wrapper crinkled in her hand. "I'm not nervous." At least she thought she wasn't once she arrived up here, but the very notion of nerves brought them back.

She popped the small ball in her mouth, only for spice and salt to coat her tongue. She almost spat it out, but Elise smiled at her, and so she handled it. All its burning and displeasing flavours.

Everything in her mouth turned sour and she stumbled towards a pillar. Elise reached for the knife in the bag and unsheathed it, turning in her palm. Veaer's vision turned fuzzy at the edges and she blinked. Sour foods tended to create tears. But her eyes were dry and soon her throat was too. Her heart beat faster and when the candy didn't seem to get any smaller and only more sour, she had enough.

She spat it into her palm, a small metal ball coated in powder and saliva landing with the weight of the world. This wasn't confectionery.

She bent over and dropped the ball, before her arms were pulled against her sides and rope was wrapped around her stomach. Every movement was just a second too late. Her head flicked back and forth but it wasn't enough to see what was going on. Her body moved on its own, being led towards the circle until she was laid on her back with no autonomy in her muscles.

Elise stood above her, the remaining length of rope being looped around her hand and then placed on top of the empty bag. She held the shiny knife tight, just by her side but awfully close, too close to Veaer's body.

"Elise... Elise?! What are you doing?" Veaer realised that Elise didn't understand her as drool pooled under her tongue and poured down the side of her face with not even a glance from the princess. "This isn't funny, I don't like this. I'm not into this—let me go!"

"I need to do this, Veaer. I need to prove that I'm willing to do this."

Tychon, help me. Tychon, help me.

"Darling, why?" Veaer cried. The knife hadn't grown any closer to her as Elise walked around to light each candle, the flickering orange at the corners of her vision telling her so, but she could already feel each stab she forced into Tychon's back, each thrust of—

"I need to. They won't care if I don't. They won't love me. They'll just treat me like everyone else, like father and Izot and, Veaer, you're the only one I can trust to do this," Elise blabbered through everything: the noise, the fire, her struggle against the tight ropes. The princess kneeled, her bare knees touching the concrete and chalk beneath them, her thighs pressing into Veaer's sides. "There is no love without sacrifice."

Veaer hiccupped, more of that horrid saltiness creeping down her throat and into her body. How could this have happened? Had she not loved Elise enough? She could've been around more, waking up by her side, bringing gifts. Instead she was always taking. Elise's attention, her commissions, her quiet time in the library, her feelings when vulnerability lingered between them. She was just another one of those people in Elise's life who turned away and left her feeling selfish for wanting love from just one person in her life. She had told Elise to be her best and that they would be good together. But she wasn't good. How could she be if all her friends wanted the world to pay for their pain?

If she were able to, she would've brought her hand up to Elise's face and told her that the world didn't deserve how much she worried.

But instead, she saw a flash of light and feathers, and an angel touched a finger to her forehead.

On a Tuesday morning, eight years ago, Veaer stood in a field of lavender and grass. The scent tickled her nose, and she pressed her palm against her nostrils to get rid of the itch.

A short distance away was a young girl, brown hair and purple cat ears and a tail, sitting on a swing.

Veaer sprinted towards her as fast as her little legs could handle until she saw two others join the swing set and start talking to her friend. She stopped behind a tree and stared. She didn't remember inviting more friends. One with long black hair and another... she couldn't quite tell with the sun glaring in her eyes, but she noticed that they had their hair tied, with the end of their ponytail chopped in strange places that made it look like the elastic would fall at any moment.

Those new friends seemed nice enough, so she took some time to turn around and pick three bundles of lavender. Her mother always said that gifts were the best way to show how much she loved someone, though she didn't really believe it. Not everyone gave gifts to their loved ones. She did it anyway, for good luck.

But when she stood up with a wonder on how she would tie the bundles together, the new friends had gotten off their swings and were holding Kitt's arms.

Veaer lifted her hand and called out, but her voice escaped her just as one of the bundles fell from the crook of her arm and scattered in the grass.

A knife appeared in the hand of the kid with a weird ponytail and their hand shook as they passed it to their friend.

She abandoned the flowers, throwing the rest to the ground with enough force to start running, reaching her arms out and calling Kitt's name. Kitt turned, her tail straightening in the air and her eyes wide with fear.

When Veaer screamed again, she was forced back, the ponytail kid hooking themselves behind her and locking her in place. The young knife wielder stepped closer and closer to Kitt, so much that the caemi fell off the swing and wooden bark stabbed her palms on impact.

Her long silky hair flew with each thrust of the knife, and her smile was just as sharp.

Conviction in her eyes, vengeance in her bones.

The way she handled the knife filled Veaer with awe, and the blood that flew out of the chest of her friend made her lurch, and she wanted to run away in case she was next, and she only kept watching because that little girl just kept going.

How could a young girl be so brave? And so cruel?

She had to go but her feet only slipped in the dirt, her captor's hold so mighty. She had to tell someone else, someone big who could do something about this.

The little girl with the knife laughed, like she finally did something right after so long of being wrong. Like she was waiting for this moment her entire life.

What is she doing to you?

Kitt wasn't moving under the little girl, and red seeped into the brown bark around her. *Did you fall asleep?*

And suddenly her body grew too big for her mind, and she was in a uniform she didn't recognise with a dirty blazer on her shoulders. Her hands were tied with rope and salty spice made her choke.

The kid behind her leaned close, his body the size of hers now, and whispered, "I'm sorry, Veaer."

～

Concrete and dust fell from the sky. Flames surrounded her before a ghost, oh so familiar, floated above her. Tychon released his touch from Veaer's forehead, and she hadn't realised that all sound had been sucked away in a vacuum, until a shriek pierced the air.

Elise dropped the knife and froze, her expression in a perpetual scream.

Veaer brought her hands to her head, then noticed that the rope had fallen away. The candles around her snuffed out in a sweep of air. She reached out to a candle close by and held it, the melted wax dripping over her hand and stinging her skin before solidifying. Stinging meant this was real, but the pain she had just felt in watching her friend...

She put the candle down and pawed her chest and legs to make sure. She was Veaer Rosell, student at Adraredon Academy, eighteen years old.

And when she was ten years old, her best friend was a little girl named Kitt, a purple cat caemi with magical potential whose life was taken too soon by a girl with long black hair and a friend who held her back. They all grew up, bigger bodies for their little minds, but that didn't come without punishment.

Today, she stared at the horrified, wide eyes of Elise Excava as she pointed and screamed at the ghost of her dead best friend, six wings sprouting from his back, his scars decorated with inked leaves, and holding a golden staff that said *holy, holy, holy* just by appearance.

An image of the Justice tarot card flashed in her mind as she beheld Tychon, glorious, tall, and angelic. He was more than lumps of wings and a grey face. More than a bug in the corner covered in webs and silk.

Veaer got to her knees and pressed her head to the floor, praying and praying, thanking and thanking. How wonderful for Angelus Caelum to grant her mercy in this time, to give herself another chance to prove her love to Elise and show her that she didn't need to do this.

The screaming stopped when Elise's throat ran dry and a coughing fit attacked her, her hand sliding across the rough ground in search of the knife.

"Why, Tychon?!" Elise wailed and hit the ground. Thump, thump, thump. "Why did you have to ruin this too?"

Tychon said nothing, his being hovering towards Veaer and gesturing for her to stand. He looked her in the eyes with no message to gather, nothing to see through his soul. His last message was a glance over her shoulder before he disappeared, and a firm hand grabbed her from behind.

Bolts of sweat slid down her face as the source of the touch made himself known with a laugh and a familiar mask on his face. "Oh, wonderful initiates. Well done!" He clapped and laughed some more.

Veaer shivered, hard, and she wondered if the poison had returned to make this even more confusing. But she wiped her forehead from cold sweat and rubbed her eyes with the heels of her palms. "Q... is that you?" But he wore a school uniform, too, one that was much too distinguishable and made his mask obsolete.

A gold and red blazer with embroidered hems and a white band around his bicep with the school's insignia. A cane in his hands but he stood just fine. No glasses in sight—no way they would fit under that mask.

"Veaer, you were so passionate!" Harq shook Veaer's shoulder.

"So willing. So willing to be sacrificed for your Excava counterpart. I see so much of myself in you!"

His laugh grew maniacal as Veaer stumbled and tried to piece her thoughts together. Was it Q or Harq with her? Was this the leader of the Ascension Order or the right-hand-man of Izot? And in a way, it saddened her to realise that they were one in the same. Just as Adair was R, Harq was Q, and for some reason he was revealing this to them now.

Elise curled up against the edge of the stone railing and rocked back and forth, muttering to herself. Veaer watched tears run down her cheeks and made a step forward. She couldn't bear to stand there and do nothing. But Harq held a hand out and took her steps instead, crouching next to Elise.

"You were really going to do it," he said, a semblance of awe in his voice. "I always thought you would but to see it... it only confirmed my beliefs. And your magic, buried under your senti heritage, it shone! The way you burned those ropes apart and extinguished those candles. The screaming wasn't quite necessary, but I can understand the emotion of it all!"

Veaer backed up until she hit a wall. Her hands shook and she was so, so cold. The sky grew darker, and evening was approaching the cathedral tower. She attempted to recall the last minutes of her memory but her inability to place Tychon in the scene made her frustrated enough to cry out in pain.

All this time she had been searching for an explanation. And when she finally figured out the mystery that had been haunting her since childhood, the answer could only be—

"Elise Excava, you have something special."

"I do?" Elise's weak voice clung to Veaer's heartstrings. Her hand hovered between reaching out and staying by her side. *Heed the angel's warning.*

"Something more special than your brother." And that put a smile on the princess' face. "You passed, and for that you will be blessed." Harq stood up and let out a breathy laugh, leaning against the tower's railing as if it were just another day, another view. "When we lost Tychon, and we knew that a Thawan was impossible to track down, we were only left with one half of the legacy. Boudreau and Carrash. But now... we might just be able to bring them back." He clapped his hands and praised Veaer and Elise again. *Oh, how wonderful your sacrifice. Oh, how wonderful your will.* "And when the time comes, you both will be very important.

PART IV

"Everything is more beautiful because we are doomed. You will never be lovelier than you are now. We will never be here again."
—— *Achilles, Troy (2004)*

CHAPTER 37
SO LONG AS WE'RE TOGETHER

1, 2, 3, 4. 1, 2, 3, 4.

H er eyes burnt no matter how dim the lights were. An incessant buzzing travelled through the walls. Music from somewhere in the manor grated her nerves and she could feel the vibrations in her bones. Her thoughts blurred together, causing her mind to wander and feed into the slush of brain she was left with. When something finally pieced together, she had returned to that cathedral tower all over again.

Life doesn't flash before your eyes when you are dying—death does. And she saw her corpse tied in rope and charred from candle flames, her chest and stomach ripped open by a blade before a flurry of butterflies burst from within her and flew into the sun.

Some of them stayed, helping to weave cocoons for new creatures of beauty and nature. They harvested her bone marrow and ran it through a loom to create silk. Her ribs were the perfect place to hang their enclosures. Her insides were still warm enough to let them grow.

A hurricane of regret and incapacitating responsibility lurched her forward and she found herself stumbling through Elise Excava's dorm room door. She fumbled with the handle to get it shut and then fell into a chair that was in her way. Her face slammed into the carpet as the chair clattered to the floor and she took relief in just laying on her back and staring at the underside of half a table while the rest of her view was off-white ceiling.

Her chest was going to explode if she didn't scream soon, just to let the flapping wings in her chest out. But her body wasn't cooperating, nor did she want to cause such a nuisance. Today was already enough, and she didn't know if she could make it through.

She turned her head when she heard a click from her left, letting her cheek relax against soft fabric. Oh, she could've fallen asleep then and hoped to wake up with no cocoons inside her. She only saw a pair of feet step out of the bathroom and then a small white towel dropping to the floor.

Veaer opened her mouth to say something, but nothing came out. Her lips were so dry and her heart so empty. She hadn't said a word when Q escorted her down to a tucked away chapel and used holy water and a cloth to clean the dirt and dust from her face. When he said that bigger things were going to happen very soon, she didn't want to know what that meant. Then a protector appeared out of nowhere and brought her back to the dorms. She tried to ask questions, but the mask stayed on and the silence continued.

"What are you doing here?" Elise asked, her voice as level as always. She walked around to pick up the chair and sat down. Veaer didn't bother to move. She could see part of Elise's face but not her eyes, not her lips.

"I don't... why did you do that?"

Elise took several moments to answer. "You know why. I had to prove that I was willing to sacrifice something I love so dearly."

Veaer blinked slowly and her gaze tracked the satin slip dress that Elise wore with the intention to sleep. She would never own anything so elegant. And if she did, she wouldn't dare sleep in it. "It's hard to believe that you still love me."

"It was only a test. Harq wasn't really going to let me do it."

A test, a test. Just like every other week. Recalling ancient artists and styles of old times. Learning and adapting to new trends. How to move her paint brush, what size and shape her canvas should be. If she used charcoal or pastels. If she drew an angel or a butterfly.

"You passed."

"Of course," Elise said, like she had received an A in her most recent folio submission.

"Because you had full intention."

"Darling, why are you on the floor? Let's not talk about this anymore. It's so morbid." Elise stood up and Veaer watched her legs move to the bed. The fluffy trim of her nightgown tickled the top of her head. "Come to bed with me. It's so late."

"I wouldn't have been the first," Veaer whispered.

"I've had others in my bed before, but that is no matter." Elise laughed, off tune, off rhythm. The sound tapered awkwardly into the quiet night.

Veaer decided it was time to get up. She grabbed the table leg as support as she turned her body over and sat on her knees, and as she stood on both feet, she pushed the table out of the way, sending cups and a jug of cold tea crashing into the floor. Elise shrieked, and Veaer looked to the side at the kitchen bench sitting on its lonesome in this pseudo-apartment dressed as a student dorm. Hardly used by how pristine it was; Elise didn't have to cook as the princess. She wondered if a knife block was housed there, sharp and clean.

"I wouldn't have been the first that you held a knife against," Veaer clarified. She moved shards of broken glass to the side with her shoe and took a step towards Elise. "And Tychon wasn't your first either."

Elise gripped her bed sheets, a look of shock and anger brewing on her features. Her delicate features contorted into something more human than beauty. "How could you say such a thing? My best friend is dead and you're accusing me?"

"Your best friend is dead and so is mine."

"What in Syriphia are you saying... Please, Veaer. Just come to bed. We'll have someone clean the glass in the morning, but you need sleep." Elise held her shaky arms out in a pathetic invitation for a hug.

"You didn't only kill Tychon, stabbing him in the back over and over again. You watched the hope light up his eyes and you still decided to do it. And I still don't know why. I still don't understand even after you tried to get rid of me next." She swayed from side to side, holding her arm that didn't appreciate fighting against rope ties and prophetic angels. "And you took Kitt away from me. She was just a little girl."

"Kitt...? Who—"

"Kitt Thawan!" Veaer screamed as she lifted her hands and imitated animal ears against the crown of her head. "Little purple cat caemi." She waved her fingers. "First Thawan, and then Galacia. You must be after the Carrash and Boudreaus next." Adair and Haiwrin, she had to protect them. Even if Elise hurt her, she couldn't let her get to the friends that still wanted her after all she had become.

"Patrons above, I didn't think this would happen." Elise's confusion, a frown and furrowed brows, washed away in place of understanding and surprise—as if she genuinely didn't know what Veaer had meant and now was completely happy to take responsibility like a child would after breaking a window with a foul ball. A slow smile, polite and courteous. "You were there. You were the little dog that Tychon had to hold back."

Veaer straightened up, holding a cautious hand forward in case Elise decided to do anything. "You admit it. You did it. You killed both of them."

"Oh, Veaer. You didn't need me to admit it if you already knew." Elise tsked and shook her head in that way that made Veaer want to crawl into the walls and hide. "You're much smarter than this. You wouldn't be here, in the academy, if you weren't."

I earned my place here, I deserve it. Veaer bristled in the shoulders and took a careful step to the side. Away from the glass, but not away from Elise. She would not back down. "I'm smart enough to know that I can't let you get away with this. I've kept your secret for too long."

"And I never asked you to keep anything for me." A serpentine smile stretched over her lips. "You were there when it happened, weren't you? You followed me when I was looking for Tychon and you watched me do it." A shrill laugh filled the room as Elise threw her head back and held a hand to her chest. "Oh, you're so lovely, Veaer. You're so kind. I never asked you to do any of that and you just did it." She wiped a stray tear from her eyes. "Have you been seeing Tychon this whole time? Has he been following you? He told me something like this would happen and I never had the mind to believe him! But look at us now..."

Elise stood from the bed, a shy creak emitting from the bed frame. The satin nightgown slid from the sheets and hovered above the floor with a flow that she could never achieve. Both of their eyes flew to the shards of glass, and she wasn't fast enough in her attempt to push Elise away as the princess shoved her hands into Veaer's chest and sent her into a wooden dresser.

Blood dripped into the puddle of iced tea as Elise clutched a large glass fragment. Veaer watched each drop run down golden skin and then disappear among fruit and leaves.

"I'm very fortunate to have taken precautions." Elise waved the fragment, cutting the air and letting red splatter here and there.

"You're going to kill me, too?" Veaer forced a level tone in her voice even as she watched the tip of glass get closer and closer. Her insides were aflame, yet her hands and legs were frozen solid. "Send me to the grave and then wait for the next one to come along and try to protect you?"

Elise stopped in front of her, their breaths close enough to mingle. The sharp point pressed against Veaer's stomach, lightly, but enough that she held her breath and let the tears well up in her eyes. For a moment, she saw the girl she still loved. Shapes cut at just the right places, freckles dotted like an artist's prized masterpiece, clothing that was entirely made for her, and, at the same time, she still would look quite beautiful in no clothing at all.

She was an intellectual mind and a visionary creative. Veaer kept a copy of each assignment in a folder in her room and liked to read them whenever she was stuck for inspiration. Elise liked the foods Veaer liked. Elise liked the art that Veaer liked. They did the same classes and followed a routine only known to them as art stream students of Adraredon Academy. They were so same and so different and that made it all the more exciting and terrifying.

Elise made her feel like they could take over the world.

Perhaps if Elise got rid of her now, she could still keep the mystery of Elise Excava in the afterlife. The unknown against the known, bursts of gold and rose and black and red. Myriads of shapes she held in her palms and composition with a heartbeat.

She could leave the world proud that she undid Elise, emotionally, physically. In will and in love. She finally knew what happened that day years ago and maybe she didn't need any more answers.

Becoming a home to butterflies didn't seem too bad. Maybe Elise would frame her too.

But instead, the pain against her stomach faded away and a burst of honey overtook her tongue, a kiss against her lips, and the texture of satin and skin against her hands. Her throat longed for air at the same time as she sighed into Elise. Everything was warm and cold, and her mind sparked with electricity and short-circuited.

Before she knew it, she was being guided towards the bed and as much as she fought to take control back, to ask what was happening and figure things out, her train of thought was washed away in place of closing her eyes and just feeling.

Maybe this was how it felt to die. To be kissed by death.

"I love you, Veaer." Elise's voice echoed in her ears between kisses and touches. "I know you won't tell anyone what I did." *What will you do to me if I do?* "I'm hopeless without you." *Do you really need me this much?* "Don't you love me, Veaer?"

"I love you, Elise."

"You're so good to me." A kiss to her forehead, a kiss to her chin, a kiss to each cheek and a kiss to her lips. "Everything is ours. The world is ours. And no one can hurt us, so long as we're together."

CHAPTER 38

CONFESSIONS OF LIFE AND DEATH

The clock on the wall read 12:12am.

She stared at the ceiling, listening to the other heartbeat that attached itself to her left arm. She noted that she could easily slide out of bed, ending up on the outer edge before the princess fell asleep, but then did nothing.

The clock on the wall read 12:43am.

She turned her head and faced a sleeping Elise. So peaceful and not dangerous at all. If Elise slept forever, then she wouldn't have to worry about watching herself at every moment, wondering what could be used as a weapon nearby. A shard of glass, a chair as a blunt weapon, pushing her off the balcony, using an actual knife and stabbing her.

When the clock's seconds hand ticked over twelve and read 1:11am, Veaer sat up and put her entire mind towards carefully pulling her arm away from Elise's grip. She avoided the broken glass on the floor and found her blazer thrown somewhere in the room.

She ended up wearing the blazer inside out in the darkness, realising when she tried to stuff her hands in her pockets to warm up but was only met with continued coldness. No one else would be able to tell, so she faced her next challenge: the door.

Elise could wake up at any moment, to a squeak, to an accidental step in spilled tea turned loud gasp, to noticing that she wasn't in bed with her anymore. She treaded along the carpet all the while wondering what it would've been like as a cat caemi, even more nimble and quiet.

She reached the door and turned the handle, which needed a bit more force than she wanted, and she almost yelled at the inanimate object for making a *chunk* sound to turn it all the way. But eventually she swung it open just enough to fit through, not too much for the hinges to reveal her, and not too little that she would trip or injure herself in the process.

The fourth floor halls, sleepy and maybe not so scary as the top of the manor, provided a perfect pacing ground. It was all she could manage after what Elise made her promise. Perhaps not an official promise that came with a pinky shake, but one weaved into a lovely confession that she held close to her heart and protected with walls and shields.

She had intended to protect the princess and redeem well-earned knowledge and answers by keeping the secret to herself, like a personal royal guard. She had dug a cavern dedicated to holding what this secret had to offer. The ghosts, the questioning, the discoveries, the riddles, the late nights, and the looks over her shoulder when she walked anywhere on the grounds.

But now things were different. Because the best and worst person to know the secret she held was the very person she was keeping the secret for. Now, more than ever, she needed the support of someone else. Or two someone elses.

The Boudreau twins would understand her. Just as she understood Adair's desire to become their highest self, and Haiwrin's wish to leave and make sure they were all safe. It would only be right for them to trust her judgement and remain open to what she had to say. The timing was perfect. The horrific reality that she didn't truly know everything about Adair's inner workings sparked feelings of betrayal and disbelief within her, but it invited her to share the misgivings plaguing her mind. Adair must have felt so relieved to tell Veaer about their journey and Haiwrin had managed to spend time outside his room. She knew they wouldn't do anything to her for keeping this secret; she had done nothing wrong, and they would've done the same for each other and her.

She stood in front of Adair's door for a long time. Her arm was beginning to get tired from almost knocking.

Then she turned around and returned to Elise's room.

"Wake up." Two hands with a vice grip shook her arm. "Veaer, wake up."

Veaer opened her eyes to Elise hovering over her, half dressed in her school shirt and underwear. Her tie was loosely hung, and Veaer had the urge to take it in her hands and pull it down, but the serious look on the princess' face awakened her senses and she sat up. The clock read 7:21am.

She rubbed her eyes and focused on breathing in and out. "What... What day is it?"

"There's a call for you downstairs. They say it's urgent," Elise said as she went back to putting on the rest of her uniform. Veaer looked down and noticed that she was wearing a nightdress. Quite pretty but she didn't think it fit her well. Out the corner of her eye, her uniform was sitting in a pile at the end of the bed. "Don't bother with the uniform. They charge per minute."

Veaer nodded slowly as she looked around. The wooden dresser that she slammed into last night was neat and unharmed. The tea table and chair were back to where they belonged, even with a new pitcher and glasses. It was as if what happened between them hadn't.

She slipped out of bed, walking past Elise and towards the door. Before she reached for the handle, Elise pulled on Veaer's elbow and turned her around enough to leave a kiss on her lips and cheek.

"I'm going to the library to get some work done before class, but the door will be unlocked for you to get ready later. Have a good day, okay?" Elise smiled sweetly and Veaer grinned.

You aren't mad at me anymore? "Yeah, I will." She watched

Elise's eyes for the slightest of changes—to reveal that she was only testing Veaer to bring up what happened or the secret. But nothing. She played with her fingers behind her back.

Elise took Veaer's face in her hands. "I love you, Veaer." Her lips twitched downwards for a moment, turning them into gentle slopes.

Veaer furrowed her brows, unsure of what to gather from her expression and words. Well, the words were clear enough, but she hadn't professed her love so many times before. Veaer's cheeks burned as she stuttered her reply.

"Good." Elise's gentle expression returned and she let Veaer go and headed for the bathroom.

Veaer left and navigated her way to the ground floor where the phone lived in the kitchen. No one spared her a glance or looked at her like they knew what she knew. Most students were still in their rooms, the shower running on each floor and chattering growing louder as more students woke up.

She saw a random student sitting by the phone before they noticed Veaer and gave her a nod. She thanked them briefly, taking their seat, more concerned for the phone sitting upright on the table with the coiled cord connected to the box. No one called her, so this was either a mistake or an emergency.

"Hey... hello?" she said into the handset. Maybe this was a joke, a viable third option.

"Oh, patrons above, Veaer!" Adair's voice emitted from the receiver, louder than she expected. She held the handset a little further away from her ear.

"Wait, why are you calling me?" Shame overcame her and she held her temple. A failed attempt at seeking Adair's counsel last night gnawed at her and she swatted her hand side to side as if it would make it disappear. "I'm just downstairs."

"I couldn't—didn't have time to..." Adair's words jumped back and forth. Coupled with the crackling that came through the line, it didn't help to get their message across, only making Veaer more concerned. She tapped her fingers against the wooden table, eyeing the students who came into the kitchen for a morning drink or breakfast. She didn't want them to hear what she'd say and became awfully aware of herself. "It's Haiwrin. He tried to leave this morning."

"Leave?" Veaer's eyes widened, and she held the phone tighter. "Like, the academy? Did he speak to someone?"

"No, no. He literally just packed his stuff and... he tried to walk out... but," Adair blubbered and their voice grew quieter. Veaer could tell that feeling anywhere.

"Where are you?" Veaer stood up and almost had the handset fly against the wall as she stretched the cord. "Are you with him right now?"

"Infirmary," Adair squeaked out and Veaer slammed the phone into the box before bolting for the admin building.

Veaer swore at herself for not grabbing her shoes before leaving. The nightdress was embarrassing enough but hopping into the building with the Library and Information Assistant staring at her trying to get grass and pebbles off the bottom of her feet made things worse.

She burst through the infirmary door and was met with a stern look from a nurse who gave her an up and down glance. The nurse shook his head and returned to sterilising equipment.

Her friend was easy to spot through the cubicle curtains and white room with their bright orange hair. They sat in a chair next to Haiwrin's bed. Small ember looking particles floated around the twins, and a subtle glow stuck to the skin of Adair.

Haiwrin was sleeping peacefully, a black sweater draped over the edge of the bed and a leg of his black pants peeking out from under the blanket. On the floor were a few bags and Haiwrin's nice shoes— ones that he wore for opening night parties.

"What happened?" Veaer grabbed a chair by another bed and dragged it over. No one else was in this section of the infirmary.

They didn't answer immediately. "Your choice of clothing is..."

Adair wiped their cheeks and smiled at Veaer. She couldn't smile back when she noticed the aura growing stronger.

Veaer made a dismissive sound and stared at Haiwrin. His chest was moving up and down under the blanket. "Didn't have time."

The orange cat caemi sat back and pulled the sheet away, revealing Haiwrin's bare chest. An intricate scar shot up his arm from his fingertips and carried across his chest, stopping at the opposite shoulder. It was hard to describe what she was looking at. Sparkly with bits of colour but otherwise dark and concerning. She imagined it running deep into his skin but couldn't bear to touch it to find out. Other than a shape similar to a lightning bolt, small runes and sigils were scattered at the edges. There had to be some sort of magic involved.

"They have enforced barriers at the edge of the school grounds, ones we can't see," Adair started to explain, following it with a humourless laugh and another wipe of their cheeks. "He made it far enough to the edge before any of the groundskeepers or other students wandering about could stop him. They said he was going to brute force his way through—they really believed he was going to with how hard he tried. At some point he even got his fox ears back. That's how much he wanted to leave. Breaking anti-magic just like his little sibling."

The two of them sat in silence for a little while, watching the glittery remnants move across Haiwrin's body like a galaxy alive.

"And then what?" Veaer asked, her gaze unmoving. In her first year she would often stare between buildings, to the expanse of land beyond the academy grounds, but she never knew anyone who wanted to try leaving. Haiwrin was the last person she would think to try.

"The magic fought back. I guess that's what happens when you test limits that you fail to consider." Their words echoed back on themselves, as if not only for Haiwrin. "The doctor said it's going to take a long time for this to heal. Constant tests and visits. Experiments, too. They don't know how bad Hai has it." They leaned closer to Veaer for a whisper. "And I can't do anything about it. I'm meant to be able to heal, but every time I try, it doesn't work. All this power, all those rituals. There's so much of *me* still trapped. Showing my form to you yesterday? Gods above, I didn't know what I was doing... it took so much out of me. I'm useless when it matters most."

Veaer turned to Adair and saw the way orange and red flickered in and out around them. Maybe her proximity did help with the magic, but she figured that Adair would've pointed something out by now if that were the case. Instead of saying anything, she reached over to Adair's knee and held it with a squeeze. Adair placed their hand on top of Veaer's.

When she looked back at Haiwrin, stirring slightly but still asleep, realisation broke her thoughts into pieces.

"Haiwrin was right." Veaer counted her fingers on her free hand. *1, 2, 3, 4.*

"What?" Adair's hand tightened around hers.

"We're not safe. Imagine if no one was watching. We'd be going to class and his unconscious body would be at the very edge of the grounds. He didn't even have to look over his shoulder for something to happen to him."

"I..." Adair's expression hardened, lips in a thin line and eyes without light. "You shouldn't say those things. I can protect you, I can protect Haiwrin. We could've... we should've seen this coming. It wasn't anything more than that."

"This all started because of what happened to Tychon," Veaer replied louder than she wanted. She heard the footsteps of a nurse around the corner, then they stopped. No one said anything until the nurse walked away.

Adair exchanged a look with Veaer, chin dipping and eyes deliberately boring into her. "We don't know what happened to him."

Veaer opened and closed her mouth. She sucked in a breath. Was this the right time to tell them? Would this fix things? Maybe if Haiwrin knew what really happened, he wouldn't be so eager to leave. Maybe if Adair knew, they could protect Elise too.

"I do," she said.

Adair took a moment to process the words, then lifted her hand from Veaer's. "What do you mean? How would you know?"

She remembered Tychon choking and bringing a hand to his mouth. Remembered the blood that covered his palms and fingers. The stumbles, desperate and reaching, and he fell when Elise stabbed him again, and again, and again.

The screams and the cries.

"I was there when it happened." Veaer shrunk into herself. *I didn't do anything wrong, I didn't do anything. We can protect her, we can save her from herself.* "I saw Elise do it. I saw her kill him and get away with it."

The world stopped spinning and Veaer was afraid that a knife would fly through the window and strike her in the head, leaving her to never speak another word. She glared at the window, framing trees and the learning centre from here, until Adair spoke again.

"You need to tell someone," they demanded, standing up and grabbing Veaer's shoulders. The chair squeaked against the lino floor and hit the bedside table. "How could you? You just let it happen, and then you let her get away with it?" Adair brought their hands to their hair and combed through over and over. The ends of their hair started tinting red and a laugh rose from their lips. "Oh, Ter and Mian, all this time. All this time you knew. I told you what he meant to me, and you didn't even tell me."

"I didn't know who you were back then!" Veaer snapped in return, pushing Adair's hands away as they lowered to her shoulders again. "Do I need to bring up what you did to me?"

"Adair, Veaer... can you stop shouting?"

Her attention flicked to Haiwrin, who groaned as he rubbed his eyes and slightly turned his head. He frowned and glanced at his sibling who was standing against the bed with their arms mid-reach towards Veaer, and then narrowed his eyes when he switched to her.

"Did I hear you right...?" he questioned in a quiet voice, a wheeze following the question. "Elise really did that?"

Veaer paled. She didn't realise that Haiwrin would've heard her, and it occurred to her that she wasn't truly ready to share this with him yet. It seemed her expression was enough.

"Come on, Ve." He brought his hand down his face and as his fingertips reached his chest, he flinched. He must not have remembered what happened and lent himself a few moments to collect his thoughts. Then he continued, "Addie's right, you need to tell someone."

"I just told you," Veaer answered pathetically, tears welling in her vision, but she blinked hard to send them away.

He shook his head, as much as he could while lying incapacitated in a bed. Then he held a hand out to Adair and they took it. "You know what we mean. We're not the ones in control here."

"This is life and death," Adair added, and their face did soften a fraction with Haiwrin seeming okay. "And aside from what she's already done, she's still out there, going to class, being among students, acting like everything's normal. She's going to do it again."

"I just want to protect her—" She was met with shaking heads and disappointed looks. Even fear lingered in Adair's gaze. "I thought you both would understand!" A glare hurled towards Adair in particular. "I thought we'd do the same for each other."

When neither of the twins answered, she shot up from her chair and kicked it with the back of her foot. The nurse came back again with an irritated look just as Veaer turned around and headed for the door.

As she pushed the door open, Haiwrin echoed, "Life and death, life and death."

CHAPTER 39
DEAD AT 18

Veaer took a deep breath as she closed the infirmary door and leaned her back against it. She let the warm brown tones of the ceiling cure the pain behind her eyes, the medical room having been too bright for her to the very last moment.

Her next course of action wasn't easily determined.

Elise was in the library—they could stay together and ensure each other's safety.

Though, as long as she stayed by the twins, she would know they hadn't told anyone.

For a moment, she considered skipping class to keep tabs on all of them; even the question of Harq's whereabouts came into mind. But her records showed that she needed to attend class more punctually, plus she had community work later.

She lowered her chin to bring herself back from paint against wood to reality, only to be met by three students standing in front of her. She flinched and looked between them. Normal students in uniform, nothing peculiar, except for how they were looking at her. They didn't say anything, so she stepped to the side and gestured to the door. Perhaps she was blocking their way.

But their gazes tracked her like portraits where the eyes appeared as if they were following you from every angle. Was it the nightdress she was wearing? In that case, it wasn't their business to stare.

"You can go in..." she prompted, reaching for the door handle in case she needed to help them there too. "It's open."

One of them, at first with their hands behind their back and then bringing them forward, revealed a uniform to her. All of them nodded at her to take it.

She frowned and stepped towards the exit, but their stares pierced through her as if to impale her against the wall. The uniform didn't look great. Perhaps it was her size, but she suspected something like paint was between the folds from the patchwork of colours. It wasn't up to the academy's standard to have a dirty uniform.

"Look, I have my own uniform at Miriam, but I appreciate it..." She peered past them, in case that assistant had anything to do with this, or some other student was watching nearby to embarrass her. No one else was in the lobby and the reception desk was tucked away enough that she couldn't see it.

The student forced the clothes into her arms. They didn't appear much younger than her—she assumed second years. Then the three of them turned and pointed towards the bathroom.

She took a step in that direction and waited for a reaction. Gentle stares, patient. They let her continue stepping in that direction until she walked into the bathroom and closed the door. When she unfolded the uniform, her suspicions were confirmed. For some reason, this uniform was covered in splashes of coloured paint. She felt the fabric between her fingers and brought it to her nose. It was rather fresh as well.

On the other side of the door, the students knocked harshly without a word.

She pursed her lips. She could put it on just to satisfy them and then head right to the manor to change again. Other than the paint, there wasn't anything in the pockets and the shirt, skirt, and blazer were indeed her size. She didn't bother with the tie for now.

She considered what she might say to the students to get them off her back, repeating the phrases to herself in her head. She had other things to do. The most important people to protect. She could do her best to be polite but firm. She didn't have time to lead around a line of baby ducks.

With a deep breath, she opened the door.

And a bat swung in her vision, meeting the side of her face.

She fell to the floor, pain searing across her temple and her arm numbing from impact. Her vision blurred and she looked up at the students, the bat being passed from one to another. They spoke quietly, in hushed tones, not minding her frantic breaths and clawing hands.

"What the fuck..." Her mind and body dropped into darkness.

She slept like a baby until her senses came back to her.

Wet touch under her fingers, her clothing sticky with the scent of paint, and a blinding light in front of her eyelids. Something like a blanket laid over her but it seemed too fragile to be anything warm and useful.

She opened her eyes and yelled at how close the source of light was to her face. A sound like wind rustling through leaves filled her ears and the light moved away. Her heart collapsed in her chest and the hairs on her arms stood. What she thought would be a ceiling was actually the sky, a few dark clouds rolling in the blue. What she thought was a blanket and bed were piles of dirt. Her legs were stuck in a hole refilled, and she struggled to sit up without proper balance.

Feathers appeared at the corner of her vision, and she risked a turn of her head, her cheek against the mud. Tychon stood tall next to her, his many eyes roaming up and down her situation. He turned out to be the light that she couldn't bear to look at. Now he seemed more person than angel in a dimmer shine, but still with wings and robes.

Then she spotted a part of the cathedral behind him, and the stones with engraved writing around her, and a shovel close by, discarded.

She screamed and desperately pushed her feet against the dirt to gain some traction in getting them out. Worms wriggled here and there, one close enough to climb her hand once she yanked it up.

She stumbled and fell like a baby deer learning how to walk, staining her hands black with mud no matter how quickly she wanted to get out. Tychon's ghost frowned at her and remained silent. A single tear ran down his cheek.

When she finally stood, knees weak and panting, she looked back at where she laid, and the stone read

VEAER ROSELL. DEAD AT 18.

She knelt down and grabbed the stone, running her hand up and down just in case her eyes were really playing tricks on her, as if this were an illusion Tychon put up to scare her. But it was etched in deeply and permanently.

Two warm hands grabbed her shoulders and lifted her to her feet. She could hear the golden rings spinning around Tychon's head right in her ears.

"Run," he says.

"What?"

"Run, as fast as you can."

And she ran towards Miriam Manor, guided by Tychon's light before he disappeared from her vision and in place was a crowd of students in the distance. Her legs pumped beneath her even while straining and sore from being held a prisoner of the graveyard, and her mind swirled in confusion. How had she ended up by the cathedral? Who dug her grave? What was happening?

As she got closer, the muttering grew louder and she watched someone heave forward with a hand clasped over their mouth before running towards the forest, their friends following close behind. Someone wailed and pointed. Someone was demanding others to get the teachers and the principal. Another, a student council member based on the band around their arm, was struggling to contain everyone and move them away.

She joined the outskirts of the group and looked upon the centre of their attention.

She froze, the world's sound drowned out by high pitched ringing in her head.

A giant painted mural covered the side of the manor, from the balcony at the top to the bricks at the bottom. Imagery of butterflies and flowers flooded her vision, skulls in the mix and bones crossing beauty. Stretching the five floors were sprinkles of feathers.

And then she noticed.

Hanging in the middle of the breathtaking masterpiece was Tychon Alastor Galacia's corpse.

Acid climbed her throat and the land she stood on tilted on its axis. Everyone turned around and faced her, wide eyes and black irises. She stumbled back and clung to a tree. She looked up again and stared at the rotting body, dripping with paint and dirt. Then she looked down at herself, almost a perfect rendition but with a beating heart.

In the bottom right corner of the piece was script writing that read

VEAER ROSELL'S ART FORM CAN REFLECT THE ARTIST'S MIND PALACE.

She burst away from the crowd as they screamed and scattered, some reaching for her and pulling her blazer off, some barely missing her short hair with gripping hands. She circled around to the front of the manor and pushed past those who were oblivious to the chaos, heading for the stairs.

But the barriers threw her away and mocked her. She wasn't welcome, she didn't belong. Her place was at the bottom of the stairs.

She cried and slammed her fists on the floor. Distraught students started coming through the front door and so she did what she knew best to do. She crashed into her room and threw open the window, climbing outside and making her way up.

She needed to get to Elise's room. She needed to get Tychon away from everyone and work out what to do. She didn't do anything wrong. She couldn't have done this.

But with each lug up the manor, she was met with her hands covered in incriminating dirt and paint. Her arms ached and her fingers threatened to slip on each hold, but she blinked through the tears and let the adrenaline in her body course through until she made it to the fourth floor.

The trip from there was easy, familiar in her mind as she planned weeks ago. It only made her more uncertain that she wasn't involved, but how may she have carried another being with her if she couldn't cross the barriers? And even then, dragging someone else up flights of stairs...

On the fifth floor, she listened out for a peep of sound. But Izot wasn't here, and she assumed Elise would be in class. The clamouring crowd outside was still loud, growing louder. She didn't like how their words weaved into the folds of her mind.

The princess' room was unlocked, and she sprinted into the room on the search for however the artist had hung Tychon's body from the top floor.

Then she paused, slowed down.

Elise was sitting in a chair on the balcony, far enough back so that those downstairs wouldn't see her, but clear enough for Veaer to walk in on the girl reading a book.

The princess rubbed her eyes and ignored her. Perhaps she wasn't really there. Several ropes were tied to the bed frame and hanging off the balcony railing. Veaer went for them and chose one to begin pulling, but gravity worked against her and she didn't trust herself enough to look over the edge to determine if pulling the ropes one at a time would do anything.

"That won't work," Elise said, taking a sip of tea.

"I know that!" Veaer snapped, her gaze following the motion towards Elise. "What are you doing here? Why are you letting this happen?"

"Just like you allowed what happened to Tychon?" Elise placed her cup in her lap and held the book up again. Veaer swallowed. "How am I to interrupt an artist's creation?"

"You need to help me, please." Veaer held two ropes together and pulled with her entire being, but she barely made progress before her hands burned and her legs gave out.

"I thought you loved me, Veaer."

"What?" She rubbed her hands against her shirt, the white disappearing with every wipe. "I do love you—I do."

"You did something you shouldn't have. I told you I have precautions."

"But I—"

Elise turned around so her deep brown eyes lit with sunbeams met Veaer's. A smile was set on her pink lips. "Tonight, I am ascending. I will complete myself and the order."

Veaer's blood turned to ice, and she rushed to Elise's side, kneeling on the cold ground. "Wait, what does that mean? What are you going to do?"

"Harq is so wise. He understands what it means to love and be loved, so well." Elise's gaze left Veaer and went to distant places where Veaer couldn't follow. The gears in her mind turned and whirled but nothing came to mind except *sacrifice*.

"No, no, no. Tell me what's going to happen. Where? When?"

"Tonight, Veaer. Tonight. The full moon." And then she fell silent and went back to reading her book.

Veaer shook Elise's shoulders until the cup of tea fell and shattered into pieces. A stampede of footsteps took up the fourth floor.

"Don't do this, please."

The door burst open behind them and solid, coordinated footsteps piled into the room. Following them was one another, with a voice she had the unfortunate fate of knowing.

Izot Excava stood among officers armed with weapons. He held his arm up and pointed to Veaer.

"Arrest her."

CHAPTER 40
AN INTERROGATION

"What was your relationship with the victim?" the detective repeated, folding her hands in front of her.

Veaer stared at the butterflies that watched her from the corners of the room. They came in all sorts of colours and sizes. Some of them had eyes on the back of their wings that made her look away if she focused on them for too long. A butterfly with red and black wings landed on top of the detective's head as she looked at her interrogation partner.

Veaer swayed in her seat and smiled as the butterfly climbed down the detective's face. "Can you let me go?" The butterfly opened its eye-filled wings again, and so she turned to the window and then looked at the dark wooden door on the opposite side.

They sat in one of the admin building offices, upstairs and away from everyone else. The desk was pushed against the wall and a new table with a lamp was brought in, fitting right in the centre of the room.

"Ms Rosell, you aren't authorised to leave until you answer a few questions for us," the officer sitting next to the detective said. "This is a very serious situation about a peer of yours."

She looked out the window again. It was approaching late afternoon. She needed more time. She couldn't leave Elise by herself. She needed to be there. But these officers didn't know what they were talking about and blamed her for nothing.

"I didn't do anything." A butterfly climbed onto her hand, and she swatted away.

The detective's gaze followed her hand. She furrowed her brows. "Okay, how about this. Can you walk us through what you did that Monday? Your classmates have told us they saw you during home-room and your morning class, but they didn't find you during lunch time and a little while after that."

Her eyes grew tired, and she swayed to the left before catching the table, making herself jump. When she steadied herself again, her mind spun, and a yawn emerged from her throat. A shining light appeared out of the corner of her eye and she noticed Tychon standing silently next to the police officer, whose expression grew more irritated by the second.

"Is this boring to you?" he demanded, slamming a fist on the table. Veaer shook her head. A yawn didn't necessarily mean she was bored. It was only a natural response to a desire for air. "Why don't we cut to the chase?" *With another question?* "We've found evidence incriminating you as the prime suspect of Tychon Alastor Galacia's murder."

"Now, now." The detective held a hand out. "Perhaps we shouldn't be jumping ahead. We don't want to scare her."

"Scare her? She's scared the whole damn school! My entire unit!" He grimaced at Veaer with a sidelong glance and then yelled a name at the door. Someone else dressed in an officer's uniform came through with a manilla folder. As though he was excusing his words with an attempt at trying to hide them, he continued under his breath, "What sick person hangs... and then forces..."

The officer passed the manilla folder to his partner who shook the contents out and arranged them on the table. Veaer frowned and batted the butterflies covering the table away.

A little plastic bag with a lock of silver hair. "We had conducted several searches of Tychon's room when he was declared missing," the officer explained in a low tone. "Yet somehow upon a recent search, your hairs—many of them—have been found on the premises."

Elise stepped closer, still staring into the mirror, and started playing with Veaer's silver locks in one hand.

Then a distinct snipping noise snapped her to a more diligent state, and she flinched this time, only to meet Elise's confused expression in the reflection and no other noises than their breaths and beating hearts.

"You may consider that we've spoken to your headmaster, and you've been reported to have broken into his room recently too, not for any reason other than emotional distress. Except that we found..."

He pushed forward a picture of Tychon's personal journal and tarot journal on her desk. "If you entered and left Tychon's room without any possessions, then how did you get your hands on these?"

Elise pulled Tychon's journal out of her pocket and held it towards Veaer.

"Hold onto this for me. I don't know when we'll need it again but I find it an ill reminder to keep it."

The officer laughed and pushed another plastic bag forward, holding a used handkerchief. "And this, well. I wouldn't know how you got one of his handkerchiefs but..."

As Veaer rubbed the tip of her nose with her palm, Elise held a handkerchief up.

Another bag, and it held the manor's master key. "A true method for how you got into Tychon's room, twice over! Maybe even more and we wouldn't know!"

Veaer walked over to the desk and opened each drawer, pressing at the bottom of each until the third one budged and moved to reveal a key.

A master key to Miriam Manor, she could get into any dorm room she wanted.

"You have no excuse for your little stunt today." The officer slammed the final photo on the table, the giant mural but without the hanging body. "You killed Tychon Alastor Galacia and made a mockery of his existence!"

Veaer cried as she held her head and bent over the table, shutting her eyes so that she didn't have to face everything set before her. Every nice gesture, every strange moment. Every casual action that went towards protecting the princess only endangered herself more. Elise was right, she was telling the truth. She had taken precautions from the very start and now it was time to pay the price. As long as Elise was covering her tracks, she was creating new ones that led back to Veaer.

Even with the darkness behind her eyelids, a kaleidoscope of butterflies didn't let her escape. She had to get out, she had to do something. Why did Elise do this? Had she really planned this all along or were these simple coincidences? Were Elise's feelings for her true or all a ruse to get away?

"That's enough, officer!" The detective stood up and her chair screeched against the floorboards. Veaer's gaze snapped up to a bright orange butterfly circling the detective's head as fire crackled in her eyes. "Badgering our suspect will do us no good. This is an interrogation, not a court. You are an officer, not a lawyer. If anything, you should be dismissed from this room. Your misconduct will make this case void if your bias continues to do harm."

Veaer blinked her tears away and watched as the detective escorted the officer out of the room. Just as he grumbled and left, and the detective returned to her seat with a sigh, Veaer bolted up and grabbed the detective's arms.

"Ah! Hey, no." The detective pulled her arms away and dusted them off. Veaer shrunk back into her seat and counted the butterflies in the room on her fingers. "You are still under custody. We just need... a recess, to sort this out." Her eyes hovered between the laid out evidence and Veaer's face. "And please, don't let his words prevent you from answering the questions. We need your help to understand this situation."

Veaer shook her head furiously. "I can't. I don't know what happened." As clever as she thought she was, perhaps she was not.

Elise did everything right in front of her and she was the one sitting with a detective right now. "I need to go. Let me go. I need to find her and stop her and... and..." She needed answers, right now. But the butterflies swarmed her vision, and she swung her arms to scare them away. They didn't listen to her. "These stupid butterflies..." Tychon sat where the officer had, staring at her with little to say. "And you! You aren't doing anything to help! This is all wrong, all wrong—"

"We can't let you go," the detective reiterated firmly. "And..." Creases in her forehead seemed to age the detective by decades. She placed a hand flat on the table, reaching but not touching. "I have some concerns about your behaviour and statements. A psychological evaluation may be helpful before we proceed."

CHAPTER 41
OVERTHINKER

Veaer didn't like this shade of brown.

Coating the walls and seeping into the floor. Creating a sky that faded into an ill colour from too much sun. And suddenly, when there was a notable enough change to cause panic, they drew the curtains together and darkened the room forever. But the pigment won't return; the brown will remain sick forever.

They gave her a little stool in the office next to the interrogation room. The desk was removed from this one, and nothing that was considered a weapon was left. She didn't even get a paper and pen.

"Paper causes paper cuts," the detective had explained as she picked up a pile sitting in a shelf that was removed, too, moments later. Veaer didn't mind the detective and the fire she had, but her words only made her want to prove her wrong. *Investigate this!* Paper didn't always cause paper cuts. Sometimes it was the person holding the paper that mattered.

The curtains remained and Veaer asked about them. The officers believed the risk of choking on thick velvet curtains was less than the risk of looking out the window and watching students. They didn't want her to get any new ideas.

It didn't matter to her anyway. The students that gave her the suspicious uniform looked like any other but part of her theorised their involvement with the order. Or they could've been the circle of underclassmen Elise kept around. She couldn't tell. Just as she couldn't tell the spiders in the corner of the room from the butterflies that started weaving cocoons between the folds of the curtains. Which were real and which were a play on her eyes in the dim light?

The detective gave the room a once over, sending a wary look to the wooden stool, before closing the door. The click of a lock resounded past her ears and into her skull.

When she heard footsteps fade away, she felt safe enough to bend over and run her finger down a leg of the stool. It was sanded down in production. There would be no splinters today. The detective didn't have to worry.

"Worry about what?"

Someone's voice, but not Tychon's. Tychon hadn't returned since the interrogation ended. This voice was familiar but fuzzy in her mind. Unpractised and needing water to wet their throat. Young and probably a student. Even the detective, while a young woman, had a distinct voice of age and experience.

But every student was partying or doing homework or relaxing by now, and they wouldn't help her. She scared them all. She had to stay in the other room.

She missed her community work today. If this investigation didn't suspend her, then the headmaster would do so himself. Perhaps this was a good time to practise her entrance interviews for her last semester before university. She didn't have paper to record her notes but if she repeated her answers to herself enough, she wouldn't need to write anything down.

"That should be the least of your concerns, Veaer."

The voice sounded like an echo, going through tunnels and coming out the other side something else than it had started as.

She pressed her palms to her eyes. She needed sleep—could the butterflies build her a giant cocoon to just disappear and never need to think or wonder or question again? Time was easily paralysed in a room of nothing except weird brown and bugs, but her breaths kept track of every second anyway.

The door is locked. I could break the lock. There should be a secret tunnel or something around here. There's one from the outside but it leads to the wrong places. Maybe I can climb out this window, but how quickly would someone be notified and drag me back? I could test it and deal with the consequences, but they may move me somewhere else without a window.

I hope Haiwrin is okay. He got hurt—because of me? But it wasn't really me. But maybe he wouldn't have felt so distressed if I told him what happened. People act out when they're confused and don't know everything. He didn't deserve what happened to him. I'll need to make it up to him. Agree to his apartment in the town if I get out of here. No, not if. When I get out of here.

I still don't understand how I woke up in the graveyard. I hope nothing went down my skirt. It wasn't even my skirt. It belonged to those students. What did they hit me with? A bat? Why was that their choice? Where did they even keep it?

What was Elise's intention? How involved was she in all this? Did she trick me from the very start? She gave me the journal to keep in a safe place; it was my fault for leaving it out on my desk. That just made it easy for them to find it. And why would Elise give me Tychon's handkerchief? Did she simply forget it was his, or was she keeping it with her until he came back, but then she saw I needed it and decided to do a nice gesture. There has to be an explanation for all this. She had to have a reason. Just not the reason everyone is assuming. She loves me, I love her. Together, we are safe. They can't hurt us as long as—

"Veaer, patrons above, shut up!"

"Sorry," Veaer said aloud as she stared at a shape in the wallpaper, but she swore the yell came from within her own head. She hadn't told herself to shut up before. Her thoughts often got somewhere, eventually.

"Just—" The voice became gentler and warmer. Much warmer.

Veaer blinked and then took off her blazer. She folded it and looked around for a place to put it. The floor would do for now. "Please. Be quiet. I can't find you if you're going on like that."

"Find me? Why are you looking for me? I didn't ask you..." She pursed her lips, as if incentivised by an invisible force. Maybe it was better that she didn't know what was happening.

"Exactly. That's exactly right. The less you know, the better I can concentrate. The fewer factors there are to worry about."

Focused voice, intense. Slightly strained on the edges. A slow pace she was familiar with in homeroom and when she used to take literature classes just for fun. She could almost see the narrowed eyes and almost hear the murmuring undercurrent of a caemi memorising quotes for an essay.

Adair.

"I'm sorry." Veaer perched her elbows on her knees and held her head in her hands. Despite everything, her lovely Adair was still looking for her. "I'm sorry, I'm sorry."

"You already said that." Their voice tapered off at the end, like a connection fizzling over a landline.

She took a deep breath and shook her head, but she knew Adair couldn't see it. Instead, she shifted off the stool and laid down on her side. It was easier to fall asleep if a wooden circle wasn't digging into her backside. The butterflies looked funny like this. Even the brown was a little different. She closed her eyes.

Then she was awoken by a flurry of urgent footsteps coming from down the hall. They weren't dragging like they didn't want to be here, or stomping like they had to show everyone who they were from their presence, or marching like they were trained to walk like they followed their commander everywhere.

It was enough of a difference for her to open her eyes and sit up. She combed through her hair with her fingertips and unfolded her blazer pillow to put it on again. The curtains beckoned her to open them, to see what time it was, but she feared that she had missed everything and the blazing sun would shock her eyes.

She was met with silence for several moments by the time she sat on the stool again, in case it was the detective there to check on her again. Had she just imagined it? There were no more butterflies in the room.

But then the doorknob started to turn, as if teasing her for not believing her senses and leaving it all up in the air for her to wonder about again and again.

The knob started shaking. The person on the other side didn't have a key, so it wasn't the detective.

"Whoever you are, get away!" Veaer yelled and contemplated throwing the stool at the door. But if it broke, then she really wouldn't have anywhere to sit. "I don't know what you want but I'm under the protection of Detective— uh..." *Shit.* She hadn't gotten her name.

There was no response, and a strong urge to shut her lips overwhelmed her. Shaking, shaking, herself and the doorknob. Until it stopped.

A thud, and something heavy rolled across the carpet from the other side of the door. Veaer backed into the wall as much as she could. Maybe she could blend in. Maybe the butterflies would really help her hide now. *Please, please, please.*

The door swung open, and a figure of blazing red and orange hair appeared with a quiet cackle.

"Adair?" Veaer's mouth hung open before it morphed into a smile, and she dashed for her friend. Her gaze was still in more than one place in case this was all a trick of the mind. She decided on placing one hand on their shoulder to confirm their existence. "You're here. How did you—" Her ears perked up in anticipation of yelling and clamouring to her office of holding, but there was only peace. "What did you do?"

"I don't know what you're talking about," Adair replied—and their tone was genuine as far as she could tell. There was no sarcasm or tricky look in their eyes. So many eyes. A blast of heat made her cough and reorient herself. The giant wings had returned, sprouting out of Adair's back. But Adair hadn't flinched even once, as if the wings, eyes, and rings were there the whole time. "The hardest part was finding where they put you."

"But—" Veaer removed her hand and stepped forward, but Adair easily blocked the doorway with their wingspan. "The detective and the officers... the faculty? How did you get past them? They wouldn't just leave me alone here."

Adair shook their head and took Veaer's hand. "Veaer, this isn't the admin building."

"I was just there!"

"If you were in the admin building, finding you would've been the easiest task. It was the first place I looked."

"Then... then..." Veaer ripped her hand away from Adair's grip and ran for the curtains, pulling them apart only to find more wall. And when the question of why curtains would come with no window came to mind, the velvet disintegrated in her palms and fell past her fingers. What was left was an excuse for a painted wall, not even with wallpaper. "Where am I?"

Adair looked to the side and Veaer asked again, more adamantly. This could change everything if she hadn't slept the night away.

"Underground." They paused and their eyes wandered here and there. "Izot announced that you were arrested, earlier. And as much as you did a horrible, horrible thing in keeping the truth from everyone, you also weren't holding the knife when it happened." A blaze ignited from the top of their being and found their feathery wings as fuel. Veaer gasped at the magnificent display until Adair screamed and fell to their knees.

"Wait, what's happening? Is this not meant to happen?" Veaer dropped to the floor and reached out, but just the outer edges of the flames hurt her, and she pulled back with a hiss.

Adair screeched like nothing Veaer had heard before and she covered her ears.

"Goodness, no. No, no. It's not, argh!" Bones cracked and muscles ripped, the sound all the more louder as it bounced off the walls outside.

"No..." Veaer echoed, realisation dawning on her. "You said you didn't have it... you couldn't do it again. You don't have the capacity —you, you... why did you take this form again when you couldn't even help Haiwrin?"

"Don't you dare bring him up now," Adair managed through gritted teeth, their wings wrapping tightly around the two of them and sharp, long fangs showing when they let out another screech. "Listen, Veaer, I did this because I'm stupid. And I'm stupid because I— I couldn't bear to know you were going to be taken away, for something you didn't do, when *she* is still out there. And I didn't know how else I could find you in time without—this." The fire began to smoulder but dark smoke took its place. "Ve... Veaer, please listen, please."

"I'm listening," Veaer cried, and a flood of tears drenched her shirt. As much as it burned, she pulled Adair's face closer in her palms. Beautiful eyes, beautiful jewels. "I'm listening, Addie. Tell me."

"Veaer, she's at the cathedral. I don't know what she's going to do, but Harq told me it would bring them back. A young Kitt Thawan and Tychon. You can't let that happen. The world always balances, it has a way to take as much as it gives." Their wings fell to dust, one feather at a time. "You must fix this. You know you must."

"Are you going to be okay?" She squeezed Adair's soft face tighter, to keep them together, to keep them from going too. "I can't leave you like this."

Adair took a deep breath and from their lips came dust and smoke. "I will be okay. With time and rest—and I have time." They lifted their hands to Veaer's cheeks, stained with dark ashes. Their eyes roamed her and peeled away layers of hurt, guilt, and grief. All that was left of the two of them were tiny, little kids, not ready for what the world had to give to them. "Oh lovely angel, I'm stupid. A stupid creature in love. And I know you may never want to accept that. You may never want to take from me. But know this, Veaer Rosell, that I did this because I love you."

"Don't say that," Veaer sobbed, messy and raw, clinging to Adair and what was left of their wings. "Don't say what you don't mean."

"I mean it, I truly do." Adair closed the gap and pressed their lips together. Ash and salt, all in one.

CHAPTER 42
THE LAST HOUR

The cathedral entrance cracked open with both hands pushing, revealing an empty lobby. Sombre classical music spilled from under the next set of doors, making everything feel all the more intrusive.

Veaer took a deep breath, incense wafting through her, providing enough courage for her to commit to revealing what came next.

The doors to the guts of the cathedral groaned in protest and a collective breath was held from the other end of the hall. Her path was lined with floating candles, dripping and forming stalagmites of wax, setting unease into her being as thick pillars towered over her. They were in throes of magic, that which shouldn't have been possible above ground, but she had witnessed enough in the last weeks that, rather than question the candles' nature, she hoped they wouldn't come after her and set her ablaze.

The carpet didn't do much to soften her steps as each one thumped loudly under her skin. High pitched singing shook her ear drums and she jolted with an urge to cover her ears. Even so, her arms remained stiff by her sides.

The song continued to play, and she passed pew after pew.

Her gaze was set on one girl with long black hair and dressed in her light robes, turned away and busying her attention with a no name order member who helped draw a circle around the altar. The chalk touched the edge of what was previously Tychon's circle in front of the altar, invisible to most but so bright and clear to her.

Harq was sitting with his back to her in one of the front pews, and a small group of anonymous protectors were standing nearby holding candles and jewels, staring right at Veaer for her unwelcome entrance.

"Elise!" Veaer screamed with her entire chest. To chase away her fear, to take up her space despite the high vaulted ceiling and sharp eyes sent her way. She staggered out of the shadows. The princess turned to meet her.

"Oh, Veaer." A bright smile beamed on Elise's face, sharp at the edges and full of shiny teeth. She held out her arms as if to pull Veaer even closer, up onto the altar platform. "You made it."

"You...!" She could barely manage another word without her throat closing up on her. All that time to prepare and she hadn't done so. Her gaze flitted to Elise's hand, peeking out from behind her back. A ritual knife. "You shouldn't be doing this."

"I had thought you got lost along the way," Elise continued in a quiet voice but her look towards Harq was undeniable. "You must give me a moment to process this."

Veaer stepped back as Elise revealed her knife in the light for everyone to see. No one gasped, no one screamed. They all watched her sway the knife before she extended her hand to the white clothed altar and placed it down.

Veaer made herself to concentrate on the girl in white, the orange glow of the candles forming a type of halo, an object anything but warming. Beautiful crystals jingled on Elise's ears, neck, wrists, and ankles. Her hair was as silky as ever, her skin calling for Veaer to bite down and devour. Veaer remembered the way her breath sat in her throat when she made her way to Elise's room and stole that necklace to prove something—to Elise or herself. She remembered when she would admire Elise from a distance, and when she was up close in a fencing mask, against a tree, among pretty bed sheets.

The day they found the crypts was the best day of her life. It was that day that told her life was worth continuing—to discover and to explore. She had savoured the warm exhales of Elise when they bent against bark and brought their lips together. When they had something in this part of the world and everything was theirs, forever and always.

"You and me, Veaer Rosell. You and me."

"Veaer, you haven't been entirely honest with me." Elise ran her finger along the altar and picked at a dot of dust. "Why must I tell you about this when there very well was a chance you weren't even going to be here?" She laughed before Veaer could even rebuke her statement. She was here now, didn't that matter? "Darling, come here."

But I want you to tell me. This is important, and aren't I important too? Yet she couldn't bring the words to her tongue as she watched Elise's arms open again, begging for Veaer to take her perfect place and be a perfect lover. No need to ask questions, no need to meet every choice with a question.

She took it a step at a time and when she joined Elise on the altar platform, everything didn't seem so scary anymore. She was tall and brave and knew how to be good so she wouldn't be sent away again.

Elise wrapped her arms tightly around Veaer and drew her lips closer to her ear. "The world is ours," she said. "There's no need to worry," she said. "We're not so tiny anymore. I don't need anything to show me how powerful we are. We can do anything we want."

Veaer held her breath. She wanted to take Elise's words and bathe in them. Scrub them in until they became a film of suds that seeped into her skin and kept her nourished. But even then, the music was too loud and there were too many eyes, and Harq walked up to them and set a firm hand on each of their shoulders.

"We need to get started." Harq squeezed Veaer's shoulder with a slight pull. "The hour doesn't give us a wide window for all that we need to do." His voice sounded distant as Veaer stared at Elise for her prompt.

The princess swept her arm against Veaer's stomach, gentle

enough to be a caring gesture but firm enough for Veaer to stumble back cautiously and find herself climbing down from the platform.

She swallowed as the protectors came forward and lit candles around the altar. A shiver crawled up her spine, her eyes darting between each order member. They all looked the same, too similar, and which ones would be involved in this ritual was impossible to discern.

Each movement towards the altar had Veaer sharpening her senses, and each glance from Harq lent barely a hint towards what she should do with herself. Completing an order, renewing a legacy, and following the footsteps of a young man who didn't live long enough to know life as his idols once did.

Everyone here had a role to play—everyone but her.

She lingered in the aisle and the events in front of her played out like a slow motion movie. The protectors positioned themselves outside the chalk circle, one of them, no name, no face, stepped up and removed their cloak to reveal a white robe that wasn't so different from the one Elise wore. The music turned bitter in the midst of chanting, low and droning, putting her in a trance.

She dug her nails into the palm of her hands as she forced the counting in her head to stop.

The lives of Kitt and Tychon. If she were able to go back with the mind she had now, would she change the past, present and future? Ensure two young souls could live on because she wasn't holding the knife, but she may as well have been. She hadn't known them very well before they left this plane of existence, and maybe she wasn't meant to know.

Perhaps she would have watched and let it happen again— because every choice, every moment, led to what was now. She feared for what an altered life would summon, how it would change the course of her childhood, adolescents, and what was placed by the universe to have her standing on prickly carpet, deprived of sleep and sense, watching a girl murder in the way justice formed in her hands and mind.

The crack of a slap across her cheek sent her crumpling against a wooden pew, pawing for the armrests to steady herself but instead finding herself staring at the spinning vaulted ceiling.

She didn't shriek, didn't gasp. Just laid on the carpet and wondered who hit her. Harq? For not doing a task she didn't have the instructions for? Or maybe a protector, for not respecting their upcoming sacrifice to the holy angels above. It could've been Elise, punishing her for even humouring the idea of a different future. Because it was them against the world, and the world was theirs.

But right now, the world seemed so big, and she was so tiny. The planet spilled through her fingers like dry, coarse dirt. It didn't obey because she didn't either.

A blast of light took her attention away from the ceiling to the base of the altar platform. Tychon's angelic spirit shook his hand in two sharp flicks, rubbing it swiftly with the other hand as if to draw the pain away.

He looked older, aged. Like he had lived his entire life in his death, coming back to the past to ensure she did right by him even if she hadn't in the first place. Redemption. Reconciliation.

Everyone else in the room stared through the spectre and into her soul.

Tychon pointed behind her. She stretched her neck and the back of her head hit the carpet as she looked under the pews. Sitting in the dark was the stone that Tychon used in his ritual.

Gasps, tackling, thrashing and screaming. A hooded boy and a girl in uniform dancing against a chalk circle, dust flying in the air and feathers catching on their clothing. Blood sparking from a dark place, a glass shattering under the weight of a mortal being. Tychon Alastor Galacia, left dead at the hands of Elise Excava, and the eyes of Veaer Rosell.

Her knees hit the side of the pew with her attempt at standing up, the song in a crescendo, clapping and ecstatic cheers joining the ritual as the protectors threw lavender. The white robed protector laid flat on the altar table. So pristine and so pure. With no mask, it was only a young girl, even younger than Elise. Her lips were drawn tight, yet her eyes bulged in fear and anticipation. She likely didn't know the feeling of a blade against skin, when it pierced the surface and brought up fresh blood. She likely didn't know what death meant.

Her gaze slipped towards Tychon before she realised he disappeared and in place was Elise flipping the handle of the knife in her palm, like waiting to put her pen down on a test.

The princess lifted her hands, and the knife reflected the flames around them. Veaer pushed past the protectors who jeered in protest, breaking the chant, and she seized Elise's wrists, making her drop the knife.

Harq screamed at her as he clamoured onto the altar platform, creating a pathway between the order members. Veaer tackled Elise to the ground, pinning her arms and legs beneath her, crystal anklets digging into her legs as she held the girl in place.

The protectors approached and grabbed at Veaer's hair and clothes. Along her arms, around her neck, her head, her ears, her eyes. They tried to throw her off, tried to yell at all her wrongdoings.

Veaer shook the creeping fingers off her back and she locked eyes with the only person who would listen to her right now.

"Stop this, Elise!" She forced the words through sobs. As if a knife had been driven through her, she doubled over and ignored the sharp tingling in her arms. "Don't you see that this won't be the last if you don't stop now?" Her crying turned into hysterical laughter that rang eerie through the largely empty hall. The music scratched along, dull without the growing euphoria of a ritual in the making. "You can't bring them back like this! You can't bring them back, you can't bring them back, you can't bring them back—"

She grabbed a hold of Elise's shoulders and shook her over and over, letting the back of the princess' head hit the platform ten times over as the protectors and Harq watched in petered off quiet. *Thud. Thud. Thud. Thud.*

"Why do you keep doing this?" *Thud.* "They don't deserve this!" *Thud.* "I'm here, I really am, so why won't you just... don't you trust me? Why won't you tell me?"

She let go of Elise and sat up, panting and wiping the sweat off her brow.

Under her, the princess stared at her with wide, shiny eyes. She took a deep breath, her chest rising as much as it could with weight upon her, before her exhalation came out as a wheeze.

"I must, Veaer," Elise whispered, for her circumstance over any attempt at secrecy. Her fringe stuck to her forehead and her white dress was stained by dirt and mud. "They told me that if I do this, that if I get rid of all of them, then I will be the one to reign true and ascend."

"Who? Who told you this?"

"The angels." A twinkle sparked in Elise's eyes as a smile crept over her lips. The freckles on her cheeks morphed into different constellations as they flickered red and bright. "They speak to me in dreams and visions."

"That doesn't—"

"They kept ringing in my ears! They kept telling me to find her. To find the little purple cat. To drive my mother's knife through her stomach. I didn't want to, but they told me, and I can't stop now, Veaer!" She cackled in the way Veaer hadn't heard since the day Tychon died. Elise's hands mobilised, grasping Veaer's arms. "Then they said Tychon was hiding something. That he wasn't truly my friend. He was only working against me, that's what Galacias do. They act on your side and trick you until they bleed you dry. They told me I had to do it first if I wanted to survive. Then there are two left..."

No, no, no, no, no, no, no, no!

"This is your fault!" Veaer freed her hands and hit the carpet next to Elise's head as frustration overtook her. "This doesn't change anything. It doesn't fix anything. You can't kill anymore, for a sacrifice, for the angels. How can you continue to walk this path? It's too much. I want to protect you but... but I can't if... you do this." Her hands went limp, her palms hovering over Elise's cheeks. "I want to protect you, but I can't when you're this."

"This?" Elise paused, then placed her palms to each side of herself and sat up against Veaer's will and strength.

Veaer tumbled to the side as Elise stood up like she was only a flimsy blanket that she had tried for a cool night only to see how useless it really was. She stayed seated on the edge of the altar platform, watching Elise bend down to pick up the discarded knife that dripped in fresh blood.

Veaer's eyes widened, and she looked to the girl who had been on the altar platform, a cut along her left forearm, staying silent at the outskirts of the group after the chaos. The protectors rushed to the girl's side and Veaer held her head in her hands, trying but failing deep breaths, tears rushing down her cheeks again.

I could've killed her. I could've killed her. I could've killed her. I could've killed her.

"Get up," Elise demanded, holding her hand out and snapping Veaer out of a spiral of regret. She grabbed Elise's soft palm and avoided the looks of the protectors, even if she could feel them on the side of her face.

Her limbs weighed heavy, and time slowed down again. She focused on Elise's face which smiled back at her.

"You must have forgotten, Rosell. I am the most powerful one here. Your words will not change the outcome of today. Life will return." Elise held up her hand and let her fingers touch the top of Veaer's head, slowly running up and down and through the strands. "It will find a way." *It has a way to take as much as it gives.* Elise stayed silent for a strange amount of time, her head tilting to the side slightly, her lips straightening, and her eyes floating elsewhere.

Veaer gripped Elise's robes and shook her, gently. "What is it?" She looked around, for perhaps a ghost only the two of them could see. Glints of gold and light that weren't there before surrounded them, but nothing tangible. Nothing she could trust to have Elise's best interest in mind. "What are you doing?"

Elise blinked and frowned, her gaze meeting Veaer's. A message of unknown factors lingered between them, and she was desperate to claw at the air to gather something, a semblance of an answer.

"Life is precious," the princess finally said in a voice that didn't sound entirely hers. "Perhaps we cannot do an exact exchange."

Veaer was taken aback, her knees turning weak and her grip growing tighter. "Then?"

"The world must balance." *The world always balances.* "And for that, I will return to the dust from which I came."

"No!" Veaer crumpled to her knees as the words hit her ears. Her palms pressed her face as she couldn't bear to watch Elise say more.

"To atone for my sins."

"No, no. There has to be another way. We'll find another way!"

"And I will bring my image everlasting love."

Veaer took a breath of air like it was the last she would ever take. "Love... everlasting love?" She uncovered her face and looked up at Elise whose gaze touched every mortal in the room.

The princess crouched down.

"I will be a saint, Ve." Elise pooled Veaer's silver hair in her palm, like prayer beads intertwined in her fingers and the pendent bared on her wrist. "Don't you understand? They will love me."

CHAPTER 43
VEAER ROSELL

With all attention beckoned towards Elise as she stood up and wiped the dirty knife on her tainted dress, she did seem like a saint for a second.

Worshipped, cherished, and beloved forever.

Veaer gripped Elise's clothes so tightly that she feared to rip it apart. But she couldn't help the waves of grief already consuming her, not after all her time and risk and effort. Not after everything she's done.

"But I love you. I love you with everything!" Veaer begged and prayed, clasping her hands together and shaking them before grabbing the princess again lest she floated away to the heavens. "Please don't listen to them. I love you more than any angel could. Please, is that not enough?"

The angels knew nothing if their solution was to take one she loved. This was punishment for all she did and didn't do. She leaned against the altar table and brought her hands to her face. All this time while Izot antagonised her, and Tychon kept secrets from her, and Elise moved through the isolated motions of the academy, she still couldn't give Elise what she was missing.

"I'm sorry, Veaer," Elise said. The princess held her against her hip and ran a hand up and down her back. "I'm sorry if this hurts you." Veaer glanced through her fingers at the gently smiling Elise. "I'm sorry that you felt you needed to do this, that you had to follow me. I'm sorry that you love me. But no, it will never be enough."

Never. "Never?" She sniffed and tried to pull Elise closer, but she formed like water in her hands, barely a pool in her palm, otherwise soaking through her. "But what about... everything?" *Everything I've done for you. Everywhere I've gone for you.*

Elise inhaled and spent time taking a seat next to Veaer, both of their backs against the altar. The protectors faded away and Harq remained idle, listening with furrowed brows and then a look at his watch. His lips parted for a moment as he caught Veaer's eye, before he pursed his lips and looked away. They had time, just a little.

The princess inched her hand onto Veaer's thigh. She squeezed gently and avoided her gaze. "I don't think I'm meant for this world. I think I've only been destined to complete something of the past, of my ancestors, before I return to Ter and Mian." Her grip tightened. "It's always been this way. My brother is a light for the world and my father a leading hand. I am a shadow in the corner and my dreams are truly haunted by something I know in my blood but nothing in my living experience. I'm technically halfway there but it doesn't feel like it." Elise swayed to the side and rested her cheek on Veaer's shoulder. Silent tears trailed down and landed in Veaer's lap. "It doesn't feel like it... and maybe it never will. Maybe all of this is for nothing, and it should all end now, just like you said. I can't keep doing this—when I don't even know why I am."

Veaer scrunched her skirt into her hands, trying her very hardest to keep the pressure behind her eyes away. Yes, Elise had to stop and let go. No, she shouldn't have to get rid of herself to do so. Yes, she took the lives of others, and this would be retribution. No, there had to be *another* way.

"Can't we start over? Leave this all behind and become stars instead of shadows?" Veaer tried to crack a smile, but her lips twisted in the wrong ways.

Elise turned her body to face Veaer and held her hand up to a blotchy face. "You're already a star. Shining bright and with so much potential. You don't need to come down just to lift me up." Her hand dropped away, and she grabbed the altar table to help herself up, Veaer watching the movement of stained white cloth like clouds moving through the dark sky.

"And—And your underclassmen?" Veaer squeaked, her hand reaching up to catch Elise, but she moved out of sight, around the altar table. Veaer stumbled up, clumsy with exhaustion on the edges of her being. The mumbled commands for the protectors were unclear, only Harq's voice breaking through the barriers in his paranoia of the time. The moon shone high and bright through the cathedral's back wall, those glass halos returning to Ter and Mian's crowns.

"What of them?" Elise answered with no mind of the protectors redrawing the circle, replacing the melted candles with fresh unlit ones, and the knife being sterilised for its next victim. Harq consulted a small notebook and glanced at his watch again. The princess moved with grace, her crystal jewellery making sweet music like hanging chimes, even while everyone else in the cathedral dragged their feet and held their heads low with the scent of decay and death among them. Elise was right—she was the most powerful here and there was nothing they could do about it.

Veaer held the foot of the altar table tightly, her mind grasped by disbelief. She pinched her hand and then pinched it again. "They follow you, they love you. It's a start, is it not?" She swallowed her tongue, disgusted by her own words of compliance and normality.

"They stay for the secrecy and special attention," Elise sang, her gaze elsewhere as a protector presented her the cleaned ritual knife, shiny and sharp. She reflected it against the moonlight, her back to Veaer. "And for the same reasons, they leave. Isolation, desire too big, trying to stretch me out as if they own me. I don't even remember half their names, half their faces. They are all meaningless and selfish."

The angels laughed in Veaer's mind. She gripped the table tight enough for the cloth to bunch in her hands. Even when the bow wasn't pointed at her, the arrows still found their way, digging deep and leaving her to bleed slowly and slowly.

"I thought that there was more than this," Veaer whispered, her eyes brimming with tears that burned her. She stepped around the table, gauging the princess' reaction, and continued forward when it was evident that she had no effect. "That I am enough to stay for. That, that—we were going to find all the answers. Understand everything."

Elise remained with her body turned towards the altar table despite Veaer's attempts to guide them towards each other. The circle was complete, and the music started playing from the beginning. Chanting filled the podium, rising high into the ceiling and low into the dirt under their feet. A collective sigh of relief pulled the tension between Veaer and Elise even tighter.

The princess tilted her head, her neck becoming exposed to Veaer as her hair followed to the other side. "Haven't we already? Haven't we found the answers we need?" And at a quiet moment in the song, Elise extended the ritual knife towards Veaer.

"What— we..." She looked between the carved blade and the side of Elise's head. The lightning pattern of common butterfly wings struck across the princess' cheek and her neck, her smooth golden skin tainted then returning pure in a blink. Veaer quickly became aware of the way her clothes stuck to her collarbone and how her skirt hung uncomfortably around her thighs. How the music clawed away at her ears and the protectors were far too close to her like insects making their way under her shirt and through the holes in her skin.

Before she even had a moment to conjure all the questions that clattered within her, to sate every hunger that ate away the stomach of her mind, Elise answered,

"Take the knife."

"The knife? No, I couldn't, no." Veaer pulled away, her heel teasing the edge of the altar platform, but Elise caught her by the hip and pressed her other side against the altar cloth once again.

"You must."

In confusion and terror, Veaer placed her palm over the back of Elise's hand, staring into the princess' eyes. The galaxy pooled in her deep brown irises, a universe reflecting the land that carried them through each step they took in life. Beyond the set lines of Elise's face and the conviction written all over her expression, a tiny flame burned. It lashed with every breath but never grew. It stayed behind, safely, not threatening to make itself known to anyone else but Veaer.

"You will be my first disciple, sweet Veaer Rosell," Elise rejoiced, the hand free from Veaer's grasp clutching her shoulder in utter trust and reverence. "In this sacrifice, I am a servant to the angelic heroes of past. I will repent for my sins and allow my soul to move onto better things. And once I do, you will honour me as a saint, so that in the afterlife I may receive a love never found—unable to be ruined, and undeniable."

Elise grabbed Veaer's hand and closed her fingers over the handle of the knife. It was cold with sharpened wood grain and just felt entirely wrong. She couldn't bear to shift her eyes, the texture of the handle burning so much that if she didn't look, maybe it would go away—both the feeling and the weapon.

A tug on her sleeve threw her back to reality and Elise laid flat on the altar table before her, her hands folded by her lap and her eyes closed—like she were asleep rather than afraid of what being stabbed would feel like.

Harq began to circle behind the protectors who danced in the same motion. He belted a prayer and a chant in words she couldn't recognise. When his gaze reached Veaer, only two words came through.

Do it.

And another.

Do it now.

A scream broke out of her like a beast ripping through her chest. She took the knife in both hands. *To stop them shaking. To do this right and well by Elise.* Her arms had been weakened in the state of her mind, yet she only held on tighter lest she wanted to watch this love die by a slip of the palm.

"Veaer," Elise's voice betrayed her fear. Death was flashing before her eyes. "Please, do the honours. I want it to be you. It can only be you."

And I want to be with *you. I want you, only you.*

"I can't do it, I can't do it."

Tychon's apparition flashed in and out of her vision, his presence holding the same weight as Harq's message to her. He was on his knees, then towering over her, then standing there, the same boy he was when he was taken away from a life of greatness.

A kaleidoscope of butterflies burst from the windows and shadows, landing upon and around Elise's body. She imagined their little hands like flies, rubbing together in preparation for a feast.

Elise chuckled as the tip of the blade caressed the soft skin in the middle of her chest. "Where has all that anger gone? Just yesterday you looked like you wanted to kill me. For taking away that precious kitty's life. For making you keep my secret for so long." Her lips wavered and her glassy eyes shone against the silver moon and golden flames. Her chest rose and dropped at the beat of the music.

Veaer inhaled, like the air had shifted to that time years ago. Struggling against the grip of someone with just as much loyalty to Elise back then. Watching Elise laugh because she had done something right by the divine. Young Kitt appeared beside Tychon, and they looked at each other as if they had already seen what would happen here today.

Veaer knew that she felt deeply in her soul, that every situation she encountered burrowed negative and positive responses into her heart and regurgitated them at the tip of her tongue.

But she had to accept, too, that these emotions only came in tides that would recede as if at the command of the moon. She feared that after today, the only feeling remaining would be grief. Grief for a saint yet to be canonised.

"I made you watch as I killed him," Elise shrieked as she grabbed one of Veaer's arms and shook it. Veaer shut her eyes so that her senses would focus on the splinters of the handle and ensure they wouldn't leave unless she willed it so. "I made you break into his room even when he was dead. I made you read his journal while he couldn't do anything to stop it. I made you steal maps from my father's office. I made you find that crypt. Join the Ascension Order. The rituals, the angels, everything!"

"Stop talking, just stop it!" Veaer's chest caved in as she opened her eyes to see tears streaming down Elise's cheeks, how her body shook in dirty fabrics, uncontrollable cries and deep yet unsatisfying breaths.

"I made you love me, so you must hate me for everything I've done to you. You hate me, Veaer. You hate me! So kill me, please!"

"I love you!"

The blade flew down and ripped Elise's skin open, past bones and flesh, into her chest, with all the power of the universe behind it.

Blood spurt from the wound and coated Veaer's hands.

Every sound drowned out. It was just blood, blood, blood, blood. *Blood. Elise's blood.* Dark red and slowly oozing, and the edge that split along Elise's chest was tender and pink—perfect, beautiful, a new butterfly's home.

She lifted the knife and drove it down again. And again. And more red. So much that she would've thought her arms were always this way. She ignored the screams of the protectors who didn't realise what was actually coming when they had chosen to be part of this cause. She ignored Harq screaming at her to stop and then turning away with a hand over his mouth.

She ignored the way the chalk circle started to glow red too, how the room became further draped in shadows.

"Oh," Elise gasped, "so this is how it feels."

Veaer wailed and crumbled against the altar table, her head finding a place to rest on Elise's stomach as a pool of blood stained the cloth. "What am I doing? What have I done?" The knife remained stuck, the blunt end of the handle pointing to the heavens.

"You love me, you truly do." Elise smiled and brought her hands to her chest, weaving her fingers around the metal blade and leaving them to be intertwined in her final moments. "I love you too, Veaer Rosell."

EPILOGUE

"Your name is humming inside my chest.
I think this is what it means to love.
I think this is what it means to be living."
—— *Emma Bleker, I am a grand, living, buzzing thing*

Years Later.

On the first Friday of May, every year, Veaer Rosell would sit in her studio with a fresh canvas and new paints.

Natural light flooded from large windows and highlighted hanging paintings along one of the walls. One in styles that overlapped as if handed around in a circle; sharp corners, soft edges, and shapes plastered on with a sense of inexperience. Another lent itself to time, being an attempt at a realistic depiction of Miriam Manor's front doors from her last year at the academy.

Otherwise, the rest of the walls were covered in muted colours, allowing creativity to bounce off the peaceful atmosphere they elicited. A rack of art supplies was in easy reach by way of wheels. When the room was empty, its home was out of the way. But when she was determined to create, most days but not all, it would hover around her stool in the centre of the room.

When others visited her sanctuary, they often described it being uneasy to understand. Charcoal drawings that were of the same subject over and over with slight changes across time were found in piles on one of the tables. On the floor were open folders of references and inspirational work. An unfinished sculpture sat in the corner. An unused pottery wheel to the side. She claimed to get to them someday, but she returned to her true artistic love: painting.

With a lift of the brush, she applied the first layer of paint. That was the easy part.

The hard part was remembering. What that moment looked like a few years ago. A young girl with long black hair, golden skin, and deep brown eyes with sun rays trapped inside laying on an altar of red and white. The perfect piece that captured what would be considered an intangible experience to others, but everything to her.

She could appreciate what context brought to art. She learnt that when she cleaned up the cathedral in the dead of the night. When she was brought in for a psychological evaluation and assigned to a psychiatrist. When she was tasked with painting over the manor mural as part of her punishment. When detectives led her to Tychon's room and then Elise's to tell them about her experience. And she would stare at the paintings and tapestries and specimen frames in both, remembering and remembering.

Eventually memories become something of a layered beast. One's memory was only the last time they remembered an instance. In this case, her painting of Saint Elise Excava on the day of her passing was only as much as she remembered from when she painted it last year, and the year before that, and the year before that.

She started in the middle, with the knife in her chest.

~

On the third Friday of May, every year, Veaer Rosell would travel to Adraredon Academy. Nowadays, rather than making Haiwrin drop her off on his way to work, she drove there herself and then parked on the western edge of the grounds, just outside the forest behind Miriam Manor.

She spun the keys on her finger as she closed the car door and moved to the trunk to pull out a canvas hidden with a cloth over it. The canvas was carried under her left arm, and she wiped the sweat on her right palm against her jacket. She brought her touch to her head where her scarlet wolf caemi ears remained even when she passed the threshold. Just like her earlier visits; maybe she had grown up enough to get past any anti-magic.

The forest was easy to navigate in the daytime as a path had been installed. When she could see the back of the manor peeking over the trees, she paused and looked among the dirt and leaves for a symbol etched into a hidden concrete slab. A hand placed upon the symbol caused it to glow, and a moment later the slab lifted itself and moved aside, revealing a small ladder downwards.

The crypt was quiet, which meant everything was normal. While only a few knew about the secret entrances around the school, she still held onto an irrational anxiety of the wrong people stumbling upon the underground and causing a chaos she couldn't control now that she wasn't a part of the academy anymore.

Days of practise and memorisation made the trip through the labyrinth of stone and sand walls easier. The crypt had become, in part, her new cathedral of comfort for the rest of her senior year, where she painted newly inspired pieces on the divine, fresh angles on the heroes that preceded the buildings and crypt itself. Her unintentional mix between Syriphian history and dedicated artistic skill helped her acceptance into some of the best institutes of arts education around the continent.

Eventually her choice of life after Adraredon Academy came down to a vision. A small house in the nearby town, living with her lover, painting her days away, but when she wasn't holed up in that studio, she was assisting in exhibitions, workshops, and special events. She liked being able to walk down the street to visit her best friend. She liked knowing that a legacy she had established wasn't so far away, but far enough that she didn't think about it all the time.

She found the large room of stone tombs that she had seen the first time she came underground. Her first stop was the room of hero statues. She stared into the eyes of each one until her eyes dried out.

Then she walked through some more corridors before arriving at an open doorway. The room inside was filled with candles, though this time they were already lit before she arrived. A figure stood deep inside, with his hands in his pockets, back to Veaer, staring at the shrine embedded into the wall.

"Izot?" Veaer called, and her voice bounced in the empty space. She hadn't seen him since graduation.

The young man spun around, his hands shifting from his pockets and his face drawn in surprise. He wore a sophisticated suit as if he had just been attending an important meeting, looking slightly out of place among cobwebs and decay.

He brought a hand to his chest and a small smile appeared on his lips. "Oh, Veaer. I wasn't expecting you."

"Wouldn't have expected you to expect me," she replied. She waited for a nod from the young man before she stepped into the room and adjusted the canvas in her hands. "What are you doing here?" She kept her gaze on the display.

A framed picture of Elise, one that didn't encapsulate her entirely as a school photo, but no picture would truly be able to achieve such a feat. The frame was surrounded with more candles, and a pot of sand sat behind it with a stick of incense upright and glowing orange at the tip. The scent of sandalwood and myrrh floated past her.

The shrine was further decorated with pieces of art, flowers, and offerings. Handmade beaded bracelets and amulets carved from metal. Two pieces of sheet music on yellowed paper provided a placemat to a tiny marble statue created in Elise's likeness.

"The same reason you are. To pay my respects." Izot folded his hands in front of him and twiddled his thumbs. He watched Veaer as she removed the cloth from her canvas and moved to the left wall. "So, you're the one who makes those?"

Veaer fixed her latest iteration next to the others. She knew that her friends considered it morbid—offering paintings of someone's demise to their shrine—but she thought this part of her duty as a disciple. It's something Elise would've liked.

"I sign these. You would know how my signature looks. At least an imitation of it." After admiring her progress, she returned to Izot's side, giving him a side glance and a smile. "How is your father?"

"He's retired."

"When?"

"The year after we finished." Izot looked down and placed a hand on the edge of the shrine. "I think he learnt how it felt to..." A pause. "He returned the administration to the Galacia family."

She straightened with a start. The path in the forest, why she hadn't heard more news about Headmaster Doallan Excava and disappearing students, how her caemi heritage persisted on the academy grounds. Safety, a new era, and magic returned at the hands of another family. Headmaster Doallan experienced a loss like no other and decided it was enough.

"And they accepted?"

"If not by a favour to my father, then a favour to their ancestors. They run this place well, maybe better." Izot wet his lips with his tongue. "I think he blames himself. He still wonders what happened. I do too, but I know—actually, I don't know—but I think Elise would want me to just grow up and be better than our dad was."

Veaer watched a single flame dance next to Elise's face. She still remembered the words said, the declarations made. She remembered that Elise sought a love only found after death. She was glad that it existed even when she doubted it.

"So," Izot cleared his throat, "I know that Haiwrin is an assistant here now. Intending to lead some new research in magical injury one day?" She raised an eyebrow and he continued, "I may not be student president anymore, but I do enjoy knowing where our cohort ends up. He's doing good work, even if it helps him at most."

She nodded in a silent agreement. He was able to receive treatment that mended anything life threatening to his heart and lungs, though his arms still suffered from pain some days, and he would ask Veaer to scribe anything important if she was available to visit him at home. That, and he had a new perspective in his participation in the theatre arts.

"I'm very proud of him," Veaer said. "I only want the best for him after what he's been through."

"And how about you? Treating yourself well?"

She feigned a gasp. Izot furrowed his brows with a nervous smile. She replied, "Is that a real question? I wouldn't have known Izot Excava to ask me such a thing."

"Of course. And tell me about that Adair."

"I'm doing quite well." She was happy to almost believe it as she said it. It was hard to know when she was genuinely doing well. "I painted that a couple weeks ago." She gestured vaguely to her painting. "I'm here today. More comfortable in my own body, doing things I enjoy with my days. Finding myself able to chat to you." Both despite their past qualms and her role in his sister's passing. "And Adair..." She held up her left hand, revealing a simple rose gold ring on her finger.

Izot blinked, his chin rising. "Engaged?"

"No, no. They wouldn't do that so soon." Veaer chuckled and hooked her hands behind her back, tapping each finger one at a time. "Just a promise."

The two stared at the shrine for a moment longer, then decided to use the forest exit together. Izot waved goodbye and Veaer rushed forward to give him a hug before he walked away.

Then they left, leaving Adraredon Academy none the wiser.

ACKNOWLEDGEMENTS

Chrysalis and Requiem has become something new and different from what it originally started as. I have carried these characters with me for almost seven years, ever since I made a world of my own to tell stories in. A time when Veaer was still a thief and Izot was still a prince, but in a world of magical, medieval mischief.

Now we are here. Obsessive murder lesbians on a gothic campus where the protagonist gets with the princess rather than the prince.

Semblances of their previous story still persist in this final version, and it makes me happy to see the growth I've experienced as a writer. For that, I have many to thank.

I would like to thank Caleb Hosalla, my cover illustrator. Thank you for dedicating yourself to my vision and executing it in the most wonderful way.

Thank you to my beta readers for their joy, shock, and passion towards my novel. Emma, Kaye, Catarina, Sophie, Sarah, Rose, Olivier, Jamie, Faith, Feifei, and Iris.

Thank you to my street team, my blurb authors, and my arc readers for their ongoing support of my publication. I have a big dream when it comes to this book and every one of you helps to make that happen.

Thank you to Happon for your continued artistic work when it comes to bringing my characters to life. You always seem to know what I'm trying to say.

Thank you to the Wranglers for being an awesome well of publishing insight and friendship in this industry. I'm so proud of us!

Thank you to my connections across publishing, such as Gideon from Room of One's Own bookstore and other amazing booksellers, librarians, and bookish vendors I keep in touch with.

Thank you especially to Feifei. You were my critique partner at the most important time of Chrysalis and Requiem's creation. You helped me form the confidence that seeps through my writing and how I share this story with others.

Of course, thank you to my partner Zak. This is only the beginning and I will fill our future bookshelves with my publications.

Thank you to my family for continuing to show excitement for my work and wanting to read my books (this one might be a bit darker than the last).

ABOUT THE AUTHOR

Quinton Li is a Melbourne-based non-binary novelist, poet, fiction editor and anthology curator. With a love for fortune-telling, angelic beings and the human condition, it's no wonder that many of their works across fiction and poetry touch on these subjects. Alongside these themes, they strongly resonate with queer and Asian diaspora works and believe that art can change a perspective or enhance it.

Find more at quintonli.com

 twitter.com/itsquinnli
instagram.com/itsquinnli